A BLANCO COUNTY MYSTERY

For Ben Sevier, with much appreciation.
Thanks for getting it all started.

ACKNOWLEDGMENTS

Here they are again—the talented advisors, editors, and early readers who make my books better in every possible respect: Tommy Blackwell, Jim Lindeman, Becky Rehder, Helen Haught Fanick, Mary Summerall, Marsha Moyer, Jo Virgil, Joe Hammer, Stacia Miller, Linda Biel, Leo Bricker, Naomi West, Richie West, Karen Ortosky, Kim Darville, Martin Grantham, and John Strauss. And a hat tip to Kathy Welsh Morrow for the line about water towers. Any errors are my own.

1

By the time he was thirty-two years old, Graham Smith had had sex with at least three dozen women over the age of seventy. He couldn't nail the number down precisely because he hadn't bothered to keep a list. But it had to be at least forty. Maybe more. Most of the relationships were brief—just enough time to determine whether any woman in particular showed promise. How trusting was she? How interested did she seem in him? Was she lonely? Did she want someone new and exciting in her life? Was she credulous, which seemed somewhat rare in that age group? Did she have children? Much better if the answer to that last one was no. He'd learned that the hard way.

The latest potential target was named Marge Slubb, and she was no more attractive than her name. Her most unbecoming physical attribute, from Graham's perspective, was her mustache. Surely she had to see it when she looked in the mirror. Why hadn't someone in her life—a friend, a sister, a daughter, or some other confidante— gently encouraged her to use a depilatory cream?

"I have to say I was surprised by your invitation," Marge said.

"In a good way, I hope."

"Well, yes."

"I enjoyed our first visit, so why not?"

She gave him a pointed look through her thick eyeglasses. "The age difference," she said. "Let's not pretend. Unless I'm mistaken about..."

"No, you're not mistaken. I enjoy your company, Marge. I want to get to know you better. There's nothing wrong with that, is there?"

"I guess not."

"So let's not even think about age. Why should we? Let's just enjoy a nice dinner together, okay?"

They were seated at a small table tucked in the corner of a dark and cozy restaurant in Malibu. One of Graham's favorite places to bring these women, but he had to take pains to ensure that the servers and other staff didn't somehow indicate that he routinely brought dates here. Sure, they could act like he was a regular, but don't ask about Doris, or Ruth, or Rita, or any of his previous companions.

"I think I'll have the lobster," Marge announced after perusing the menu for several minutes.

"As well you should. An excellent choice."

"You've had it?"

"Several times. It's heavenly. That's the only way to describe it. In fact, I think I'll have it, too. See, we have similar tastes. Another reason we hit it off."

Graham hated lobster. One time he got sick after eating it, and he'd wondered if he was allergic.

"Shall we have a glass of wine?" Graham asked.

"That would be lovely."

"Or perhaps a full bottle?"

"Even better."

"Sauvignon blanc? Riesling? Something else?"

"I love a riesling."

"Riesling it will be."

Frank the waiter came by, and Graham ordered the wine and the lobsters.

After Frank left, Graham said, "When we chatted outside the art gallery, you said you were a bit of a painter yourself. Tell me more about that."

Graham had known that well before they'd met. He'd known quite a bit about her, chiefly because he'd sent her a Facebook friend request from a fake profile he'd created. He was Gwen Bernbach, a woman who'd attended the same high school as Marge, but three years after her, hence the reason Marge probably didn't remember Gwen. Marge accepted the request, of course. In Graham's experience, very few people declined requests from fellow high school alums. It would be interesting to see if Marge said anything on Facebook after their date. Would she post anything later tonight, or even tomorrow, depending on how the date went?

"Oh, I piddle around with watercolors," Marge said. "I'm not very good."

"I'm sure you're being modest. I'd love to see some of your work."

"I have a few photos," Marge said. She took her phone out and showed him several examples. One was a painting of a poodle she'd owned several years ago. He looked more like Baby Yoda. She'd painted sunsets, mountains, flowers, and all of them were terrible.

"These are really nice," Graham said. "Have you contacted any galleries about a showing?"

"You think I should?"

"Absolutely."

"I never even thought of that."

"These have a lot of…nuance, I would say. You can feel the emotion coming off each one. They touch me."

"Oh, my." She brought a hand flat to her chest. "That's the nicest compliment I've ever received."

Frank brought the bottle of wine and poured them each a generous glass.

After he was gone, Graham said, "May I ask about your husband—if the memories aren't too painful?"

She posted about him often on Facebook, so he knew she'd be willing to talk.

"Harry was a prince," she said. "The love of my life. We met when I was only fourteen. We got married when I was seventeen. He was the best person I ever knew. Just so loving and kind to everybody."

"I'm so sorry you lost him."

"He was also brilliant. He succeeded at everything he did."

"That's wonderful. Like what?"

"Well, business, for one. He built one of the most successful travel agencies in the state. Built it from the ground up, starting with a thousand dollars he managed to save over several years. This was back before the internet, of course, when people still used travel agents."

"That's really amazing. I've never been business-minded myself. Some people just seem to have a knack for it."

"That was Harry—with business and anything else. He could fix anything around the house, or master any sport. He could finish the Sunday New York Times crossword puzzle in an hour!"

"How did he learn so much about business?" Graham asked, to keep the conversation on the track he wanted.

"Well, he didn't go to college, but that didn't stop him from learning. He got a job with a cruise line right out of high school and worked his way up to a management position in less than three years. He was twenty-one and the next-youngest manager was thirty-four. Can you imagine that?"

"Sounds like he was a good provider."

"He certainly was. He was a saver. And a planner. *And* he taught me how to enjoy nice things—cars, vacations, a beautiful home— without overextending yourself. 'Never touch the principal.' That was one of his rules. Well, it became a rule after we'd achieved financial independence. Before that, it wasn't realistic, but by the time we'd reached fifty, there was no reason to touch the principal. Live off the interest. That was plenty."

The question was, had she continued to follow that rule? Being childless, there was less of an incentive to hold on to that money. Graham had encountered several women like Marge who had squandered everything they owned. What a waste of time.

"Honestly, I'm not even sure what the term 'financial independence' means," Graham said.

"Well, if you earn enough money that you can cover your expenses for the rest of your life without working, that's financial independence. Why would you touch any of that money and risk your independence?"

"Makes sense to me," Graham said. "Do you still live by that rule, now that Harry is gone?"

"Absolutely. He made me promise. I keep my promises."

"That's good to hear," Graham said. "I'm sure Harry would be proud."

Right then, the lobster arrived.

2

Six years later.

Jimmy Lee Jackson was ogling a nude woman on a postcard when he heard the explosion. He felt it, too, as a matter of fact. The vibration came up through the four metal legs and lightly shook his deer blind.

Weird.

The way the woman on the postcard was photographed, you could tell she was naked, but you couldn't really see all that much. There were a lot of shadows, but just enough bare skin to make the photo totally hot.

Jimmy Lee had been kind of obsessed with the postcard since it had arrived in his mailbox the day before, but now he reluctantly set it aside and waited a moment, simply listening. A minute passed. He could ignore the explosion, right?

But what about Lonnie? He must've felt the blast, too, right? And probably even more intensely, since it had come from the direction of Lonnie's blind, more or less, although it was difficult to pinpoint how far away it had been. It could've been a big blast that was far away or a smaller blast that was closer.

It had been an explosion, for sure, not a gunshot or fireworks or a car backfiring or anything like that. Dynamite? Possibly.

By now, another three minutes had passed.

Jimmy Lee decided it was time to send a text to Lonnie.

The hell was that?

Jimmy Lee knew for a fact that Lonnie kept his phone propped on a little shelf directly in front of him, so he would see the text come in.

But two minutes passed and Lonnie didn't answer. Maybe he'd gone to look for the source of the explosion. But wouldn't he have texted back first?

Or maybe he'd fallen asleep. Lonnie was partial to naps, and he could take one just about anywhere. Lonnie and Jimmy Lee had been out late the night before, dancing at Mercer Street, and they hadn't gotten home until nearly one in the morning.

Jimmy Lee sent another text. *Did that shake your blind?*

Five minutes later, Lonnie still had not replied.

It was now 4:57 p.m. on Sunday. A beautiful January afternoon. Forty degrees. Jimmy Lee's deer feeder would throw corn in three minutes. Well, shit. He couldn't really hunt now, could he? Not without knowing what that explosion was, and why Lonnie wasn't answering.

Jimmy Lee grabbed his .270, opened the blind door, and carefully backed down the ten-foot ladder. For just an instant, he caught a whiff of something burning. Or burnt. Wasn't cedar brush, either. This had a nastier smell, like burning lumber or construction debris.

Jimmy Lee was starting to get a bad feeling.

He set off in the direction of Lonnie's blind, roughly two hundred yards to the north, but then he stopped and sent a third text.

I'm coming to check on you. Don't shoot me.

He paused for half a minute, just in case Lonnie might reply, but there was no response. So he started walking again, following a deer path that meandered through the cedar and oak trees. After eighty or ninety yards, Jimmy Lee reached an opening from which he could usually see the top of Lonnie's blind poking out above the brush line.

But now he saw nothing—except a thin plume of black smoke swirling toward the sky. That stopped him cold. What the hell was going on?

"Lonnie?" Jimmy Lee called out, which was silly from this distance.

He began walking again, faster now, keeping the muzzle of his rifle pointed at the ground.

"Lonnie?" he called again, louder this time.

He had to go around a dense grove of cedars, and when he came to the other side, he simply couldn't process what stood before him. The majority of Lonnie's deer blind was gone. All that remained was a smoldering floor, part of one wall, and the four legs that had held the structure up.

Nothing else remained. Certainly not Lonnie, or the chair he'd been using, or his rifle, or any of his other gear.

"Lonnie?" Jimmy Lee said again, quieter, because he was no longer expecting to hear a reply.

Red O'Brien was kicking back in his recliner, watching a *Green Acres* rerun, when he heard Billy Don's Ranchero approaching on the county road. Then he heard it idling at the mailbox for half a minute. Then it slowly climbed the long caliche driveway to the trailer.

Red took a long drink of beer and resigned himself to the fact that his peaceful afternoon was about to be ruined. Billy Don Craddock had been his housemate for quite a few years now, but there were times when a couple of hours alone was pure bliss.

Red heard Billy Don park and kill the engine. The Ranchero door slammed shut, and five seconds later, Red felt the vibration as Billy Don mounted the steps to the front porch, opened the door, and stepped inside.

"You got some interesting mail," he said with an unusual grin on his face.

"Just put it on the table," Red said.

"You ain't gonna like it."

"Ain't gonna like what?"

"The mail."

"Why's that?"

"You'll see."

"The 'lectric bill? I told you to quit running that damn space heater in your room all the time. You always forget it's running and just leave it on. Gonna burn the damn place down."

"You're gonna wish it was the 'lectric bill."

"Then what is it? Did you open my mail or what? You wanna move out of the way so I can see the TV?"

"No, it's a postcard. So I didn't have to open it."

"From who?" None of Red's friends or family members ever traveled anywhere, so who'd be sending a postcard?

"More like a what," Billy Don said.

Red was getting irritated with this guessing game. "The hell are you babbling about?"

"It's not from a person, it's from a place. A business."

Red held his hand out. "Well, pass it here."

"Hang on," Billy Don said.

He went into the kitchen and returned with two beers—Red's beers—and handed one to Red.

"No, really, help yourself," Red said. "And give me my damn mail."

"Not yet. I'm having fun with this."

"You're the only one," Red said.

"I'll give you a hint. It involves Mandy."

"It what?"

"It involves Mandy."

Mandy was Red's girlfriend, more or less, who was plenty sassy and had a killer body. He'd kind of stumbled into a relationship with her when her husband got shot and killed, and at first it appeared Mandy had done it, partly because she was having an affair with this Spanish-speaking Dairy Queen manager who had a foot fetish. But the cops later determined that Mandy's shot had been a clean miss and she hadn't killed her husband after all. At one point, Mandy tried to extort some money from Red, so it was weird to be hooked up with her, but he couldn't resist. It had all turned out okay so far. Red especially enjoyed the fact that Mandy liked to send him private photos on his phone. She wasn't all hung up on being ladylike and didn't really care what anybody thought of her. His kind of gal.

"Mandy sent me a postcard?" Red asked.

"Nope."

"Damn it, Billy Don, would you just hand me the friggin' card?"

"Think about it for a second, Red," Billy Don said. "What would Mandy have to do with a postcard—one that she didn't send?"

"Don't make me get up out of this chair," Red said.

"And do what?" Billy Don asked.

Billy Don stood six-four and weighed roughly three hundred

pounds, so anything physical was out of the question.

"Put a lock on the fridge," Red said. "Tally up the amount you owe me in rent. Hide all my lingerie catalogs. That's just for starters."

Right then, they heard an explosion. Not nearby, but close enough for them to stop talking for a moment and wait. They heard nothing else. Whatever had blown up, it didn't really concern them. This was the country, and people out here could do whatever the hell they wanted. If somebody wanted to blow something up, that was his God-given right as an American.

"You want another hint?" Billy Don asked. He was obviously enjoying himself, and that pissed Red off.

"Oh, sure," Red said. "In fact, I'm hoping we can keep playing this little game for a couple of hours."

"Remember what Mandy told you a few weeks ago?" Billy Don asked. "About being a model?"

"Oh," Red said, suddenly remembering now. Mandy said some dude had seen her in town and asked if she might want to be in some ads for his wellness retreat, which had been open for a few months.

"What the hell's a wellness retreat?" Red had asked Mandy at the time.

"You know, a place people can go to relax and get away from stress and just basically hit the reset button."

Sounded to Red like Mandy was repeating what the dude had told her. "Hit the reset button?" Red said. "That's what beer joints are for."

"He said the photos would be tasteful. Plus, he's gonna give me two hundred bucks and a free membership."

Up to that point, Red had wondered if the wellness dude was just trying to use flattery to get into Mandy's pants, but if he was putting up some cash, that was a different ballgame.

That was the last Red had heard of it until now.

Billy Don said, "Turns out this place is a retreat, all right—the kind where you retreat from your clothes."

"What?"

"She ain't wearing no clothes. See for yourself." Billy Don finally handed Red the postcard.

Red looked at it. The front showed a beautiful sunrise—or sunset—over the Texas hill country, with the words "Rebuild your spirit."

Then he flipped it over. There was Mandy. A lot of Mandy. More Mandy than Red would've thought anyone could legally send in the US mail.

"Son of a bitch," Red said.

"She's nekkid," Billy Don said.

"I can see that for my damn self," Red said.

"But the way she's sitting sideways and got her arms crossed, she covers up all the good stuff."

"Still too much," Red said.

He could feel his temperature rising. He didn't like this at all.

"Gotta admit the photographer did a hell of a job," Billy Don said. "Not that he didn't have plenty to work with."

3

"I ain't trying to be difficult, but what I wanna know is, how am I s'pposed to fill that tag out after I shoot a deer, and then I gotta track him, and by the time I find him, the sun's been down for thirty minutes. That's what happened tonight. Look how tiny that type is on the back of that license. How am I s'pposed to read that in the dark? Even with a flashlight, hell, my tired old eyes just ain't up for it."

Blanco County Game Warden John Marlin knew from years of experience that many hunters had no idea how to properly fill out a hunting license after they'd harvested a deer. Sure, they were good at applying for the license, and most of them remembered to have it on hand when hunting, but when it was time to record their kill, they hadn't taken the time to understand what was required, as simple as it was. However, most of them were skilled at generating excuses.

"That's why you should look at it in the daylight when you first get it," Marlin said. "It's really not that difficult. You have to cut the numbers out, and then—"

"Cut 'em out? Those little things? I can't hardly even *read* the numbers."

The man's name was Edward Glomb. Fifty-three years old. Lived in Houston. Had been leasing this ranch for three years, but this was Marlin's first interaction with him. Glomb was holding a large Bubba mug containing a mixed drink of some kind, and it apparently wasn't his first of the evening. His speech was mildly slurred and he swayed from side to side. Just another guy having too much fun at deer camp.

"Then bring a magnifying glass," Marlin said. "Or have a friend read it for you. Or use your phone to zoom in. Get creative."

"My tired old eyes just ain't up for it," Glomb pleaded.

"You already said that."

"Cuz it's true!"

"A lot of people manage to get it done without any problems," Marlin said.

They were standing near a campfire next to an RV that acted as headquarters on the hunting lease. One other hunter was present, seated in a lawn chair, quietly drinking a beer. An eight-point buck was hanging by a rope from a nearby oak tree, field dressed, but not yet skinned.

"They need to print those numbers bigger," Glomb said.

"Then there's the deer log on the back," Marlin said.

"I've never eaten a deer log before," Glomb said. "Is that anything like a pecan log?"

Marlin couldn't help but laugh—not because the joke was funny, but because Glomb *thought* it was funny. The man in the lawn chair snickered, too, most likely for the same reason.

"Right after you kill a deer, you need to enter it in the log. That way there's a record of every animal you harvest."

"That's the first I'm hearing about it," Glomb said.

"See where it says 'white-tailed deer log instructions'? That spells it all out for you."

"I never was much good at spelling."

"Just remember to cut out the dates and fill out the log."

"I don't see why we need a license to hunt on private property," Glomb said.

"That's a different conversation," Marlin said.

"I mean, I can drive my truck around this place without getting pulled over by a traffic cop," Glomb said.

"What's your point?"

"What makes a game warden so special?"

"Mostly my sparkling personality."

"You're a charming fella, I'll give you that. How tall are you?"

"Six four."

"And you look pretty solid for a guy your age. I bet that comes in handy when you're hassling hunters who aren't as laid-back as I am."

Yep, this guy was definitely drunk. Pretending to joke, but mouthing off just the same. Trying to be clever about it.

Marlin said, "Normally I just give a warning for these kinds of mistakes, but if you want me to bump it up to a citation…"

The man in the lawn chair let out a laugh and said, "Quit while you're behind, Ed."

Marlin's phone pinged with an incoming text.

Glomb said, "Hey, I'm just kidding around. You wanna stand here and watch me fill everything out the right way?"

He was being sarcastic, but Marlin said, "Absolutely."

While Glomb was grumbling and getting his license and tag straightened out, Marlin glanced at his phone.

He'd gotten a text from Sheriff Bobby Garza. *Give me a call when you get a minute.*

Five minutes later, after Glomb had his buck properly tagged, Marlin got back into his truck, and as he drove off the ranch, he called Garza.

"Did you happen to hear an explosion just before five o'clock?" Garza asked.

"I did, yeah, but I didn't hear any kind of follow-up on the radio. What's up?"

"That was over on Hidden Hills Ranch," Garza said. "A deer blind exploded, which makes no sense at all. Unfortunately, Lonnie Blair was in the blind at the time. He was DRT."

Cop lingo for *dead right there.*

Marlin was disappointed to hear that. Lonnie had always been a little rough around the edges, with a tendency to skirt hunting and fishing laws, and to chase women who weren't available, but he was a likable young man nonetheless.

"Any idea what happened?"

"At the moment, none whatsoever. Can you come to my office and talk for a minute?"

Red called Mandy, but she didn't answer, so he sent a text.
Got some interesting mail today.

He waited twenty minutes, but she didn't reply. So he sent another one.

Wanna guess what it was?

He realized he was playing the same silly game Billy Don had played with him earlier, but Red couldn't help it. He wanted to see what Mandy had to say for herself. But she still didn't reply.

"What's she saying?" Billy Don asked. He'd taken his regular spot on the couch, where the springs were so shot his knees were almost as high as his shoulders. Red was still in his recliner.

"Nothing yet."

"She's ducking you."

"No, she ain't."

Red sent a third text: *I bet this particular piece of mail is already hanging on refriggerators all over Blanco County.*

He studied the postcard more closely. By now, local tongues would be wagging—not just about the model, but about the new wellness retreat.

Billy Don said, "If it wasn't Mandy on that card, you'd be all for it. You'd be talking about how hot the model is, and saying she's got a couple of the nicest—"

"Why don't you grab us a couple of fresh beers?" Red said.

"You know I'm right," Billy Don said, but he extracted himself from the couch with a grunt and went into the kitchen.

Now Red remembered the name of the wellness dude. Drake. Seriously. Drake. Who names a kid Drake? It was almost like the parents were wanting him to grow up and be a douchebag.

Just then, Mandy replied: *What are you talking about?*

Red said: *You don't know?*

She said: *Know what?*

He said: *What do you think I'm talking about?*

She said: *No idea. Can we talk later?*

What the hell kind of answer was that? What was so important that she was putting him off?

So he got right down to it: *You seen that postcard your on?*

Yes, I've seen it, but I didn't know it had been mailed yet. What do you think?

So now she could talk? When it was about her, she could talk?

How come you didnt tell me its a nudist collony?

He wasn't sure he'd spelled all those words correctly because he'd turned off the spell-check feature a long time ago. He didn't like his phone bossing him around.

Are you drunk? she replied. *It's not a nudist colony.*

He wasn't drunk, but Billy Don returned just then with two Keystone tallboys, one of which he handed to Red. Red popped the top and drank about half of it in several big gulps.

Then he dialed Mandy's number again. She didn't answer, but she texted again instead.

Can't talk because I'm getting a facial at the retreat. Phones have to be silenced.

Why didn't you tell me about any of this? Red asked.

About my facial?

No the postcard.

I did tell you.

You never said you were gonna be naked.

I'm not naked.

I can see most of a boob and half of a butt cheek.

That's a long ways from naked. It's tasteful.

But they can see your face and everyone will know it's you.

So what? I'm proud of it.

So you knew they were gonna show all that?

Of course I did.

And you were okay with it?

Why wouldn't I be? You can see more than that anytime a girl wears a bikini.

He said: *Right under your picture it says they got a clothing optional area. How is that not a nudist colony?*

Quit being a drama queen. I'm turning my phone off now so I can enjoy myself. We'll talk later.

Red let out a growl of frustration. What the hell was it with women? Half the time they complained if you looked at their bodies, and the other half they put them on display. Make sense of that.

"What'd she say?" Billy Don asked.

"She said she understood why I was upset and she'd make it up to me later. She realizes now it probably wasn't a good idea."

"Uh-huh," Billy Don said.

Red took another long drink of beer and tried to settle down, but he was pissed. He was beginning to think he might need to have a talk with this Drake douchebag.

4

"By the time Ernie got there, Jimmy Lee had found some remains," Garza told Marlin in person thirty minutes later. "In several places. Ernie said he'd never seen anything quite like it. Once he realized it was an explosion, he backed out of there—taking Jimmy Lee with him—and called me."

Ernie Turpin had been the first deputy on the scene. He was intelligent and experienced; he would've known to be concerned about additional explosive devices on the scene. Some bombers used an initial explosion to draw first responders and curious bystanders to the scene, then used a second explosion to create as many casualties as possible. But those types of incidents didn't usually happen on ranches; they happened in cities.

"Was Lonnie Blair hunting alone?" Marlin asked.

"In that blind, yes, but Jimmy Lee was in a blind a couple hundred yards away. He's the one who called it in. He's pretty freaked out, which is understandable. Oh, one piece of good luck…as they were walking away from the scene, Ernie found Lonnie Blair's cell phone, about forty yards from the blind."

"In one piece?" Marlin asked.

They were seated in Garza's office with the door closed. The sheriff was a handsome guy, but the stress from this incident was already showing on his face.

"Believe it or not, yes. It had one of those super-tough cases around it. I haven't tried to power it on yet—not until I get a warrant."

"We're sure it was an explosion?" Marlin asked.

"I don't know what else it could've been."

"Any chance it was some kind of accident?"

"Jimmy Lee said Lonnie kept one of those small propane heaters in his blind, but there's no way it could've caused that amount of destruction. I guess there's a chance he might've taken a larger tank up there—like a barbecue-grill-sized tank—but why would he? Guess we'll know soon enough. The APD bomb squad will come out tomorrow morning to clear the scene, and then I've got an investigator coming from the Austin Fire Department."

Like most sparsely populated rural counties, Blanco County simply didn't have the resources to tackle this type of investigation without outside assistance. The AFD investigator would manage the collection and custody of evidence, coordinate any lab testing that might be required, and provide written reports to the sheriff.

"Who uses a bomb to kill some poor guy in a deer blind?" Marlin said. "If that's what happened."

Garza simply shook his head in reply.

Most bombings were acts of terrorism. Or a mob hit. Or some random nutjob, like the bomber in Austin a few years earlier. There had been five package bombings in the span of three weeks, killing two people and injuring five. More than five hundred FBI and BATF agents assisted the Austin Police Department with the massive investigation, and when the team eventually identified the suspect and pulled him over, he killed himself—with a bomb. A fitting end, some might say. His motive was never clear.

Garza said, "I hate to say it, but if this was somebody with a grudge against Lonnie Blair and this is the end of it, I guess we'll consider ourselves to be fortunate. I sure as hell don't want to hear about another bomb tomorrow, or next week."

"Did Jimmy Lee give you anything useful?"

"He told Ernie that somebody tried to run him and Lonnie off the road a few weeks ago on 1320."

"Does he know who it was?"

"Nope. Just a dark truck, probably a Chevy. Then a few days later Lonnie found a bullet hole in his trailer. Went in the front wall and out the back. He never heard the shot and neither did any of his neighbors.

But it's hunting season, and maybe it was just a stray. Lauren is interviewing Jimmy Lee right now, but after seeing what he saw, I don't know if he'll be able to focus."

Lauren Gilchrist was the chief deputy and a skilled interviewer, with an easygoing but persistent manner of questioning. She also happened to be one of Marlin's old flames from his college days. Fortunately, that hadn't caused any issues in their working or personal relationships. In fact, for quite some time now, Lauren had been casually dating Marlin's best friend, Phil Colby, whose ranch, coincidentally, was next door to Hidden Hills Ranch, where Lonnie Blair had been killed.

"You looking for some help on this?" Marlin asked, although this meeting had already given him the answer to that question.

Garza said, "You know all these hunters and ranchers better than my deputies do. You got time to nose around, now that deer season is almost over?"

Marlin always enjoyed helping the sheriff's office with larger investigations. As a fully commissioned peace officer, he was free to enforce any state law, not just those pertaining to hunting, fishing, and boating.

"I can make time," Marlin said. "You got anything specific for me in mind?"

"No, just do that unleashed maverick thing you do so well."

Marlin had to grin. "I'm an unleashed maverick?"

"You're a renegade. A rebel. A man who plays by his own rules. Go out and shake the bushes. Talk to some of Lonnie's friends, or talk to the ranch manager, or the neighbors, and see what you can dig up. You're always good at that. And just keep me and Lauren posted along the way, so we don't duplicate your efforts. Mostly Lauren, because I'm gonna be tied up getting ready for the budget planning sessions. What a pain in the butt. I used to actually fight crime."

"You still do."

"I'm trying. I'm not stepping away from this case, but Lauren will be the lead."

"Noted," Marlin said. "Let me know what the APD and AFD folks say tomorrow."

"Absolutely. Cross your fingers there's a simple explanation. We're working on warrants for the phone and Lonnie's trailer. I'll let you know if those go anywhere."

"I'm very sorry about Lonnie," Lauren Gilchrist said.

"I appreciate that. It was god-awful to see something like that. I've gutted my share of deer, and I've got a strong stomach, but that was terrible, knowing what I was looking at."

"I'm hoping you can answer some questions and we can figure out what happened."

"I'll do my best. Did someone blow him up or what? I mean, that couldn't have been an accident, right?"

"We've got some experts coming tomorrow to figure that out. Was Lonnie the type to mess around with explosives?"

"Not that I ever knew of."

"Any chance he might've been playing some kind of prank and it went wrong? Maybe he wanted to blow the blind up and make you think he'd died, but something went wrong."

"Nah, that wasn't Lonnie. He wasn't that kind of a jokester."

"Can you think of anyone who might've wanted to hurt him? Anyone with an ax to grind?"

Jimmy Lee let out a rueful laugh. "Did you know him?"

"We never met."

"He was one of a kind, and not everybody liked him."

"Why's that?"

"Okay if I'm blunt?"

"Absolutely."

"He was loud and obnoxious and basically a pussy hound. Pardon my language."

"Not a problem. You talk however you need to talk."

"He was always chasing women. Well, when he wasn't hunting, fishing, or working. I don't mean to be out of line, but if he was in a beer joint and saw a woman who looked like you? He'd be buying you beer, asking you to dance, telling you how nice you look—all that stuff. He came on strong, for sure."

"Did it usually work?"

"Plenty of times. He was a good-looking guy, and he was pretty smooth, so he could get away with almost anything. The problem was, he didn't really care if they were single or not."

"Meaning there might be some angry husbands out there?"

"And wives, too, for all I know. I know for sure there was one woman who swung both ways. Lonnie told me all about her."

"Any recent hook-ups?"

"The last one was a few weeks ago, the same night that truck tried to run us off the road. Or maybe he was just drunk."

Ernie had already filled Lauren in on that, although the details were sparse.

"Tell me about that night," Lauren said.

"We were at the dance hall in Albert and he started hitting on this cute blonde gal. They went out to his truck and, uh…" He hesitated.

"You're not going to embarrass me," Lauren said. "I've heard it all."

"I'm worried about embarrassing *me*. How much detail you want?"

"Everything you can tell me," Lauren said.

Jimmy Lee's face was turning red. "Okay, well, Lonnie said she gave him a blow job and then rode him in the driver's seat."

"Did you or Lonnie know her before that night?" Lauren asked.

"Never saw her before."

"What was her name?"

"I think it was Tracy. Pretty sure. Or Stacy."

"Any last name?"

Jimmy Lee laughed. "I'm sure she has one, but I don't know it."

"Who was she there with?"

"Some friends, but I didn't get a good look at 'em. Also, to be honest, I was pretty hammered. My memory is a little foggy."

"Female friends or male friends or both?"

"Two other gals. That's all I remember."

"No boyfriend or husband with her?"

"Nope."

"Did she seem like a regular at the dance hall?"

"I've got no idea. I never even talked to her."

"Think Lonnie would've gotten her phone number?"

"He wouldn't have asked for it, and if she gave it to him, he wouldn't have kept it."

"So he wasn't the type to see a woman twice?"

"That pretty much sums it up. He saw this one girl for a few months a year or so ago, but she split up with him, and he said he was done with that kind of situation."

"What was her name?"

"Jemma."

"You know her last name?"

"Sorry, I don't remember. She lives in Marble Falls."

"When Lonnie was seeing her, was he seeing *just* her?"

"Kinda."

Lauren grinned. "That's a pretty wishy-washy answer."

"I'm pretty sure Lonnie messed around behind her back, but he never admitted to it. Just some things I heard."

"Can you remember anyone ever threatening Lonnie?"

"He's definitely had a few close calls when we're out partying, but nothing I'd call threats. Besides, Lonnie wasn't a fighter. If some dude got really mad, we'd just leave, or he'd buy the guy a beer and try to smooth things over."

"Did he have any specific enemies?"

"Nobody I can think of."

"Do you think the person who tried to run you off the road had anything to do with this woman Tracy or Stacy?"

"I have no idea. I don't remember anything happening that night that would've made me think anybody had it out for Lonnie. Or me."

"You think that person might've shot the hole in Lonnie's trailer?"

"Again, no idea. Sorry. I have no idea who did that or if it was even intentional."

"Where did Lonnie work?"

"He runs his own fencing company. Ran, I mean. It was doing real good. He mostly did ranch fencing, not, like, residential. Miles and miles of ranch fence."

"He have any employees?"

"A couple of guys that worked on an hourly basis."

"Any problems with either of them?"

"Not that Lonnie ever mentioned. They're good workers."

"He paid them a fair wage?"

"I don't know the specifics, but Lonnie always knew the value of hard work. He played hard, but he worked hard, too. Long hours."

Lauren questioned Jimmy Lee for another full hour, exploring every possible avenue, but he didn't have much more to add.

"I'm going to need you to make a list of all the women you can think of that Lonnie hooked up with in the past year or two. If you have full names great, but if you can only remember first names, that's fine, too. Or just a description if you can't remember a name at all. And make some notes about where Lonnie met each one, how long ago it was—things like that. Can you do that for me?"

"Sure can, but I gotta warn you—that's gonna be a long list."

5

"If people was talking about Mandy on Facebook, would you wanna know?" Billy Don asked later that night, looking at his phone.

They'd moved from the trailer into the backyard, where they were seated around the fire pit. Several large cedar stumps popped and crackled and hissed with orange and blue flames. The heat felt good, considering it was about 35 degrees outside right now. Fortunately, the air was dry and there was no wind at all. The moon was rising bright and nearly full.

"Don't you see the problem with that question?" Red asked.

"No, but I bet you'll tell me."

"Just by the fact that you asked, I know people are talking about her on Facebook."

"Okay. Well, then, would you wanna know what they're *saying*?"

"Depends on who's saying what," Red said. "If it's somethin' dumb enough that I wanna track somebody down and knock his teeth in, then no. I ain't up for it right now. Just don't even tell me."

Billy Don didn't reply. Red looked at him. Billy Don shrugged.

Red said, "See, now it's the fact that you're *not* saying anything that gives me the answer."

"Mandy is a good-looking lady," Billy Don said. "You know it. I know it. Everybody knows it."

Red looked at him. "What's your point?"

"Ain't nothing wrong with a good-looking lady posing for a

postcard. Ain't like she's twirling around a pole for dollars. Not that there's anything wrong with that, either, come to think of it."

Red didn't say anything. He was irritated that he still hadn't heard back from Mandy after her facial.

"Think about all of them pictures Mandy sends to your phone," Billy Don said. "You never have a problem with that."

"Those are just for me!" Red said. "They don't show up in every mailbox in the county."

He got up and threw another stump on the fire.

Billy Don said, "Okay, then I want you to ponder a hypodermical situation. Let's say you got that postcard in the mail and you didn't even know Mandy. Then you happen to meet her in town, and you work up the nerve to ask her out, and she says yes, even though you're a skeevy old redneck. You wouldn't care about the postcard then, would ya? In fact, you'd be bragging about getting a date with the hottie on the postcard."

"I don't remember asking to have this conversation," Red said.

He drained the last of his beer and flung the empty can backward, onto the porch. This situation was already getting out of hand. People were talking about Mandy on Facebook? Of course they were. What else were they going to talk about in Johnson City? The latest city council meeting? Who got the biggest buck this season? Those things were boring in comparison to the postcard and the new wellness retreat.

Billy Don said, "They're talking about her on Facebook 'cause there's more pitchers of her on the website. For that wellness place. Four of them. I figured you'd wanna know."

Red was not happy to hear that.

"They show more or less than the one on the postcard?"

"I'd say about the same. Or maybe a little more. But there's one in particular you ain't gonna like because it's got some dude in it with her."

Red looked at Billy Don in the light from the fire to see if he was kidding. That was the kind of joke he'd make to jerk Red's chain real good. But Red could tell that Billy Don was serious.

"I'm not worried about it," Red said. "Probably just some model, and most of those guys are gay, anyway."

"No, under the picture it said it was the owner guy," Billy Don said. "I can't remember his name."

"Drake?" Red asked.

"Yeah, that's it. He looks like a model, though."

"Who does? Drake?"

"Who else are we talking about?"

"He looks like a model?"

"Yeah, like one of them underwear models. He's got a serious six-pack, and I'm not talking Keystone Light."

Marlin grilled some chicken that night, then called Phil Colby after he and Nicole had eaten.

"Well, looky here, it's my long-lost friend, finally finding the time to call me," Phil said.

"I deserve that. How've you been?"

"Oh, I'm not done chastising you yet."

"In my defense, you know what time of year it is? Have you been hearing shots lately? Have you seen any of those animals with antlers on their heads?"

"Yeah, yeah, it's deer season, so you've been busy."

"Next time, just poach a ten-point. Then I'll come see you right away," Marlin said.

"How do you know I didn't?"

"Good point."

Marlin was on the couch in the living room with the TV volume down. He could hear Nicole in the kitchen, loading the dishwasher. Geist, the pit bull, was curled in a tight ball on the floor, enjoying the warmth from the fireplace.

"I bet you're calling about Lonnie Blair," Phil said.

"As a matter of fact…"

"I heard the explosion," Phil said. "I was putting a new starter in my truck. I didn't think much of it, and then I heard what happened."

"How did you hear?"

"Alford Richter called me. He said Carissa had heard about it online, so he called the sheriff's office, but they wouldn't tell him much. They probably didn't know much at the time. Of course, neither did I. Still don't."

Alford and Carissa Richter's ranch was two tracts over from Phil to the east. Between them was Hidden Hills Ranch, where Lonnie Blair had died. But Phil actually shared a fenceline with the Richters, too, because their ranch was shaped like an L, and a small portion of their land extended along the rear property line of both Hidden Hills Ranch and Phil's place.

"None of us do," Marlin said. "We'll know more tomorrow."

"Meaning the public, too, or just you special law-enforcement types?"

"That I can't tell you. Guess it depends on what they find. Some of it they might hold back. Hell, they might not even tell me."

"But Lonnie was blown up?"

"That's what it looks like, but we don't know the source of the explosion."

"We got a mad bomber running around?"

"Sure hope not. Got no reason to think that right now."

"But you got no reason to think there *isn't*?"

"What're you, a reporter?"

"Think Lonnie was targeted?"

"Don't know yet."

"Lonnie was a player, but you already know that. You should be looking at angry husbands, boyfriends, dads, uncles—hell, anyone with a woman that Lonnie might've, uh, spent some time with. Or maybe a woman did it. You never know."

"You thinking of anyone specific?"

"Not really, but there's bound to be some pissed-off people when you throw a guy like Lonnie into the mix. Oh, and then there's Mason Cross—the Richters' new foreman. Newish. They hired him about six months ago. Met him yet?"

"Nope. I dropped in there right before deer season to introduce myself, but he wasn't around. I left a note saying he could call me if he had any problem with poachers—or anything else. Never heard from him."

"Doesn't surprise me. He isn't what you'd call the gregarious type. I had a little chat with him in November, right after the season started, and it didn't go well."

"What happened?"

"He didn't like the location of one of my blinds, so he asked me to move it."

"Which blind?" Marlin knew every inch of that ranch, and he'd hunted in every blind hundreds of times, going back to his childhood.

"Deep Draw," Phil said.

That blind was at least a hundred yards from the fenceline, and the window facing the Richter place was nailed shut, so nobody could shoot in that direction.

"What was the problem?" Marlin asked.

"There wasn't one, but he said where he comes from, if the neighbor can see the blind, it's too close to the fence. It wasn't like a friendly request, either. He was a jerk from the word go—like he was trying to start something."

"So what did you do?" Marlin asked.

"Nothing, at first, because hell if I was gonna move a blind just to please him. But then I came back the next morning and found a bullet hole through the back wall and out the front, meaning it came from the Richter property."

Marlin recalled that somebody had fired a bullet through Lonnie Blair's trailer—possibly a warning of some kind. Seemed like a similar situation here, but Marlin kept that theory to himself for the time being.

"Why didn't you call me?" he asked.

"Because I'm a hardheaded son of a bitch," Phil said, laughing.

"No argument there."

"But what could you have done, really? He'd just deny it."

"At least he would've known it was on the record," Marlin said. "And there's always the possibility somebody else might've fired that shot. Maybe he could've helped me figure out who it was."

"Okay, true, but that doesn't seem very likely."

"Either way, it would've been good for me to ask him about it."

"I hear ya. Anyway, the next time I saw him, I told him I'd move the blind—because other people hunted there, not just me, and I didn't want anybody getting hurt on my account. But I told him if I found out he fired that bullet, I was gonna kick his ass for a week."

Marlin didn't have to ask if Phil had really said that. He knew from decades of friendship that Phil never embellished or exaggerated this type of story. Plus, Phil had a short temper and was known, in times of anger, to say exactly what was on his mind, unfiltered, and with little concern for consequences. Marlin had seen it firsthand many times.

"What did Mason Cross say?"

"Not much. Oh, and I told him I'd do it with one hand tied behind my back, to keep it fair. I meant that literally, because there's something else you need to know about Mason Cross, if you don't know already."

"Which is what?"

6

Two months into his relationship with Marge Slubb—just as Graham Smith was about to raise the possibility of an exciting new investment opportunity—she had a stroke. Or maybe it was an aneurysm. Or were they the same thing? He supposed he should care about the difference, but he really didn't.

That was because, as he had known from an early age, he wasn't "normal." Not in the way most people used that word. He never had been. He was missing the portion of his psychological makeup that would cause shame. That absence allowed him to behave as he did, without any remorse whatsoever. No regrets. Ever. Didn't matter what he did.

He also never understood why anyone would consider it wrong to take something from someone who has more than enough. If you steal one dollar from a man who has a thousand, is that wrong? Even better, what if that person gives it to you willingly? What if that person *wants* you to have it? Does it matter what you told them to make them feel that way? Why on earth would it? They *gave* it to you just the same.

Take the elderly women he dated. After he made sure each relationship was on solid footing, he would begin to tell them things designed to invoke compassion or even pity. Make them think he had suffered a tremendous financial blow. Maybe describe how he had been suckered in some kind of shady investment scheme, and now he was in danger of losing his house. Silly old Graham. He felt so stupid, but he had always been the trusting type. He might end up homeless if he didn't figure something out.

A few years after Marge Slubb, there was one woman in particular—Lorene Spatch—who practically insisted that Graham let her cover his loss. She had inherited ninety million dollars at the age of sixteen and had nearly doubled it by the age of seventy. Of course, simply investing it in a decent index fund would've doubled it in about seven years, during a decent run of the market.

Lorene heard his sob story and immediately offered to help. He resisted. She pushed harder. He had to pretend it was out of the question. Besides, he would feel indebted to her, and he feared that would sully their relationship.

"Absolutely no strings attached!" Lorene said. "In fact, after you take it, I don't want to hear a single word about it."

"That's…that's truly selfless of you," Graham said, and he even managed to make his eyes moisten. "That sort of kindness and generosity is amazingly rare."

Lorene said, "When you get to be my age, you'll understand that money isn't really all that important. But if I can do this—if I can restore your faith in your fellow human beings—*that's* making a difference. That means I'm really leaving a mark on the world."

Mark. Hilarious. The perfect word choice. She was definitely a mark. An easy mark, for sure.

So he took the money. Of course he took the money. That was the point. One hundred thousand dollars. He had been hoping Lorene would offer even more, but that was the amount she came up with, and Graham wasn't dumb enough to push it.

Three weeks later, there was a knock on his door. A man roughly Graham's age was standing on his front steps. Big guy. Short brown hair. Broad shoulders. Graham wasn't expecting anybody.

"May I help you?"

"I'm Sid Spatch. We need to talk."

Lorene's son. She'd mentioned him many times. He lived in Seattle, and as far as Graham knew, Lorene hadn't been expecting him in town anytime soon. But Mother's Day was coming up, so maybe that explained it.

Graham gave Sid his warmest smile. Sid didn't smile back, but he did shake Graham's offered hand, as he was sizing him up and down.

"Come on in," Graham said, swinging the door wide. "It's really great to meet you, although I'll admit it's a bit of a surprise. Lorene didn't say you were coming to town."

"She doesn't know I'm here," Sid said. "I came down to talk to you, face to face."

Uh-oh. There was no possible scenario in which this was a good development.

Graham closed the door.

"Would you like something to drink? Coke? Cold beer? Whiskey?"

"Nothing."

"Let me get you a beer. You look thirsty. Hell, I could use one. Hang on a sec."

Graham went into the kitchen and came back with two beers in ice-cold bottles and handed one to Sid.

"It's really great to meet you," Graham said. "Your mom has told me all about you."

Namely that Sid was a loving son, but he didn't have his father's business skills. Not even close. Sid had lost a lot of money over the years. Lorene kept him afloat. She always spoke about Sid with a certain reservation, if not quite disappointment. He hadn't lived up to the family name.

"How old are you?" Sid asked.

"I'm sorry?"

"How. Old. Are. You."

He wasn't even pretending to be friendly.

"Why do you ask?"

"I know how old you are. I checked. I'm three years older than you are, and my mom had me when she was thirty-seven. That means she's old enough to be your grandmother."

"I afraid I don't see the point you're making."

"Any way you look at it, that's weird."

"I understand your concern. I really do. But I want to assure you that—"

"What did you do with the money?"

This was getting worse by the minute. Sid knew about the money.

"I realize it doesn't look good from your perspective," Graham said.

"You kidding? It looks like you're preying on a lonely old lady."

Sid's voice was rising. He was several inches taller than Graham, and probably forty pounds heavier. Was he planning to get physical?

"I assure you I'm not doing anything remotely—"

"You took *money* from her," Sid said. "Yes or no? I want to hear you admit it."

"I did, yes. That's not *admitting* anything."

"What kind of person does that?"

"She insisted. I honestly begged her not to give—"

"Is that a joke? She *made* you take it. Is that what you're saying? She *forced* the money on you?"

"It would be nice if you'd stop interrupting and just let me answer your questions. I mean, if you came down here to talk to me, why not let me talk?"

"Okay, then talk. Explain yourself. Why are you dating a woman forty years older than you are—who just happens to be wealthy? You telling me you're sincerely interested in her?"

"Absolutely. Of course I am. She's a wonderful woman. Surely you agree."

"And that's what it's about for you. Nothing else. Certainly not the money."

"It's true, but I realize how it looks. I don't blame you for thinking otherwise. If you knew me, you'd know—"

"That you're a con artist," Sid said.

Graham realized by now that he wasn't going to be able to smooth this over. Sid wasn't going to buy any of his excuses.

"I think you should probably leave now," Graham said.

Sid set his beer bottle on the coffee table. Without a coaster.

"Or what?" he asked.

"You'll wish you had."

Graham had trained for situations like this one. Not a lot, but enough to handle a guy like Sid Spatch. The size difference wouldn't matter.

Sid said, "As tempting as it might be to kick your ass, that's not why I'm here. Instead I'm gonna tell you what I could do next. For starters, I could get the cops involved. Tell 'em you conned my mother out of a hundred thou. She's a little confused half the time, and you took advantage of that. And once they start digging around in all your finances, I'm sure they're gonna find all kinds of great shit. Like the emails you sent to my mom, where you explained that she didn't have to declare the money as a gift and pay the taxes, because you were gonna make it look like an investment on her behalf. Yeah, it was sort of a wink-wink between you two—a tax dodge—but do you think they're gonna give her any heat for that? Hell, no. That's all gonna fall on you. And once they have access to all of your records, what else are they gonna find? How many other women have you ripped off? They're gonna tear you wide open and—"

"Okay," Graham said. "I get it. You want me to give your mother the money back."

"Nope. I want you to give it to me. In cash."

Graham looked at him for a long, knowing moment.

"What?" Sid asked.

"Bullshit."

"Bullshit what?"

"You're taking the money for yourself."

"It's my mother's money, and that makes it my money."

"Right. Try that one on the cops."

"If you give it back to her, I'll have to explain that you're a con artist, and that'll break her heart."

"Sort of like it would break her heart if she knew what you were doing today?"

"Look, you little fucker. You don't have a choice. Either you give me the money or I call the cops. Better yet, I might go straight to the FBI. You realize they got a web page specifically about elder fraud, complete with phone numbers for all the field offices in the state? They call what you did a 'romance scam.' They *want* to find scum like you. And if they jump in, that makes it federal, my friend. Talk about an endless nightmare. They'll plant their teeth in you and never let go. Even if you finally get away with it, it'll take ten years and you won't have a penny left. You're gonna need a goddamn *team* of lawyers. And after they're done, you'll be on their radar for the rest of your miserable life. Have fun with that."

It was a brilliant con, really. In fact, it was nearly flawless. Sid Spatch would be stealing from someone who wouldn't report it. He didn't really care about his mother. He just wanted her money.

"Or I can avoid the unpleasantness by giving the money to you."

"Yup. You give the money to me."

"I'd say splitting it is fair," Graham said.

"Ain't gonna happen. You need to let that delusion go. You're lucky I don't ask for more."

Graham saw no easy way out of this mess. Not without losing all that money, which wasn't acceptable.

Maybe it was time to do something a little more drastic. Maybe it was time to take the money and start fresh somewhere far away.

7

The morning after Lonnie Blair's blind exploded, a Texas Tech freshman named Justin and his girlfriend Claire were traveling from Austin back to Lubbock when the engine in his Audi Quattro began to make an odd clattering sound. Just great. One of his dashboard warning lights had turned on several days ago, followed by a second one yesterday, and he'd been meaning to check into it, but he hadn't had the time. Maybe he could make it to a repair shop.

Right now, they were following a small county road that would take them to Johnson City. Claire had insisted they go this way because it was such a pretty drive. Justin wasn't much into pretty drives, but he loved driving his car fast on winding back roads, so he readily agreed. Now he was regretting it. Better to be on the highway if they had car trouble.

"What is that noise?" Claire asked.

If *she* noticed it, that meant it was getting bad. Now it was banging.

"I think the oil is low or something. I'd better pull over."

"Where?"

The road was narrow in this particular stretch, with no shoulder, so Justin pulled into the first available spot, a gated ranch entrance, and called AAA. They were waiting for roadside assistance when an aging Chevy truck approached slowly on the other side of the ranch gate.

"Oh, great," Claire said. "He can't get around us, Justin. We're blocking him in."

Her mood always went south fast when problems cropped up.

"There's not much I can do about it, Claire."

"Well, why did you park here, Justin?"

"What was I supposed to do, Claire—just leave it in the road?"

Each of them had the habit of saying the other person's name with dripping condescension whenever they argued.

"Maybe you should've checked the oil before we left, Justin," Claire said. "Don't you know anything about cars?"

"More than you do, Claire," Justin said. "There's probably a leak or something."

The Chevy came to a stop on the other side of the gate, and the man driving emerged from the truck.

"Well, why don't you get out and look under the hood, Justin?" Claire said.

Justin did get out, but it was to speak to the man, who appeared to be in his forties. He was wearing a feed-store cap, a denim shirt, blue jeans, and work boots. Every item was faded and stained. He reminded Justin of the oilfield workers he encountered in Lubbock. Some were friendly enough, but with others, you were wise to steer clear. Justin's dad warned him to stay out of the roughneck bars.

"Morning," Justin called, with his left hand resting on his open car door. "Sorry about this. My car broke down."

"It ran out of oil, Justin," Claire said from the passenger seat. "It didn't break down. If you'd checked it before we left..."

Justin leaned into the car. "Can you be quiet for just a minute and let me take care of this, Claire?"

She crossed her arms and pouted, but at least she shut up.

Justin turned his attention back to the man beside the Chevy. "I didn't want to stop in the road, so I pulled in here," Justin said. "Triple A is on the way."

He was hoping the man would be friendly and willing to help—or at least not be a dick about the situation—but the man was simply staring.

"You don't happen to have any oil, do you?" Justin asked. "Maybe I could add some and that would help."

He had never checked the oil level in any vehicle before, but how hard could it be?

The man stared a moment longer. Then he said, "Move it."

"Pardon?"

"Move your car."

His voice was deep and raspy.

"I can't," Justin said. "Because it—"

"You can't leave it there," the man said. "You're on private property."

"I'm outside the fence."

"It don't matter. You're on private property."

"Okay, but if you need to get past me, you might be able to squeeze by without—"

"I don't need to get out," the man said.

Justin was confused. "Then, uh, why do I need to move? We won't be here long."

The man walked toward the gate, and as he got closer, Justin noticed three things about him. First, the right side of his face was scarred, perhaps from a burn from several years earlier. Second, he was missing several fingers on his right hand. And third, he had a revolver holstered on his left hip.

"You got some kind of hearing problem?" the man asked.

Uh-oh. This was getting ugly fast. But why?

"No, sir. I just—"

"You comprehend the English language?"

"Yes, sir."

"Then move your fucking car."

"Wow," Claire said.

Justin was getting nervous. "But there's nowhere to pull over, and my engine was making all kinds of—"

"Ain't my problem," the man said. "You move that car or I'll come move it for you. You follow what I'm saying?"

"Justin," Claire said in a sing-song voice, and her tone was saying *Let's get out of here before this psycho kills us and dismembers our bodies.*

Justin got into the Audi, closed the door, and started it up.

The man stayed where he was, glaring.

"What is wrong with that jerk?" Justin muttered. He started his car and quickly backed onto the county road, then proceeded north, frantically searching for a better place to park.

They'd gone no more than sixty yards when the engine made the worst sound yet and stopped running.

"Transform your soul and rejuvenate your spirit. What does that even mean? You got a soul or a spirit, Red?"

"I got a pit full of snakes and broken glass. Does that count?"

"Realize your full potential and—"

"Would you stop looking at that website?" Red said. "You got some kinda obsession?"

"I can't figure out if this guy Drake is some kinda new-age hippie or a total bullshit artist."

"Seeing as how he talked Mandy into taking her clothes off in front of a camera, I figger it's the second one."

"Yeah, but she—"

"Just move on, Billy Don. Or I'm gonna pull over and dump you out."

It was ten o'clock and they were in Red's truck, heading toward a potential job site outside Round Mountain. The landowner wanted a bid to clear cedar trees off three hundred acres, so the first step was seeing just how overgrown the place was. Turn your head for a couple of years and the damn cedars would take over. Choke out all the good trees and suck up all the water. If the ranch was totally covered with cedars, that could be several months' worth of work.

"So have you talked to Mandy yet?" Billy Don asked.

"Nope."

"Not even by text?"

"Nope."

"She's ghosting you?"

"She's what?"

"Ghosting you. It means when someone stops talking to you out of the blue. No texts or calls or Facebook messages."

Red had never heard that phrase before. "I know what it means," he said.

"Then why'd you ask?"

"I didn't hear what you said."

"I said why'd you ask?"

"No, I mean earlier."

"Well, it sounds like she's ghosting you."

"I don't know what she's doing. Don't really care."

"Right," Billy Don said, but he was being sarcastic as hell.

"She can do whatever she wants," Red said. "She's a grown woman. Same here."

"You're a grown woman?"

"No, I mean I can do whatever I want, and there's plenty of other women out there."

"Not many that will put up with you," Billy Don said. "Plus, she's sweet and funny and kind of a hoot. The more I think about it, the more I wonder why she's slumming with you."

Red turned left on Ranch Road 962 and headed west. When he was a kid, this was a great road for poaching deer with a spotlight, all the way to Highway 71, or maybe turn on 3347 and head toward Willow City. Nowadays, well, there weren't *any* good roads for spotlighting. Too many people ready to call the game warden, instead of minding their own business. What the hell was the world coming to?

"You still got the ring?" Billy Don asked.

"What ring?" Red said, knowing full well what Billy Don meant.

Not that long ago, a hitchhiker named Garrett—who may or may not have shot and killed a mafia hit man at a zoo south of Blanco—had given Red a diamond ring he'd found on the side of a highway. That was Garrett's way of paying for the damage he'd caused by firing two bullets into Red's truck after an argument. Red took it, of course, and it hadn't taken him long to start wondering if he should give the ring to Mandy. Not just give it to her, but get down on a knee and ask that one particular question.

"You know damn well what ring," Billy Don said.

"The one you left around the bathtub?"

Billy Don grunted.

"Maybe that isn't such a great idea anyway," Red said.

"What isn't?"

"Giving Mandy that ring."

Billy Don didn't offer his opinion.

"Hell, if she's ghosting me, why would I give her a diamond ring?" Red added.

Then there were the photos, of course. He'd finally broken down and looked at the ones on the wellness center website, and he'd just about come unglued. Mandy looked like she could be on the cover of *Playboy*, if they still printed it, and the only reason she wouldn't be on the inside pages was because none of the pictures quite showed everything. There was always an arm or a leg positioned in such a way as to cover up the best parts.

Then there was the one with Drake. He was facing the camera, trying to look all sexy with his stomach flat and rippled. Mandy was right beside him, standing sideways to the camera, with one of her boobs smooshed up against Drake's bicep. Bet he enjoyed the hell out of that. You could only see Drake and Mandy from the waist up, so there was no telling if they were both completely naked.

To be honest, the photo looked like one of those cheesy romance book covers with some shirtless dude—like a blacksmith or a pirate or a cowboy—and a woman who just can't keep her hands off of him. Mandy would read one of those books now and then, and one time Red had a peek inside to see what it was all about. What he found was basically porn, but in words instead of pictures. Red couldn't read more than a few pages without shaking his head about how silly it was, and then reading a few more pages to see if it continued to be as silly, which it always did, so he would read a few more pages. Okay, sure, some of these authors could paint a pretty good picture, with all kinds of body parts "throbbing" and "heaving" and "pulsating," but ultimately Red couldn't read more than three or four chapters at a time.

Red took a left on Smith West Ranch Road, which was another great drive—a narrow little road with wide-open ranchland on either side. Lots of low-water crossings and cattle guards. It had probably been five or six years since Red had driven this stretch, and that was a shame. When he was younger, he used to ramble all over the county, poaching or partying or just driving. Where had those years gone?

"Whoa," Billy Don said, looking at his phone again.

Jesus, what now? Red figured Billy Don was reading something else about Mandy, or finding more photos, but either way, Red didn't want to hear about it.

"This is crazy," Billy Don said.

Red wasn't going to take the bait.

"Can't believe we're just now hearing about this," Billy Don said.

Red *really* wanted to tell Billy Don to shut the hell up, but he managed to hold his tongue.

"You know Jimmy Lee?" Billy Don asked.

"Jimmy Lee Standifer or Jimmy Lee Jackson?" Red asked.

"Jimmy Lee Jackson."

"Yeah, I know him."

"Then you probably know Lonnie Blair."

"Of course I know Lonnie Blair. He's an asshole."

"Well, he's a dead asshole now."

"Lonnie Blair is?"

"Yup."

"What happened?"

"Somebody blowed him up."

Red looked at him. "What're you talking about? Blowed him up how?"

"It don't say how. He was sitting in his deer blind yesterday afternoon, minding his own bidness, and it blew up. Hey, you 'member we heard that explosion? You figure that was it?"

"Maybe so. Jesus."

"I know, right?" Billy Don said, which was another expression he'd picked up online. "Getting blowed up is almost as bad as having your girlfriend nekkid on a postcard."

8

John Marlin pulled through the gate of the Richters' ranch at eleven-fifteen and followed the winding driveway through the gorgeous property, which had at least a mile of frontage on Miller Creek. Marlin could remember when this place was a working cattle ranch operating under a different owner, and that family lived in a small house close to the county road. Nothing fancy. Ranching was a hard life that didn't pay much. Drought years could be brutal.

Then, maybe fifteen years ago, the parents passed away and their children had no further interest in the ranch. They sold the property to a man in Houston who never set foot on the place once, as far as Marlin knew, and then that man sold to the Richters three years ago.

The Richters built a large modern home on a creekside bluff, with a remarkable view to the west. Alford Richter was an award-winning architect, and it showed. The design was sleek and contemporary; enormous limestone rectangles formed the walls on the first floor, whereas the second floor was almost entirely glass. An area around the house—perhaps an acre—had been fenced off and landscaped impeccably, with a rectangular pool in the backyard.

Marlin had been to the house once before to introduce himself to the Richters and ask them if they planned to allow hunting on their ranch, but he didn't expect them to remember him now. So he was surprised when Alford Richter opened the door with a smile and said, "John Marlin. Good to see you again."

Alford led him through the house to a den, where Carissa Richter was waiting. She also greeted Marlin warmly, and they sat in matching upholstered chairs around a square coffee table.

Last night on the phone to Alford, Marlin had said he wanted to speak to them about a hunting incident on a neighboring ranch. He'd kept it vague. For the time being, he didn't want anyone, including the Richters, to know he was working on the Lonnie Blair case. Phil Colby's run-in with the Richters' foreman gave Marlin a good excuse to arrange this meeting and try to get more information about Mason Cross.

The Richters—both in their forties—were dressed in casual but stylish clothes. He was tall and slender, with short black hair and a goatee, neither of which showed any traces of gray. She was average height, with long strawberry blonde hair and large green eyes.

After some small talk, Marlin said, "I wanted to talk to you about something that happened a couple of months ago, but I only heard about it recently. I believe you know your neighbor, Phil Colby."

"You bet," Alford said. "We've stopped and chatted on the road a couple of times. Seems like a great guy."

"You're right. He happens to be my best friend. I've known him since we were kids."

"Is that right?" Alford said.

"We've been meaning to have him over, but we've just never gotten around to it," Carissa added. "Plus his girlfriend, the deputy. I've forgotten her name."

"Lauren," Marlin said.

"Right," Carissa said. "I like her. It was kind of funny—she pulled me over once when I was leaving the wellness center. She was coming from my left, and I simply didn't see her, so I pulled out right in front of her. But she didn't even write me a ticket, and before we were done talking, we'd decided we should grab lunch sometime. I need to get on that. Actually, I need to invite her out to the center."

"We're partners in the new wellness center," Alford explained. "We believe strongly in taking charge of one's own health. Being proactive. I mean, sure, it's important to have a good health care team, but ultimately, you have to take care of yourself."

"We think this kind of wellness center is going to play a big role in health care in the coming years," Carissa said.

Marlin thought both of them sounded like they were repeating text from a membership brochure.

He said, "That's interesting. I hope it all goes well for you."

"But back to Phil Colby," Alford said, grinning. "Carissa and I tend to ramble, but you obviously have something you want to discuss."

"I do. Right after deer season started, Phil found a bullet hole through his deer blind—in one side and out the other."

"Jeez," Alford said. "That's careless on somebody's part."

"Absolutely. So I'm just trying to determine where that bullet might have come from. Phil sent me some photos, and I could tell which direction the bullet was traveling from the way the wood was splintered."

"Which direction did it come from?" Carissa asked.

"It was traveling from north to south," Marlin said.

It was obvious from their expressions that they were going to need more information.

"It came from the direction of this ranch," Marlin said. "Specifically the portion that runs behind Hidden Hills Ranch and then Phil's place."

"This news concerns me," Alford said.

"So you think it came from our property?" Carissa asked Marlin.

"Right now, I can only say it came from this direction."

"Couldn't it have come from someplace even farther north?" Alford asked.

"Honestly, I can't be sure, but since there were holes on both sides of the blind, I could judge the trajectory, which was fairly flat, and since both ranches are fairly wooded, I'd say the bullet didn't fly far, meaning no more than several hundred yards. Probably four or five hundred at the most, but that's just a guess. In other words, I don't think it traveled from, say, a mile away, because the trajectory would've been much different."

"We do have hunters on our place," Alford said. "You probably already know we lease it out. It never occurred to me that one of them might fire a weapon that irresponsibly—if it was one of them. I hate to think of the potential liability involved—and the safety concern, of course. Somebody could've been killed."

"How many hunters on your lease?" Marlin asked.

"I believe it's four. Mason handles all that. He could give you their names and contact information. I've never met any of them."

"Do either of you hunt?" Marlin asked.

Carissa laughed.

Alford was grinning when he said, "We find it a lot easier to buy meat at the store. Honestly, I hunted one time when I was a teenager, but it wasn't for me. We both like to shoot, but we don't like to kill things."

"Where do you shoot?" Marlin asked.

"We have a range at the back of the ranch, but it's nowhere near the property line with Phil Colby," Alford said. "It's a very safe set-up, with berms all around."

"People underestimate the therapeutic value of going out and shooting a bunch of rounds," Marlin said, to keep this part of the conversation going.

"Oh, I totally agree," Carissa Richter said. "It's great for stress."

"You prefer handguns or rifles?" Marlin asked.

"Both," Carissa said. "Although there's something about making a long shot that's more rewarding. You should come out and shoot with us sometime."

"Does anyone else hunt or shoot out here?"

"We've told Mason he can hunt, but I don't know if he has," Alford said. "He sort of does his own thing, and that's the way we want it. We go days at a time without talking to him. He takes care of basically everything on the ranch—from the cattle to the fences to clearing cedar and maintaining the roads—and so far, he seems to be doing a good job."

"And he takes care of my horses," Carissa added. "I have two. He didn't know much about horses, but he's a fast learner."

"How long has he worked for you?"

"Since last summer."

"Would you say you know him well?"

"Not really," Alford said. "He's a quiet guy. Sort of, uh…"

"Taciturn," Carissa said. "Bordering on unfriendly, but I think that's just his way. He doesn't mean anything by it."

"The only person I've ever seen him warm up to is Carissa," Alford said.

"Well, I think 'warmed up' might be a stretch," Carissa said with a laugh, "but I'm patient with him and respect his boundaries, and I think he appreciates that."

"If Mason knew who fired that shot, do you think he would tell anybody?" Marlin asked.

"I would certainly hope so," Alford said. "But if your friend Phil never told anybody about it until now, Mason wouldn't know it had happened, would he?"

"Well, it turns out they did have a discussion about it back then. Did Mason mention that?"

"He never said anything to us about it," Alford said. "When was this exactly?"

"Mid-November."

"So Mason had been working here for just a few months at that point. What exactly did their conversation entail? Did Phil tell Mason he thought the bullet had come from our place?"

"Let me give you the backstory first," Marlin said. "Mason asked Phil to move one of his deer blinds because he felt it was too close to the property line. That particular blind is roughly a hundred yards from the fence, so Phil was a little puzzled, and he politely refused."

"Hmm," Alford said. "I don't really know much about deer-hunting etiquette, I guess you'd call it. Was Mason's request out of line?"

"Most hunters would agree that a hundred yards from a fenceline is plenty, especially here in central Texas, where most properties are fairly wooded and rolling. Phil also pointed out that the window facing your ranch was nailed shut, so nobody could shoot in that direction. Any hunter in that blind would never even be looking this way."

"How did Mason respond to that?"

"Phil said he was kind of argumentative. The next morning, Phil found the hole in the blind."

"Oh. That doesn't look good." Alford said.

"Just to be clear, are you saying you think Mason might've done it?" Carissa asked.

"Right now, I'm just trying to figure it out. Mason might not know anything about it."

"When Phil Colby talked to Mason about the bullet hole, did he deny doing it?" Alford asked.

"He did, yes."

"I wish he had mentioned this to us at some point," Alford said. "Just so you know, we ran a criminal background check on Mason before we hired him, and he didn't have a record. So if he did anything illegal, it's probably the first time."

Marlin didn't point out that Alford's assumption was incredibly naïve.

"In case you're wondering, Phil did move that blind," Marlin said. "After he found the bullet hole, he decided it would be best to move it."

"I can understand why," Alford said, "but I hate to think he might be angry with us over here. How come he never told you about it until now?"

"He likes to handle things himself."

"I'd say Mason is cut from the same cloth, from what I can tell," Alford said.

Marlin had saved the most important line of questioning for last.

"I understand Mason is missing three fingers," he said casually.

Alford said, "Yes, and I'll be honest—at first we were hesitant to hire him because of that. I mean, let's be realistic—ranch work isn't easy with two hands, much less a limitation like that. But we talked to his former employer, and she said she'd never had a harder worker."

"Why did Mason leave that job?"

"Her son moved back home and basically took over Mason's job," Alford said.

"Where was that ranch located?"

"South Texas, down near Laredo."

"Do you know how long he worked there?"

"I recall that it was about ten years."

"Any idea how he lost his fingers?"

"All I can gather is that it was some kind of accident or injury from his time in the military. You can tell he doesn't like to talk about it."

Carissa grinned. "Like I said earlier, he doesn't like to talk about anything. I once had a gardener who was way too chatty, and I have to say I prefer Mason over that."

"When did he serve?" Marlin asked.

"I'm not sure," Alford said. "I assume it must've been at least fifteen or twenty years ago, considering his age."

"How old is he? Do you know?"

"I'd guess 45 or so."

"I think he's closer to 40," Carissa said.

"Any idea where he is right now?" Marlin asked.

"I think he went out for some supplies," Alford said. "A couple of days ago, he mentioned that the metal roof on his house needed some work, and I think he was going to town today for those materials."

"Okay, then, if you'll give me his number, I'll get together with him later and have a chat. I'm going to ask that you not talk to him about our conversation. Right now, I'm just gathering the facts, and that might be the end of it. Let's not make this a bigger deal than it is. Phil wants to keep it all neighborly."

"That's good to hear," Alford said. "I knew I was right about him."

"You mind if I drive to the back of your ranch for a few minutes?" Marlin asked.

"No problem, but what for?"

"I'd like to look for evidence of trespassers, just in case somebody else was back there. Maybe Mason and your hunters had nothing to do with that bullet hole at all."

"Absolutely," Alford said. "Look around all you want. We want you to find out exactly what happened. While we're at it, let me give you the gate code. You should feel free to come on out anytime."

"I appreciate that," Marlin said.

He was moving toward the door when Carissa said, "Have you heard anything about that bizarre incident on Hidden Hills Ranch? That poor hunter who died yesterday afternoon? You know, I heard that explosion all the way up here at the house."

"I haven't heard much on that yet," Marlin said.

"Carissa called me at the wellness center and told me what happened," Alford said. "Some kind of freak accident?"

"We just don't know," Marlin said. "Investigators might be in touch to ask you some questions about that. His name was Lonnie Blair. Did either of you know him?"

"I'm afraid not," Carissa said.

"We haven't met as many people around here as we'd like," Alford said. "But we'll certainly help if we can."

9

Alford Richter peered through one of the living room blinds as the game warden walked out to his truck, got inside, and drove away.

Alford turned to face Carissa, who was doing her best to appear unconcerned.

"Well, that's not good," Alford said.

"He was only here about the deer blind," Carissa said.

"Well, sweetie, if you believe that, you're sort of blind yourself. All that stuff was just cover. A good excuse for him to poke around without tipping us off."

"Okay, but even if that's true, it doesn't matter."

Alford crossed his arms and stared at her.

"I didn't kill Lonnie Blair," she said. "And I don't know who did." He didn't say anything.

"For God's sake, you believe me, don't you?" she asked.

"Yes, but you've certainly surprised me before."

"I've made some mistakes, okay? I acknowledge that. You've made mistakes, too. But I thought we were trying for a fresh start. That would include you not speaking to me that way, wouldn't it?"

He couldn't help it. She always knew how to push his buttons.

He said, "The bottom line is, if they dig deep enough, you're not going to look so innocent."

"There's nothing I can do about that."

"It would help if you had an alibi," he said.

Carissa sat on the edge of the couch with her spine straight. That was how she sat—totally tense—when she was stressed out.

"There's nothing I can do about that, either," she said.

"You said you stayed home all day yesterday while I was meeting with Drake?"

"Yes. I didn't go anywhere."

"You didn't go for a ride?"

"Not yesterday."

"But you went to get the mail. I found it in the kitchen."

He could see from her expression that she had forgotten about that.

"I think that was Saturday," she said.

"No, it was yesterday," Alford said. "We both forgot to get it Saturday, remember?"

She nodded slightly, reluctantly admitting he was right.

He said, "That's the kind of inconsistency they'll be looking for, and they won't think you forgot, they'll think you're lying."

"But I'm *not* lying," she said. "Plus, we're getting ahead of ourselves. The man was a *game warden*."

"Mark my words, the sheriff or one of his deputies will be out soon enough, and they'll be digging into all kinds of stuff. You ready for that?"

Now she looked like she might cry, and damn it, Alford couldn't help but feel sorry for her. She had always been able to manipulate him one way or another. He always fell for it, too, and he knew that, but he couldn't stop.

"Maybe we should talk to an attorney," Alford said. "Considering the way things look."

"I don't care how it looks!"

Just like that, her mood swung like a pendulum. Her infamous temper.

"All I'm saying is, you might have to *prove* you didn't do it."

"That's bullshit."

"Just the way it is. If you've kept anything from me, now's the time to—"

"I haven't. I promise. You think I'm some kind of mad bomber? That's insane. I can't believe we're even talking about this."

He sat in the chair across from her.

"If you even suspect anything…"

"Like what? What does that even mean?"

"It means there's Mason to consider."

"What on earth are you talking about?"

"Is there any chance he knew what you were doing? Because if he did, there's no telling what he might have done about it. For you. He may be a strange man, but it's obvious he likes you."

Carissa started shaking her head in that dismissive way that indicated she'd had enough of a conversation.

Alford said, "We have to face the possibility he might've done it. We don't really know him, do we? I mean, how could anyone really know him? He doesn't want to be known."

"That's ridiculous," Carissa said, standing now, "and I'm done talking about it."

Lauren Gilchrist spent the morning researching the names on the list Jimmy Lee Jackson had given her—women that Lonnie Blair had slept with in the past few years. Sixteen names. Damn. And those were just the ones Jimmy Lee knew about or could remember. Lonnie had been a busy boy.

Eleven of the names were complete—first and last—but three were first names only, and there were two women Jimmy Lee couldn't name at all. He had called them "Tall redhead in Luckenbach" and "Brown-haired girl at the chili cookoff." Lauren was pretty sure she would never ID those women.

Lauren managed to make contact with seven of the eleven by phone. Some had heard about Lonnie's death, and some had not, but judging by the reactions, none knew anything about it, and they weren't able to name anyone who might've had a grudge against Lonnie. Two of those seven were married, and had been when they'd hooked up with Lonnie. They had only been willing to talk after some reassurance from Lauren that she would do her best to keep the situation private— meaning their husbands would not find out. Then they talked, but they had nothing useful to share.

Lauren found a woman named Jemma Dodson on Lonnie's list of Facebook friends, and she lived in Marble Falls, which meant she was likely the woman who'd dated Lonnie a year earlier, as Jimmy Lee had mentioned. Lauren sent Jemma a message through Facebook at ten o'clock, and Jemma replied with her phone number a few hours later.

Lauren called her, told her why she was calling, and Jemma said, "Yeah, I heard about that last night. I can't believe it, but I also can, because Lonnie is such a dog. Was, I mean. A loveable dog, but a dog."

"Oh, I've known those types," Lauren said with a laugh.

"But you knew that going in. It's not like he pretends to be this sweet, sincere guy who wants to get married. So you can either take him for what he is, or not. You play his game or you don't."

"And you played it?" Lauren said.

"For a while, yeah. It was fun."

"But then you broke up."

"I wouldn't say we broke up, because we always kept it pretty casual, but it ran its course and I decided it was time to move on."

"Did you stay in touch?" Lauren asked.

"Oh, sure. Not a lot, but we text now and then, especially when he's drunk. He likes to drunk text and see if I'm ready to hook up, but I ignore him until the next morning. Usually. Sometimes I tell him to stop being an idiot."

She was speaking of him in the present tense again. The loss hadn't sunk in yet.

"When did he last text?"

"Hang on a sec." A moment later, she said. "It was two weeks ago this past Saturday night."

That was when Lonnie and Jimmy Lee Jackson had been at the dance hall in Albert.

"Mind me asking what he sent?"

"Actually…uh…this isn't really cool, but he sent me a photo of a blonde girl and he asked if she was cute enough to bang."

Despicable behavior, but Lauren kept her opinion to herself.

"Did you recognize the girl?" she asked.

"No. Just some rando. It looked like they were at a club somewhere, but it was hard to tell. The photo was blurry. I don't think she knew he was taking it."

"Did you answer him?"

"I said he was a dog, and he said, 'What am I supposed to do? She's mad at her boyfriend and totally wants me.'"

Interesting. This must've been the woman named Tracy or Stacy, according to Jimmy Lee.

"How did you reply?"

"I sent an eyeroll emoji. I didn't hear anything else after that."

"You still have that photo?"

"I haven't deleted that conversation, so yeah."

"You mind sharing it with me? And your text messages?"

"Okay, yeah. I'll send screen shots. You think the boyfriend of this woman killed Lonnie?"

"At this point, we're just trying to gather all the information we can. Can you think of anyone else who might've wanted to hurt him? Any other jealous husbands or boyfriends that might've held a grudge, even for months or years?"

"I can't think of anybody."

"Do you know any other women who hooked up with Lonnie?"

Jemma provided two names, but both of them were on Jimmy Lee's list.

Lauren said, "Did Lonnie ever mention being in danger, or anyone threatening him or following him? Anything like that?"

Lauren knew she was being repetitive, but sometimes that's what it took to jar someone into sharing a relevant detail.

"No, I'd remember that," Jemma said.

"Did he mention someone trying to run him off the road a few weeks ago?"

"Jeez, somebody did that? He never mentioned it."

"And a few days later, somebody fired a bullet into his trailer."

"Whoa. I had no idea. That's scary."

"Any idea who might do something like that?"

"Sorry, no. I really can't think of anybody."

"If you hear any rumors or gossip, will you let me know?"

"Absolutely. It sucks what happened to Lonnie. If somebody killed him, they need to pay for it."

10

Mandy finally called Red at noon, while he and Billy Don were eating lunch at El Agave. He was tempted to let it go to voicemail, just to let her know how it felt, but he couldn't resist the impulse to answer. He had to hold the phone tightly to his ear to hear over the restaurant noise.

"Hey, baby," she said.

Hey, baby? She was acting all casual and breezy.

"Hey," he said, and that was all.

"What're you doing?" she asked.

"Nothing," he said, and that was all.

There was silence on the line for several seconds.

"You're literally doing nothing?" she asked.

"Having lunch," Red said.

More silence.

"Is everything okay?" Mandy asked.

"I guess," Red said.

"Red," she said.

"What?"

"Are you still pouting about those photos?"

"I'm not pouting."

"Then what would you call it?"

"You really wanna know?"

"Let's hear it," she said, and now there was some attitude in her voice, like she was prepping for an argument, and she was going to hand him his ass.

"I'm pissed off that you made those pictures sound all innocent, but they're basically just this side of porn."

Billy Don, who was hearing only one side of the conversation, muttered, "That was dumb."

Mandy said, "Oh, you didn't just say that. Porn?"

"I said *just this side* of porn," Red said.

"Stop digging," Billy Don muttered.

"They're *art*," Mandy said. "Like Venus de Milo."

"That tennis player?" Red asked.

"You're being an ignorant redneck," Mandy said.

"Damn right I am."

"That wasn't a compliment. You're seriously pissing me off."

"Okay, I'm sorry, but let me ask—"

"Are you really sorry?"

"Huh?"

"Are you really sorry, or are you just saying that?"

Red couldn't imagine anything positive would come from the truth, so he said, "I'm really sorry."

"Okay, then. Thank you."

"You know how my temper is. But I have a question."

"What?"

"When you agreed to be the model, are those the kind of pictures you had in mind?"

Billy Don had stopped eating with a chip halfway to his mouth.

"Not exactly," Mandy said.

Red wanted to jump on that answer immediately, but he kept his cool. "What did you think they would look like?" he asked.

Billy Don was leaning forward, hoping to hear anything Mandy might say.

"I don't know...more like a..."

"What?"

"Not so...sexy, I guess. Not that I have a problem with it. I think I look great."

"Of course you do, but did you *want* to do those pictures, or did he talk you into it?"

"Nobody talks me into shit," Mandy said. "Especially a man."

"I know, but—"

"You should know that by now."

"Oh, I know it."

"I do what I want, when I want to do it."

"I know you do."

"And maybe sometimes I make bad decisions, like we all do, but that's my business and nobody else's."

"That's true," Red said.

"You're the king of bad decisions," Mandy said.

"Can't argue with that."

"And I'll admit I'm more likely to make a bad decision myself if booze is involved."

Okay, now they were getting somewhere. Red had an idea where this was headed. Mandy had a fondness for vodka, usually in a screwdriver, but also in cranberry juice or tomato juice or grapefruit juice. Just about any juice would do.

"We've all been there," Red said, which was true.

"It wasn't that big of a deal," she said. "Drake brought a bottle of vodka to the shoot just to loosen us both up."

There it was. Red wanted to shout that he was right all along, but he resisted. Instead, he said, "Guess you had a drink or two."

"Yes, and it helped me relax. I was pretty nervous, this being my first time to model."

"You pour your own drink?"

Red couldn't hear her reply in the loud restaurant.

"What?"

"Drake did," she said.

Red could tell from her tone of voice that she knew what Red was getting at, and maybe she agreed a little, but she didn't want to admit it. Or maybe he was mistaken about that, because it wasn't often that a woman thought he was right about anything.

"Think you woulda done pictures like that without the vodka?" he asked, trying his best to sound curious and concerned, rather than judgmental.

She didn't answer right away, and for a moment, Red thought she might've hung up on him, or maybe the call had disconnected.

Then she said, "I don't know. Maybe not." Then she quickly added. "But that doesn't mean I regret it. I did it, and anybody who doesn't like it can kiss my ass."

Or just kiss that postcard, Red thought. *Nearly the same thing.*

Judge Hilton signed search warrants first thing that morning, and Bobby Garza sent Ernie Turpin and Callie Young to Lonnie Blair's trailer. Callie was the newest deputy in the department. She'd proven herself to be intelligent and capable.

After several hours at the trailer, Ernie and Callie didn't have much to report. They'd found a value-pack of condoms and several types of personal lubricant in Lonnie Blair's nightstand, and a pair of red panties under the bed. They'd sorted through mail, bank statements, and other documents, but found nothing that might reveal why Lonnie would have any enemies. Likewise, they'd found nothing to indicate he'd purchased any explosives or had any interest in creating a bomb.

Meanwhile, Garza began to sort through Lonnie's phone, which, fortunately, seemed undamaged from the explosion and was not protected by a passcode. Garza went to the camera roll and found dozens of photos of women, some in various stages of undress. A few of the women seemed to welcome the camera's focus, whereas quite a few were obviously moving to cover their faces or breasts or other exposed portions of their bodies. Garza could imagine the conversations that followed.

"You'd better delete that!"

"I will."

"Right now!"

"It's already gone. I was just playing around."

He was disappointed, but not surprised, to learn that Lonnie used Snapchat, which meant any text sent through that app was deleted permanently—both from Lonnie's phone and Snapchat servers—as soon as the recipient viewed it. No help there. There were a handful of texts within the Messages app on his phone, most of them to family members.

There were no stored voicemails, and the call log from Lonnie's cellular provider didn't include anything that appeared useful. Lonnie didn't make many calls, and he'd made none at all on the day he died.

At noon, Lauren Gilchrist called with an update on what she'd learned from Lonnie's former girlfriend about the woman named Tracy or Stacy.

"I believe I have that photo on Lonnie's phone," Garza said. "Hang on a sec. Yeah, this was taken on that Saturday night."

"Just the one photo of her?" Lauren asked.

"Yep, and I don't see any texts from that night to Jemma. Was it on Snapchat?"

"No, she said he used the regular Messages app, so he must've deleted that thread," Lauren said.

"How about you try to ID the woman in that photo—and her boyfriend—and I'll work on the rest of these photos?" Garza said.

"Will do. Gotta admit I'm having a tough time picturing an angry boyfriend or husband using explosives, as opposed to maybe a shotgun or a baseball bat. Why get so elaborate?"

"I've been thinking about that. Assuming there was a timer involved, not simply a trip wire..."

"Oh, I gotcha," Lauren said. "An alibi. If the killer knew when the bomb was going to detonate, he could be a hundred miles away when it went off."

"That's a pretty good reason to do it that way, if you know how to handle explosives."

"I guess the bomb squad is still out there?" Lauren asked.

"Yep. Hoping they'll be done shortly, so the investigator can take over with some light left."

To Garza, it seemed like the bombing had taken place days ago, but in reality, it had been less than twenty hours. The APD bomb squad had been on the scene for less than five hours.

Lauren said, "I'm heading to the dance hall in Albert right now. Will touch base later."

•

11

Marlin drove slowly along the caliche road that would eventually take him to the northeast portion of the Richter ranch. This road was likely following the same path cattle and deer had followed a century ago, winding around groves of trees, over rugged ridges, and across deep draws that were likely impassable in heavy rain.

He wasn't sure what he was looking for. Recent tire tracks? Even if he found some, hunters routinely drove all over this place. So did Mason Cross.

Then what was the point? Not likely he'd find anything related to the explosion. No matter who was involved—Mason Cross or somebody else—the person would have to be incredibly stupid to leave any evidence behind, even hundreds of yards away from the crime scene.

Ten minutes later, Marlin reached the north fenceline and the caliche road turned west. It took him around a large cedar brake, then began to ascend a small peak, at the top of which sat a tower deer blind. The windows were closed and there were no vehicles parked anywhere nearby, so Marlin pulled up close to the blind and grabbed his binoculars.

The view to the south was wide open. In the valley below, on the Hidden Hills Ranch, a large marked truck from the APD bomb squad was parked in a grassy area. Fifty yards north of the truck stood the skeletal remains of Lonnie Blair's deer blind. Marlin estimated that the blind was three hundred yards from where he was sitting. Certainly no farther.

This deer blind would be a perfect spot to watch Lonnie's blind with binoculars and know when he came and went. It might also be close enough to send a signal to a detonating device. Marlin's knowledge of bombs was limited, but it certainly seemed feasible.

He took his phone out and snapped a couple of photos.

Then he called Holly Griffin, the game warden in Webb County for many years, and after they'd caught up for a few minutes, he said, "Does the name Mason Cross ring a bell?"

"Oh yeah," she said without any hesitation. "He was the foreman on a big place twenty miles south of Laredo. Is he up there now?"

"Yep."

"I wondered where he went. You having a problem with him?"

"Possibly," Marlin said, and he described the shooting of Phil Colby's blind and the death of Lonnie Blair.

"Wow," Griffin said. "I had a similar situation down here."

"Let's hear it."

"Two years ago, a hunter shot a buck on his lease and it hopped the barbed-wire fence and died on the ranch where Cross was working. So the guy shimmied under the fence and dragged the deer back—without making contact with Mason or the landowner first."

That meant the hunter had trespassed. Even if you shot a game animal legally, if it crossed onto someone else's property, you couldn't track, trail, or retrieve it without permission from that landowner or someone authorized to speak for that landowner.

"Cross caught him on the wrong side of the fence?" Marlin asked.

"Not at the time," Griffin said. "You know how big the ranches are down here. The hunter figured it was no big deal to just grab that deer real quick. I mean, it was right there, maybe twenty yards from the fence. He could see it. Between you and me, I couldn't really blame him. There wasn't another hunter, or even a deer blind, for maybe a mile. So he went and got it. But somehow, Cross found the trail of blood and the drag marks later and figured out what had happened. He called the landowner—a man named Haney—and told him one of his hunters had crossed the fence, but Haney sort of shrugged it off. A few days later, that blind burned to the ground. We knew for sure it was arson, because they left an empty gas can there to make it clear."

The similarities in the three incidents were striking. All of them involved deer blinds. The blind in Webb County had been burned, Phil's blind had been shot, and Lonnie Blair's blind had exploded.

Marlin said, "That's pretty bold. And stupid."

"Yeah, I checked every store within fifty miles for cans from the manufacturer, but nobody carried it. So then I contacted the manufacturer, and when I sent a photo, they said they hadn't made that type of can for nearly twenty years, and they never sold it in Texas at all. Basically a dead end. There wasn't much point in getting location data on Cross's cell phone, because even on the ranch where he worked, it would've pinged off the same tower."

"Would he talk to you?"

"I drove to his place and we talked for maybe five minutes before he shut it down. Said he didn't do it and wasn't going to answer any more questions. Guy gave me the creeps. I remember checking his history at the time and he was clean, which surprised me, to be honest."

"Did you cite the hunter for trespassing?" Marlin asked, more out of curiosity than anything else.

"Gave him a warning."

"Did he ever have any face-to-face interaction with Cross?"

"Nope. After he got his buck, he decided he was done for the season."

"Did Haney have any run-ins with Cross after that?"

"Not that I heard of."

"Who was the rancher employing Cross?"

"Madeline Powell. That place has been in her family for something like a hundred years."

"You happen to have her number handy?"

"You bet. I'll text it when we're done talking."

"I appreciate it. Was she helpful two years ago?"

"She tried to be, but she didn't really give me anything useful."

"What did she say about Cross at the time?"

"Not much. Said he was a hard worker and reliable. Quiet. Just did his job without any issues."

"I don't suppose you learned how Cross lost his fingers."

"I never really asked at the time, because there was no reason. But you've got a pretty good reason now, huh?"

"So what're you gonna do?" Billy Don asked.

Red didn't reply. He didn't have an answer yet.

"On the one hand, Mandy ain't got no problem taking care of herself," Billy Don said, "but on the other…"

He didn't finish his comment.

"On the other hand what?" Red said.

"I don't wanna mess around in Mandy's bidness, but it sounds like this douchebag Drake got her drunk on purpose."

They were in Red's truck, heading back to the trailer. They'd just stopped at JC Liquor for a bottle of Wild Turkey. Red had made Billy Don spring for it, and lunch, too.

"Sure as hell did," Red said. He was steaming mad. He tried not to think about the times he'd served Mandy an extra-strong screwdriver so she'd be a little friskier in bed. But that was different—right? There wasn't any big secret about it.

"Even if she wants you to butt out, that don't mean Drake gets a pass," Billy Don said.

"He sure as hell don't."

"And if she won't do nothin' about it, that means you gotta do it," Billy Don said.

Red looked over at him.

"Just me, huh?"

"She's your lady, not mine," Billy Don said.

"Sure, but she's your friend, ain't she? And I'm your friend. Not that I can't take care of him myself, but I figured you might enjoy tagging along."

"Okay, you talked me into it. What're you gonna do? I mean we."

"Don't know yet, but it's gonna be more than just talk."

"We could beat the hell out of him."

"And then what?"

"That's it. Just beat the hell out of him."

"I figure we can come up with something a little more creative than that."

"Why?"

"Why what?"

"Why be creative?"

"The situation seems to call for it," Red said. "Don't know why, but it does. Maybe it's because he's a con man. He suckers people. I mean, look at the kind of place he's running. A 'wellness center.' What the hell is that exactly? You know what a detox is? And I'm not talking about where movie stars go to stop drinking."

"I got no idea."

"I saw it on the website, and they set you up with this special diet that's supposed to clean all the bad crap out of your body. But you know what the problem is?"

"Enchiladas are forever?" Billy Don said.

"No, it's all bullshit. It don't work."

"How do you know?"

"Hey, you're the guy who's always checking shit on his phone nowadays. Get on there and tell me what you find. See if I'm not right."

Red turned on the little county road that led to the trailer. Billy Don was busy searching his phone.

"I'm not getting nothin'," Billy Don said.

"How you spelling it?"

"D-e-t-o-c-k-s."

"No, it's with an x," Red said.

"Instead of the s?"

"D-e-t-o-x," Red said.

A minute later, Red turned at his driveway and began bouncing and swaying up the long caliche hill.

"Mayo Clinic," Billy Don said. "I've heard of that place. Isn't that where they make—"

"No sandwich jokes," Red said. "Just read."

Red crested the hill, pulled into his regular spot in front of the trailer, and killed the engine.

Billy Don, reading in a halting voice, said, "'Do detox diets offer any health benefits? Detoxification diets are pop'lar, but there is little evidence that they eliminate toxins from your body.'"

"See there? Now keep reading and call out some of the bad stuff that can happen if you get on one of those diets."

Red waited, and then he waited some more, because Billy Don was a slow reader.

Finally Billy Don said, "Fatigue…mineral deficiencies…cramping, bloating, vomiting…"

"And Drake *sells* this bullshit to people," Red said. "They *pay* him to do this stupid shit, which is double-stupid, because even if they want to do that kind of diet, what do they need *him* for? They can just do it on their own."

Billy Don read some more, and then said, "Four hundred bucks? That's what he charges?"

"That's if you're already a member. And that's without the food!" Red said.

"Bullshit. No food?"

"Not one bite. Just a recipe book and some little bottle of vitamins they're supposed to take, which they'll probably need, since the diet sucks so bad."

"That's crazy as hell."

"No kidding."

"You know what?" Billy Don said.

"Huh?"

"This dude is a genius."

12

Back in his office, Marlin called Madeline Powell, Mason Cross's former employer, and got no answer, so he left a voicemail.

"This is John Marlin. I'm a state game warden and I would appreciate the chance to ask you a few questions. Could you return my call when you have a minute?"

Then he spent thirty minutes online trying to learn everything he could about Mason Cross. Alford Richter said he'd run a criminal background check on Cross and it had come up clean, but Marlin ran one himself, because he had access to more detailed data. A few speeding tickets and a citation for public intoxication eighteen years earlier, but that was all.

Marlin dug deeper.

Cross was forty-two years old.

He had no readily identifiable presence on social media.

He was registered to vote.

He had never been sued.

He had been married two decades ago for seven years. No children.

Marlin was able to find Cross's ex-wife on Facebook. He bookmarked her page in case he might want to access it later. Many of her posts were visible, going back twelve years, and as far as he could tell, she'd had no interaction with Cross in that time.

Marlin had just closed that site when Bobby Garza called.

"The bomb squad is done and the scene is clear. They didn't find any other devices. Check that. I said 'other,' which implies there was a first device, but apparently there wasn't—not technically. Or there might not have been. One of the guys on the squad had a theory, off the record."

"Which was..."

"Ever heard of a product called Boom Town?"

"No."

"I hadn't either, but it's similar to Tannerite."

"Oh, you're kidding."

Tannerite was a well-known brand of binary explosive—a two-component product that was mixed together to create an exploding target.

"He found a fragment of a red-and-black plastic bucket, and apparently that's how Boom Town is sold—in five-gallon buckets. Mostly bulk quantities."

Binary explosives were perfectly safe and stable before the two components were combined, and even after they were mixed, the powder could only be set off by a bullet with a velocity of 2,000 feet per second or more. The resulting boom could be enormous, sometimes heard several miles away.

The ATF didn't regulate the sale or distribution of exploding targets, which helped make them widely available and exceedingly popular with recreational shooters.

Marlin wasn't fond of exploding targets, for several reasons.

Many shooters seemed to simply enjoy being a nuisance. Annoy the neighbors! Rattle their windows! Giggle like a toddler when you find out they're angry! Marlin had once seen someone online tell an 85-year-old rancher—a Blanco County native born and raised in the cedar-covered hills—that if he didn't like the explosions, he should go back to the city where he came from.

Some hunters used large quantities of the mixed powder to kill wild pigs, because one shot could wipe out quite a few at once. Marlin was firmly against that practice, because so many pigs were inevitably wounded or maimed. Feral pigs were an enormous problem in Texas, resulting in billions of dollars in agricultural losses every year, but that didn't justify addressing the problem in a manner that resulted in carnage and suffering.

Marlin had also seen a video in which a man had used 164 pounds of binary explosive in a plastic tub to destroy an old barn. It had certainly gotten the job done, and Lonnie Blair's deer blind was much smaller than the barn.

"Where did he find the bucket fragment?" Marlin asked.

"Just a few yards from where the blind was standing," Garza said.

"How quickly will the arson investigator be able to confirm it?" Marlin asked.

"She's already out there and she says later today, with any luck. I'll keep you posted. Let's keep it quiet about the Boom Town for the time being. I don't want word getting around, and there's also the chance the bomb-squad guy is wrong. Maybe that bucket fragment was already out there. You got anything good?"

Marlin recounted what he had learned from Phil Colby, the Richters, and Holly Griffin in Webb County.

Garza said, "You know I don't like jumping to conclusions, but damn. Talk about an MO. Three incidents involving deer blinds."

"I was planning to talk to Mason Cross about his run-in with Phil, but if you'd rather I hold off…"

"You know what? Go right ahead with that—but don't get into any of this Lonnie Blair stuff. We don't want him to know he's a suspect in the Blair case."

"Will do. How's your budget stuff coming?"

"Been putting it off. I don't remember signing up for this bullshit."

At two o'clock, Lauren Gilchrist arrived at the dance hall in Albert and spoke to the manager—a man named Artie Glass. After identifying herself, she asked, "Were you working two weeks back from this past Saturday night?"

"I work every Saturday night, so yeah, I was here."

Glass was in his thirties and very tall. Six-six, at least. Clean shaven, with a crew cut. He wore a denim shirt, jeans, and lizard-skin boots. He was stout enough that he probably served as a bouncer, too, or he could if he needed to.

"Did you have any problems that night?" Lauren asked.

"Such as?"

"Fights? Loud arguments? Shoving matches. Overflowing toilets. Anything, really."

"I don't remember any problems. We keep a pretty tight rein on things. People get too rowdy, we tell 'em to hit the road. Not if they're drunk, of course."

"Was it busy?"

"Saturday night always is."

"Do you know most of your customers?"

"There's a lot of them I don't know, and there's a core group of regulars I recognize, and then an even smaller group I know by name who're here almost every weekend."

Lauren took out her phone and showed him the photo Lonnie Blair had sent to Jemma.

"That's Tracy," Glass said. "You mind telling me what's going on? Is she okay?"

"She's fine," Lauren said. "I just need to ask her some questions. What's her last name?"

"Stillman."

"Did you see her much on that Saturday night?"

He hesitated, then said, "Is she in trouble for something? She's kinda wild sometimes, but she's not a troublemaker. Just loud and fun. Good girl."

"Artie, here's the deal. Right now, we're investigating a possible homicide and we're looking for witnesses. The victim was in here on that Saturday night, and we know he interacted with Tracy. We also know there was an incident after he left. So I just need you to shoot straight with me, okay?"

"Yes, ma'am. That's terrible. Who died?"

"I'll get to that, but tell me what you remember about Tracy from that Saturday night."

"Okay, well, I remember she was here with a couple of her friends."

"What about her boyfriend?"

"Barton? I didn't see him."

"Is that his first name, Barton?"

"Yeah."

"What's his last name?"

"I don't know it. I don't know him very well. He's a quiet guy."

"What does he look like?"

"Six feet, black hair, mid-twenties. Kinda skinny. Decent dancer."

"He ever cause any trouble?"

"None whatsoever. He seems pretty mellow—the opposite of Tracy."

"You never saw him that Saturday night?"

"I don't think so. There was, uh, another guy hanging around her that night. At least for part of it."

"What did he look like?"

Glass described Lonnie Blair.

"Had you ever seen him before?"

"I didn't remember him. Definitely not a regular."

"Ever hear the name Lonnie Blair?"

"That doesn't ring any bells."

"I'll give you a minute. Think about it."

"That's not gonna help. I don't know that name."

"How about Jimmy Lee Jackson?"

Glass shook his head. "Sorry."

Lauren said, "I notice you have some security cameras inside and outside. Those work?"

"They do."

"How about we take a look at some video from that night?"

"Don't you need a warrant?"

"Not if you volunteer to show the video to me."

"Oh, right. I didn't know how it worked. I don't mind showing you at all."

13

George Besserman had been employed by a women's clothing company for more than thirty years, but that didn't mean he wasn't a tough guy. He was plenty tough. Masculine as hell. He hated the stereotypes that plagued every male in his industry, whether you were a designer, an accountant, or a shipping manager, like George was. Oh, sure, maybe the forklift operators in the warehouses were exempt, but every other man in the business got painted with the same broad brush.

For example, if George was at a dinner party and another man asked what he did for a living, George would say, "I'm in charge of shipping in three states for a large company."

"Which company?" would be the inevitable follow-up question.

"A clothing company you've probably never heard of," George would usually answer. Sometimes that would do the trick, but many times it wouldn't.

"What's the name of it?"

"Sarah's Intimates," George would say. "We make a damn nice product."

"What is it?"

"Sarah's Intimates."

"Oh. Okay. So that's, uh…"

"Bras and panties, mostly," George would say, because it was so obvious. Everybody knew what "intimates" were, right? And why shouldn't he give an honest, straightforward answer?

"What, uh, drew you to that line of work?" the man would ask.

At that point, George could see that they were wondering about him in a way they wouldn't wonder if his company sold men's clothes, or even if they sold women's coats or shoes. But intimates? They pigeonholed George right away, even if it wasn't accurate. And what did it matter anyway?

George contemplated this unfair cliché as he drove west from Austin toward Blanco County in his red Tesla coupe. It was time to have a talk with the gentleman who had forced George's son, Justin, to drive his overheating Audi, thereby destroying the engine. George intended to hold that man accountable. The man was a rancher, or he worked on a ranch. Justin said he would be easy to identify, because he had a scarred face and was missing several fingers on one of his hands.

George had admittedly taken some comfort in the assumption that a man with missing fingers wasn't likely to want any sort of physical confrontation. Not that George wanted that, either. He had never been involved in a fistfight in his life. But considering what this man had said to Justin, George was going to demand that he pay for the damages to the car. Or, at a minimum, they would split it. George was a reasonable man.

When George arrived at the entrance to the ranch, he found the gate closed. There was a keypad, with an intercom button to contact the house. A small sign read as follows:

Visitors for Alford and Carissa, please press the button.
For deliveries or anything else, please call Mason Cross.

Mason Cross had to be the man in question. An employee of some sort. George dialed the number provided at the bottom of the sign. After three rings, a man answered with a very curt "Yeah?"

"My name is George Besserman."

No reply.

"I think I need to speak with you about my son's car."

Still nothing.

"Are you the man who insisted he pull out of your driveway this morning when his car was clearly not operable?"

After a pause, the man said, "You parked at the gate right now?"

"I am, yes."

"You need to move along. You're on private property."

"I'm outside the gate," George pointed out.

"Don't matter. That area beside the keypad is all private property."

"I drove out here from Austin," George said. "We need to have a conversation about the damages to my son's car."

"Ain't my problem," the man said.

"But I'd like to know why—"

"Your son was parked on private property, just like you are right now. The law requires me to warn you twice, which I have, and now I'm free to come remove you."

What in the world was wrong with this guy?

"I think maybe I should speak to your employers," George said.

"I wouldn't advise it."

"You're not giving me any other choice."

A long moment passed, and George wondered if the man had simply hung up.

"Hello?" George finally said.

"You stay where you are," Cross said. "Don't go anywhere."

George set his phone down and put his car in park. Turned the engine off and waited. With each passing minute, he questioned whether this was a good idea.

According to the time stamp from the camera mounted on the northern corner of the building, Lonnie Blair's truck slipped into a parking spot outside the dance hall at 7:47 on Saturday evening. Lonnie and Jimmy Lee didn't emerge from the Ford until 8:18. Lauren had the feeling they had polished off a few beers in that half-hour.

As the two of them made their way from the truck to the front door, Lauren was struck by the difference in body language. There was nothing wrong or odd with the way Jimmy Lee carried himself, but in contrast, Lonnie moved with the confidence of a man who had the world at his feet, and knew it. Pure swagger. He walked toward that dance hall like he owned the place and everybody inside was waiting for him to arrive so the party could start.

"Is that time stamp correct?" Lauren asked.

Artie Glass was seated at a desk inside a small office inside the dance hall. He had opened an app on a desktop computer to access the stored video. Lauren was standing behind him.

"It is, yeah," he said.

He switched to a camera just inside the front door.

Jimmy Lee entered first, followed by Lonnie. Now it was much easier to see their faces.

"You recognize them?" Lauren asked.

"Nope. Sorry."

Fast-forwarding occasionally, they spent fifteen minutes tracking the two men's movements in the dance hall throughout the evening. At 9:21, a petite blonde woman obviously caught Lonnie's eye.

"Tracy?" Lauren asked.

"That's her."

Not long after that, Lonnie approached Tracy, made some conversation, then escorted her onto the dance floor. They danced well together—a smooth, loose jitterbug.

Afterward, he went to the bar and bought her a beer, and one for himself. Then another round. Then they danced again. Lonnie swayed a bit on the way to the floor. The band took a break at 10:07. Lonnie leaned in close and whispered something into Tracy's ear. Then he strolled casually around the dance floor and out the front door. Tracy went to the ladies' room, and when she came back out, she also exited the building, without telling her friends.

Artie Glass switched to the outdoor camera again, and the video showed Tracy making her way to Lonnie's truck and getting inside. Twenty minutes passed. Vehicles came and went in other parts of the parking lot.

"Uh oh," Artie Glass said.

"What?"

He pointed to the upper left portion of the screen. "I think that's Barton's Jeep."

"You don't know his last name, but you know what he drives?"

"What can I tell you? I've seen him come and go. If he ever paid for anything with a credit card, I might know his last name, but a lot of people pay cash."

The Jeep parked in a dark spot under the limbs of an oak tree, and now it was facing directly at Lonnie Blair's truck. Then the driver's door to the Jeep opened and a man emerged, but it was difficult to see him well. A moment later, however, as he mounted the steps to the dance hall, he was much easier to see.

"Yep," Artie said. "Barton."

Barton went inside, slowly roamed the crowded dance hall, and eventually found Tracy's friends. A brief conversation ensued, and both friends looked around for Tracy.

After a few minutes, Barton took his phone out. Sending a text to Tracy? He appeared to wait for a reply, or an indication that Tracy had received his text, but a moment later, he put his phone back in his pocket.

Barton spoke with the friends for a few minutes, then roamed the dance hall some more, looking for his girlfriend. When he reached the front door again, he spoke with the woman taking the cover charge. She said something and gestured toward the door. Had she just told Barton that Tracy had walked outside earlier? Seemed that way. So where was she?

Artie switched to the exterior camera again, and they could see Barton exiting the dance hall and walking amongst the parked vehicles. The farther he got, the harder it was to make out what he was doing, but they could see that he stopped at a dark SUV and looked inside.

"That's Tracy's Tahoe," Artie said.

Barton wandered farther away from the hall, out of frame, but he returned a few minutes later and went to his Jeep. Got inside. Ten minutes passed.

Then Tracy emerged from the passenger side of Lonnie Blair's truck. Barton had to have seen her. Lonnie's truck was right in front of him. There was no way he missed seeing Tracy unless he was sleeping or looking down at his phone.

A minute passed, and then Lonnie exited his truck and went back inside the dance hall. Likewise, Barton couldn't have missed that, either. And he would've easily concluded what had just happened between Tracy and Lonnie.

Three minutes passed. Then Barton stepped from his Jeep and began walking briskly toward the dance hall. Any reasonable observer would've concluded that Barton was either in a hurry or angry. A showdown was coming. Maybe a fistfight. An ugly scene, for sure, one way or another.

Then, halfway to the door, Barton stopped abruptly. Just stopped. Stood motionless for ten seconds. Then turned around and went back to his Jeep, walking more slowly now. Got inside and…nothing happened. Not for twenty minutes.

Then Lonnie Blair and Jimmy Lee Jackson left the dance hall, no doubt giddy and drunk, and piled into Lonnie's truck. Lauren figured Lonnie had probably bragged to Jimmy Lee by then about what had happened in the parking lot. Maybe Tracy's perfume still hung in the air inside the truck.

Lonnie backed up, put it in forward gear, and drove away.

Ten seconds later, Barton's Jeep followed.

"Uh oh," Artie Glass said again.

They watched for a few more minutes, but neither vehicle returned. Tracy and her crew left a few minutes later.

"I'm going to need two things," Lauren said.

"A copy of this video," Artie said. "And what else?"

"I need you to keep all of this to yourself—the video, our conversation, everything."

"I can do that."

"I'm counting on it."

14

The man in the dirty Chevy truck parked on the other side of the gate and stepped from the driver's door as the gate swung open. He was wearing faded blue jeans, work boots, a baseball cap, and a light vest. He was also missing several fingers on his right hand, just as Justin had said, so George knew he had the right man. Mason Cross.

Then George saw that Cross had a gun in a holster on his left hip—a revolver—also as Justin had warned.

George pulled on his door handle to get out of his car, but the door was locked, so he had to fumble around to find the unlock button, and by the time he did that, Cross was standing beside the driver's door. He rapped on the window with his knuckles.

George lowered the window. Before he could speak, Mason Cross reached inside the car with one hand and dropped something heavy into George's lap, and George let out a short yip of surprise.

For some reason, George knew exactly what it was. He didn't know *why* he knew, but he knew. He looked down and saw a black handgun. A semi-automatic. George owned a gun a lot like that—a gift from his brother—but it had been stored in his closet for years. He wasn't what you'd call a gun guy.

Out of sheer instinct, George grabbed the gun, and he simultaneously knew that was a mistake. When he looked up again, Cross was aiming his revolver at George's nose.

"The hell're you doing bringing a gun with you?" Mason Cross asked.

"What are you talking about?" George asked, and he hated how weak and whiny his voice sounded. "You dropped it in my—"

"Don't raise it. You point that thing at me and you're a dead man."

"I won't. I wasn't."

George put the gun back into his lap. He could feel his heart banging in his chest. Mason Cross was insane. No question.

"I thought you came here to talk," Cross said.

"That's exactly what I—"

"But instead you're trying to threaten me."

"That's not true."

"You starting to realize what kind of trouble you could get yourself into?"

"Yes," George said. "Absolutely. I understand."

"Your idiot boy burned up his own damn engine," Mason Cross said. The right side of his face was scarred, as if from a burn.

"I agree. He did."

"Ain't nobody to blame but himself. Ran it out of oil."

There was anger in Cross's voice. Or resentment.

"You're exactly right," George said.

"But you're trying to teach him to blame his problems on other people."

"I'm not a good parent. I never have been. His mother is much better."

"But not good enough."

"Of course not. We're both terrible. Justin deserves better."

George could hear a vehicle passing behind him on Miller Creek Road. Surely they would see that Mason Cross was pointing a gun at him, and then they'd do something to help. But the vehicle kept going. Cross didn't seem concerned about it at all.

"Long as we agree that the engine ain't my problem," he said.

"We sure do. We agree."

"And you ain't gonna drive down the road and call the sheriff."

"No way. I wouldn't. I won't call anybody."

"Because I'm gonna have that gun in your lap back by then, and your prints are all over it now."

"I understand. I'd be stupid to call."

"And they'll notice that you filed the serial number off it. Or somebody did. And you'll have to explain why you had a gun like that, and why you came out here with a gun."

"I wouldn't even know what to say."

"I don't understand why men like you always have to cause trouble. I could just shoot you right now. Self defense. It's tempting. Gotta admit. You wouldn't be the first."

"Please don't. Please, please don't. I didn't understand the situation until now."

George was suddenly aware that he was pissing in his pants. He had always thought that was a myth—that nobody really lost control of his bladder from fear—but he'd been wrong.

"You understand it now?" Mason Cross asked.

"Very much so. My son ruined his car and blamed it on you. I believed him, but I shouldn't have."

"And you shouldn't have brought a gun."

I didn't bring a gun!

"It was a huge mistake. Dumbest thing I've ever done."

Mason Cross didn't say anything for several seconds, although it seemed like years to George. Was he deciding whether to shoot George?

"Now hand me that gun," he finally said.

Was this a trap? Maybe Cross wanted the gun in George's hand when he pulled the trigger.

"I don't want to," George said.

"Pick it up."

"You'll shoot me."

"Give me the damn gun."

George couldn't do it. He couldn't move. He was frozen with fear.

Cross lowered the revolver and slipped it into the holster. This was George's chance! Now he could raise the semi-automatic and shoot Cross right in the face. It would be justified, too! He had been threatened! And framed!

He was just about to make his move when he realized *this* was the real trap. This right here. Giving George the chance to shoot him. That meant the gun in his lap wasn't loaded. Of course not. Why would it be? Why would this maniac hand him a loaded gun? If George raised the unloaded gun, Mason Cross could pull the revolver again and fire away. The gun would fall from George's hand, and the crime-scene people would later determine that George had been armed.

George remained perfectly still.

Cross shook his head—*You're not much of a man, are you?*—then he reached through the open window again and retrieved the gun from George's lap.

"Don't come out here again," Cross said, before he walked back to his truck.

Madeline Powell returned Marlin's call at four-thirty, saying, "I thought I knew all the game wardens in Webb County. Are you new?"

"No, ma'am, I'm in Blanco County."

"Oh. Okay. I misunderstood."

The change in her tone was unmistakable. She'd immediately gone from friendly to guarded.

"Do you have any idea why I'm calling?" Marlin asked.

"Well, I know only one person in Blanco County, and that's Mason Cross, so I'm guessing you want to ask me something about him."

"I do, yes. I understand he used to work for you."

"He did, but let's stop there for a minute. Did he do something?"

"There was an incident that took place on the ranch next door to the one he manages."

"That doesn't really answer my question."

Marlin laughed. "No, you're right. We don't know who's responsible, but considering what happened next door to your place, I figured it was worth talking to you."

"What happened up there?"

"A deer blind exploded."

"Whoa. It *exploded*?"

"A man was killed."

"Good Lord."

"At this point, we don't know much more."

"Was it an accident?"

"Sure doesn't look like it."

Marlin waited to let her speak. Sometimes it was better to wait and see what a person might say, especially someone who seemed reluctant to talk.

"They never proved Mason burned that blind down," she said. "It was all speculation."

"I understand that."

"I realize he's a...I'm not sure how to describe him. He's not friendly. He's a loner. In fact, he seems to go out of his way to get into disagreements. But that doesn't make him guilty of anything."

"No, it doesn't. It very well could be that anything you tell me might rule him out. That would be progress in itself."

"Let me think about this for a minute," she said. "This makes me nervous, to be honest."

"Talking to me does?"

"My father was a prosecutor for years. He taught me the value of evidence. And he taught me the risk in reaching conclusions *without* evidence."

"He sounds like a wise man."

"He was. He's been gone for several years now."

"I'm sorry to hear that."

"I realize Mason was the obvious suspect when that blind burned down. He'd had a problem with the hunter who used it, and with my neighbor to some degree, but there was no evidence to prove anything."

"Understood."

"Do you have evidence in your case?"

"I can't really get into that, but I can assure you everybody working this case will follow the evidence where it leads—whether it's toward Mason Cross or someone else entirely."

"I'm not sure I have anything that will help you, but if we talk some more, can it remain confidential?"

"I'm afraid I can't guarantee that, but the odds are slim that Mason will ever know we talked, and I'll do my best to keep it that way."

Madeline Powell didn't answer right away. When she did, she sounded more reluctant than before. "What would you like to know?"

"I realize the value you place on evidence, and I do, too, but I'm still going to ask—do you think Mason burned that deer blind?"

"I asked him if he did it and he said no. I believed him, and still do, because I'd never caught him in a lie before."

"That's not a bad way to operate. Did you ever see a photo of the gas can that was used?"

"Yes, and as far as I could recall, I had never seen it before."

"Were you at home—meaning anywhere on the ranch—on the day the blind burned?"

"I was not. I'd driven to Laredo to have lunch and do some shopping with a friend. I was gone all day."

"You mind me asking if you live alone?"

"I did then, yes."

"Was Mason on the ranch that day?"

"He was."

Marlin wanted to ask her if Mason Cross had ever bought or shot any binary explosives, as far as she knew, but Garza had asked him to keep that quiet for now. However, if she happened to mention that on her own...

"Is Mason much of a hunter?" Marlin asked.

"A meat hunter, yes. He couldn't care less about hanging a trophy on the wall."

"A decent shot, as far as you know?"

"I've seen him shoot feral pigs at three hundred yards. A lot of them. Without missing."

"Using his own rifle or one of yours?" Marlin asked.

"His own."

"What does he use?"

She hesitated. "Was the man in the deer blind shot from a distance?"

"He was not," Marlin said, which was technically true. "I'm just gathering as much information as I can, so I don't have to bother you later."

"No bother at all. You can call me back if you need to. I don't take this kind of thing lightly. To answer your question, he shoots a Remington model seven hundred."

"What caliber?"

"Three-oh-eight."

A basic hunting rifle, but a time-tested classic that was known for accuracy right out of the box. Variations had been used by law enforcement and military.

"Did he do much target shooting?" Marlin asked.

"Quite a bit. He would go to the range at the far end of the ranch, so as not to bother me, but I could still hear him."

"What would he shoot—just paper targets?"

"That's what we use."

"Paper targets, deer, wild pigs. Anything else?"

If Mason Cross ever shot binary explosives, surely she would mention it now.

"An occasional coyote, but mostly we leave them be, unless they're coming around the house regular or if they seem to have rabies."

Marlin changed tactics. "Why did Mason leave the job?"

"My son got divorced and moved back home. With his extra help around here, I didn't need Mason anymore. I hated to let him go, but it was the only practical choice. My son is planning to stay for the long term."

"How did Mason respond to that?"

"He's not the type of person to show much emotion, so he said he understood and that was pretty much it."

"He wasn't angry?"

"Mason wouldn't get angry with me. Or if he did, he never showed it. He was always very respectful."

"Would you say you knew him well?"

"Oh. Hmm. No, I guess not. We had a working relationship."

"You gave him a good reference to the Richters?"

"I did, yes. I had no reason not to."

"Did the subject of that burned blind ever come up?"

"With the Richters? Of course not. As I've said, there was no evidence Mason did it, so why would I mention it? That wouldn't have been fair to him—or to them for that matter. They might've decided not to hire him, so they would've missed out on a hardworking foreman who knows how to get stuff done. Those types aren't easy to find."

Marlin was running out of questions to ask. He appreciated the fact that Madeline Powell was reluctant to implicate Mason Cross without evidence, but he wondered if she might be withholding some important facts solely because she viewed them as irrelevant.

"I understand," Marlin said. "Just one more question. Any idea how he lost his fingers?"

"He went into the Army straight from high school. I'm not positive, but my understanding, based on a few of his comments, is that he lost them while serving."

"In combat or training?"

"I couldn't tell you."

"I appreciate your time," Marlin said. "And your candor."

15

Phil Colby was on his way to Johnson City, driving on Miller Creek Road, nearly to Highway 281, when he glanced to his left and saw a vehicle parked in the paved area that was previously an official rest stop next to the highway. Now it was just a place where construction workers and other laborers sometimes parked to catch a ride with a coworker to a job site. Those parked vehicles were usually trucks, backed up against the fence that separated the old rest stop from the private property adjoining it.

But this vehicle—the one Colby saw now—was a red Tesla coupe parked, or stopped, parallel to the highway, facing away from Colby. A middle-aged man was standing beside the car, and judging by his body language, he was angry or excited or otherwise overcome with emotion. He was pacing and muttering to himself, and occasionally gesturing wildly, with windmilling arms. Was he talking to someone on the phone? Not as far as Colby could tell. Maybe something else was going on. Colby could see through the rear window of the car, and nobody else was inside it, as far as he could tell.

Then Colby noticed that the crotch of the man's pants was wet. Had he spilled a drink? Was that the reason he was angry? Or had he soiled himself? Maybe the man thought this was still a rest stop, and that there would be a men's room here, but he'd been disappointed, and then he couldn't hold it any longer.

Or he was having some kind of breakdown. Mental or automotive.

Colby had reached the stop sign prior to entering the highway, but he backed up about ten yards, then swung a left into the old rest stop. As he got closer to the Tesla, the man saw him coming and his behavior changed immediately. He settled down. Stopped muttering. Reached for his door handle just as Colby eased to a stop on the passenger side of the Tesla. Colby's truck was high enough that he was looking over the roof of the Tesla at the man.

"Hey, there," Colby said.

"Hi."

"Everything all right?"

"Yep, all good."

"Got car trouble or something?"

"No, I was just stopping for a second."

It wasn't convincing. The man was twitchy and distraught, or embarrassed that Colby had seen the way he had been behaving.

"I thought you were talking to someone for a second," Colby said.

"No, I was just—I was mad about something. I needed to pull over for a minute. I'm better now."

"You sure?"

"Yes, thanks. Nice of you to check."

"Nothing wrong with asking for a little help," Colby said. "We all need help now and then. God knows I do. So you just let me know what you need."

The man didn't say anything, and he wasn't making eye contact now. Just shaking his head, like he was frustrated, and watching cars pass on the highway. He was about to spill it.

"You need to talk about it?" Colby asked. "Sometimes that's what it takes."

"Maybe so," the man said.

"What's your name?"

"George."

"I'm Phil. Good to meet you."

"Same here."

"So what's going on?" Colby said. "Let me help."

The man didn't answer right away. Then he pointed west on Miller Creek Road. His voice was controlled, but furious. "Right down there—there's a lunatic living about a mile that way. An absolute lunatic."

Colby said, "I bet I know who you're talking about."

The man looked at him now, interested and maybe relieved. "You do?"

"I live in that direction. About a mile down, as a matter of fact."

"So you think you know him?"

"Yep. He's a nutcase. His name is Mason Cross."

"That's him!" George said.

"Want to tell me what he did?"

Marlin was driving back to the sheriff's office when Phil Colby called.

"Seeing as how you're so big on me sharing stuff, I've got something for you," Colby said.

"What's up?"

Marlin could tell from the road sounds that Colby was also driving with his phone set to hands-free.

"Keep in mind that I'm telling this to you first, instead of Lauren, so I get bonus points for that. She's gonna give me a hard time."

"You'll survive," Marlin said. "This better be good."

"You know that old rest stop at Miller Creek and 281? I just saw a guy parked there who seemed to be kind of losing it, so I pulled over and asked if he needed help. Turns out he'd just had a run-in with Mason Cross."

"And?"

Colby filled in the details. The man, George, had a son named Justin who'd had an overheating car that morning and had pulled into the Richters' gated entryway. Mason Cross had shown up and forced Justin to move on, thereby burning up his engine. George had driven out this afternoon to have a word with Cross, and it had not gone well.

According to George, he talked to Cross on the phone and explained why he was there. Cross told him to leave, so George raised the idea of calling the Richters instead.

"So that gets Cross down to the gate," Colby said, "but the first thing he did was drop a semi-automatic into George's lap, and of course George grabbed it out of instinct."

That meant George's prints were on the gun.

"What a set-up," Marlin said.

"When George looks up, Cross is aiming a revolver at him, and playing the whole thing up like George had come out there to shoot him. So George puts the handgun back in his lap so that Cross won't shoot."

This man George had placed himself squarely in the sights of an experienced predator—but who would expect that kind of reaction? How would George have known what was going to happen?

"Where did it go from there?" Marlin asked.

"Cross tried to make him pick the gun up again, but George wouldn't do it. So Cross holstered his own gun and gave George a chance to shoot him, but George was smart enough to figure the gun in his lap wasn't loaded. Eventually Cross grabbed the gun out of George's lap and told him to hit the road."

"You think all of that was accurate?" Marlin asked.

"I guess George could be a wacko, but based on what we know about Cross so far, I'd say it happened just the way George told it."

"What was George's last name?"

"He didn't want to give it, and he didn't want me to call the sheriff. Said Cross had warned him against doing that. The dude was terrified, I can tell you that much. I pushed him hard to report it, but he wouldn't. By the time we were done talking, he'd calmed down, but he wanted nothing more to do with Mason Cross."

"It was good of you to try to help," Marlin said. "And thanks for letting me know."

"I got his license plate, in case you want to talk to him."

"Text it to me."

"Will do. I think at this point Mason Cross needs a long-term attitude adjustment."

"You stay away from him," Marlin said. "He's not worth it."

"He needs to get his ass kicked."

"Resist that urge. You know, like an adult."

"Aw, that's no fun."

"He *wants* trouble. He seeks it out. You said that yourself. Don't give him an excuse."

"Then *you* nail him."

"Working on it."

A moment passed.

Colby said, "Hey, Lauren and I were thinking we should grab some dinner soon. The four of us. Maybe that new place in Dripping Springs."

The two couples had spent time together at parties and other group events, but they'd never gone on a double date. Decades had passed since Marlin's relationship with Lauren, but in some ways, it seemed like yesterday. Ever since Lauren had relocated to Blanco County, he found himself thinking about those times more often. But that was to be expected, right?

"Which one?" Marlin asked.

Colby named the new restaurant everyone had been raving about. It was a small, intimate place—candles on the tables, white tablecloths, fine stemware, the works.

"Sounds good," Marlin said. "Let us get this case sorted out first, okay?"

"Yeah, that's fine. Now I'm gonna call Lauren and tell her the same story I just told you. I'll probably say I called her first."

"Wise man," Marlin said.

16

Twenty minutes later, Lauren was pondering the story Phil had just told her when her cell phone rang. After her meeting with Artie Glass, she'd left a voicemail for Tracy Stillman. Now Tracy was calling her back at nearly five o'clock.

"I was waiting for my boss to leave," Tracy said. "If I make any kind of non-business call, he bitches about it. And it's not like I'm hourly, I'm on a salary. What's the big deal?"

"Where do you work?" Lauren asked.

"At a real estate agency in Blanco. Basically I'm an administrative assistant right now, but I'm planning to get my license. There is so much opportunity in this business. This county is booming. Can you, uh, tell me why you called earlier? I'm guessing you aren't shopping for a new home."

"No, I called about something else. You were at the dance hall in Albert two weeks ago this past Saturday night, correct?"

"I think so, yeah. With some friends."

"And you met a man named Lonnie Blair that night?"

"I met a guy named Lonnie. I don't know his last name. We danced a couple of times."

"Have you been in touch with him since then?"

"I don't even have his phone number. What's going on?"

"Unfortunately, he was killed yesterday afternoon."

"My God. That's terrible. What happened?"

"We're still trying to figure that out."

"Like, a car wreck or something?"

"Right now it's being investigated as a homicide."

"Oh," Tracy said, but that one word said so much. It was a mix of surprise and sudden guarded apprehension. Or maybe Lauren was reading too much into it.

She said, "So we're talking to anybody who interacted with him over the past couple of weeks."

"I understand. We only danced twice."

"Did you get a chance to talk much?"

"A little bit, but it's pretty loud in there when the band is playing."

"What did you talk about?"

"Just your basic small talk. He told me he lived a few miles outside Johnson City and that he owned a fence company. I don't remember much else."

"What was he like?"

"A total player, but likable."

"Did he mention any arguments or disagreements with anybody, or say anything about anybody being mad at him?"

"Nothing like that at all. This is all so sad. How was he killed?"

"We're working on that, too."

"I mean, like, was he shot or stabbed or something?"

"I can't really get into that right now."

"Okay, well, I wish I knew something important that would help, but I don't."

Lauren believed her, but she needed to push Tracy harder, in case she was keeping anything to herself. "Tracy, I already have a pretty good understanding of what happened that night between you and Lonnie. So I just need you to be straight with me and tell me everything you can. If you have something useful that might help me figure out who killed Lonnie, that would be great, but if you don't, that's fine, too. I really couldn't care less about anything else that happened between consenting adults."

Lauren didn't mention *how* she knew that Tracy had hooked up with Lonnie—the video footage—because she didn't want Tracy, or anyone else, to warn Barton there was video. If Barton learned about it, he'd realize the investigators knew he'd followed Lonnie that night. It would be better to question him without divulging that.

After a short pause, Tracy said, "Can you hang on a minute?"

"Yeah, sure."

Another moment passed, and then Lauren heard a door click shut. Tracy had gone somewhere for more privacy.

"This is embarrassing," Tracy said.

"You shouldn't feel that way on my account."

"I can't help it. I didn't make the best decisions that night."

"I've done that plenty of times myself, especially when I was younger. And the good news is, as I've gotten older, I care less and less what other people think."

"If anything, I'm usually the opposite—almost too uptight. Well, except when I've been drinking. Then I'm more laid-back, but I'm not so sure that's a good thing."

"You were drinking at the dance hall that night?"

"Well, yeah. We were out dancing."

"Enough that it affected your memory?"

"No, nothing like that."

"Without drinking, would you have hooked up with Lonnie?"

"No way. I honestly don't do things like that, but between the drinking and the argument I had with my boyfriend—now my ex-boyfriend—I said to hell with it."

"What was the argument about?"

"That night was sort of the last straw. He just wasn't putting anything into the relationship because he works all the time. That's fine, but it was time for me to move on. It wasn't like I was gonna marry him. I think we both knew that."

"What's his name?"

"Barton Scott."

"Where does he work?"

She named a vodka distillery on Fitzhugh Road, twenty minutes east of Johnson City.

"Was he at the dance hall that night?" Lauren asked.

That question would be a good test to see how forthcoming Tracy would be.

"He was supposed to meet us, but then he worked late, and when he did show up..."

"You were outside in Lonnie's truck."

"Unfortunately."

"Did Barton know what you were doing?"

"No, and my friends didn't even know where I was. In hindsight, that was really stupid, to just go outside with a stranger."

"So you never saw Barton that night?"

"No."

"Did you talk or text?"

"He texted that he was at the dance hall, but I never texted him back, and then he left. I didn't reply until the next morning."

"Earlier you said ex-boyfriend…"

"Yeah, we broke up that next day."

"Who did the breaking up?"

"Actually, he did, but only because he beat me to it."

"Was it ugly?"

"I've been through worse."

"And it was all by text?"

"Yep."

"Did you tell him about Lonnie?"

"God, no. Why would I tell—oh, I just figured out why you're asking about all this. You want to make sure Barton didn't kill him, right? Because if he knew what happened between Lonnie and me, he might've gotten pretty mad. He absolutely didn't know. Besides, even if he had known, he wouldn't do something like that. He's a very quiet and gentle guy. Is he a suspect?"

"I wouldn't say he's a suspect, but we need to rule him out, and you're helping me do that."

"Okay, good. Are you going to talk to him?"

"I probably will, yes."

"What about my friends?"

"Possibly."

"Are you going to tell them everything that happened—between me and Lonnie?"

"Right now, I don't see any reason for that," Lauren said.

"I would hate for word to get out," Tracy said. "I know that sounds, like, so self-centered, considering that Lonnie died and everything, but I don't want everyone thinking I'm a skank. I'm not. It's just that I don't know what happened to him, and I can't imagine how my hooking up with him had anything to do with it."

Because you haven't seen the video, Lauren thought.

"Did you have any contact with Lonnie after that night?" she asked.

"No. We didn't even exchange numbers."

"You didn't look for him on Facebook or Instagram or anything like that?"

"Honestly, I didn't want to see him again, and I was really hoping he wouldn't try to get in touch. I didn't think he would, and he never did."

"He was there with a friend that night. Do you remember the friend's name?"

"No idea."

"Did you talk to him at all?"

"Not one word."

"When you were outside, including when you were in Lonnie's truck, did you notice any other vehicles coming or going?"

Lauren believed everything Tracy had told her so far, but that didn't necessarily mean it was truthful or complete. Witnesses sometimes lied convincingly or left facts out. There was always the chance Tracy knew that Barton had shown up and discovered what Tracy was doing with Lonnie—and that Tracy didn't want to implicate him in a murder case—so this was another chance for Tracy to come clean or perhaps contradict herself.

"Well, I mean, I remember headlights, but I wasn't paying much attention to that. I see what you're asking, though. I never saw Barton's Jeep, but anybody coming into the parking lot would've been driving behind us, not in front of us."

"How long were you outside with Lonnie?"

"I don't know for sure. Maybe thirty minutes?"

"Do you still have the texts from Barton that night and the next morning?"

"I'm sorry, I don't. I deleted that whole thread."

"When did you learn he was at the dance hall?"

"When I got out of Lonnie's truck and was walking inside. Barton had sent a text saying he was there, and that he couldn't find me, so he left. He said he was too tired to hang around."

Tracy didn't appear to know that Barton had been parked just fifteen yards from Lonnie's truck. But was she being sincere?

"From some of the other statements we've received, I'm pretty sure Barton was still outside when you got out of Lonnie's truck."

"Well, if he was, I didn't see him. Or his Jeep. And obviously he didn't see me, because he didn't say anything. I guess that whole scene could've been pretty ugly, but luckily we missed each other."

17

Mandy came over at seven that night, and by then Red had decided he wasn't going to say another word to her about Drake. He had also warned Billy Don not to say anything either. Not one damn word—unless, of course, she brought it up. If she did, Red had told him to play it cool. Just act like it wasn't important. They weren't even thinking about it anymore. They'd moved on. No reason to get all worked up about a few photos. Of course, he *was* going to deal with Drake, but Mandy didn't need to know that.

Now they were in the living room, watching TV, after eating some barbecued ribs from a wild hog, washed down with beer and other adult beverages. Billy Don was in his usual spot on the couch. Red was in his recliner, the footrest extended, and Mandy was sprawled across his lap, her arms around his neck. She was always the affectionate type, but this display was a bit out of the ordinary. He was enjoying it, even though one of his legs was going numb and he had to take a leak. He'd tried to slide his hand up her shirt a few times, but she'd stopped him. He had to admit that her face looked fantastic after the facial she'd received at the wellness retreat. She was glowing.

By nine o'clock, the strategy of not saying anything about Drake had worked out just fine. She hadn't brought it up, and he figured they weren't going to talk about it at all, which was okay with Red.

Then she whispered into his ear, "You know what?"

She was a little bit tipsy from drinking a couple of strong

screwdrivers.

"What? You ready for bed?" Red was hoping the answer was yes. Not to sleep, either.

"No, I've been thinking about the photo shoot. And Drake. And the vodka."

"What about it?" Red asked.

Red was wondering if she was about to apologize. He had, after all, been right about everything. Or almost everything. At least some of it.

If she said she was sorry, then maybe, just maybe, he wouldn't carry out his plan to do something terrible to Drake. Maybe all Red would do under those circumstances was have a talk with Drake and threaten him with a severe beating. A guy like that would crater in half a second. Red would warn him about shooting any more photos like that, even of women Red didn't know.

But what Mandy actually said caught Red totally by surprise. "I've been thinking about it, and I'm wondering if there was something other than vodka in my drink."

She was speaking quietly enough that Billy Don wouldn't be able to hear, especially with the TV turned up loud to *The Good, the Bad and the Ugly.*

"You mean some other juice?" Red asked.

"No, I mean, like, *something else*. Like maybe a drug."

Red pulled his head back so he could look at her better. "*What?*"

"I wonder if my drink was spiked with something," she said.

"Are you friggin' kidding me?"

"It's just that I know exactly how vodka affects me, and this was different. I mean, the vodka was there—I could feel it—but there was something on top of it."

Red was having trouble processing what he was hearing.

"That son of a bitch," he said.

"What?" Billy Don asked.

"I can't be sure though," Mandy said. "That's the problem. And if he did…"

"He's a dead man," Red said. He could feel his temper building.

"What are y'all talking about?" Billy Don asked.

"I knew I shouldn't have told you," Mandy said.

"What would he have put in there?" Red asked.

"I've got no idea. I'm not even sure he did."

"Who put what in where?" Billy Don asked.

"Can I tell him?" Red asked. "I'm gonna tell him."

"Just hang on," Mandy said. "Be cool for a minute."

"It's damn hard to be cool when some sicko put something in your drink," Red said.

"He *what*?" Billy Don asked.

"I told you, I don't know for sure," Mandy said. Now she cupped Red's face with one hand. "Please relax, baby. Okay? Don't get all crazy. Not any more than normal."

"But what if he did do it?"

"*Then* you can get crazy, if we ever know for sure. And I'll be right there with you."

"Was there anybody else at the shoot?" Red asked.

"Just the photographer, but he had nothing to do with it."

"Did Drake make your drink there in the same room, or did he bring it in from somewhere else?"

"There was like a little kitchen around the corner from the room we were in. He went in there to make it."

"To make what?" Billy Don asked.

Red started to say something, but Mandy shushed him. Then she turned to Billy Don and said, "I don't know for sure, but when I did that photoshoot with Drake, I think he might've put something in my drink. Like a drug."

"Whoa," Billy Don said. "Holy hell. Like Bill Cosby used to do?"

"But I don't know for sure," Mandy said.

"What'd it do to you?" Billy Don asked.

"I just felt very relaxed. Uninhibited. Happy."

"Ain't like you're normally hibited," Billy Don said. "I don't mean that in a bad way."

"More so than normal," Mandy said. "I just felt…free. Drake asked me to strip down and I had no problem with it at all. I mean, normally I would've thought about it some, then probably went ahead with it—but maybe in a more modest way."

"What does that mean?" Red asked. He really had to piss now.

"You're gonna get mad. Madder."

"I promise I won't," Red lied.

"I think you will."

"Just tell me. I'll do my best."

"Okay, well, I stripped right in front of them—Drake and the photographer."

It took every ounce of Red's self control, but he didn't say anything. He didn't let his anger show on his face.

"Then what happened?" he asked with his teeth clenched.

"We shot the photos and that was it."

"Drake never touched anything he wasn't supposed to?"

"No. Hell no. I might've been a little bit loosened up, but I wasn't out of my mind. I would've kicked some ass if Drake had tried anything."

"And you remember everything?" Red asked.

"Yeah."

"You're sure?"

"I think so."

"How would you know if you didn't?" Billy Don asked.

Nobody said anything for a long moment.

"I mean, if you didn't remember something, you'd also forget not remembering it," Billy Don said.

Red figured Billy Don was right, which didn't happen often.

"Do you even know if you got to see all of the pictures?" Billy Don asked.

"Oh, damn," Red said, because this conversation was opening up all kinds of bad possibilities.

"Y'all need to settle down," Mandy said. "We've got no reason to think anything like that happened."

"We've also got no reason to think it didn't," Red said.

During supper, Marlin recounted the story Phil had told him about the man named George and his experience with Mason Cross. Nicole simply stared for a long moment, then said, "That's insane."

"I know."

"I mean totally off the rails. Who keeps a throwdown handy for situations like that? Assuming it was all accurate."

They were both seated on the L-shaped couch in the living room. Geist was snoozing soundly on a blanket in the corner of the L. The temperature outside was in the thirties, but it was snug and warm inside the small cabin. Marlin had built this room himself with his own hands before he'd met Nicole, bringing the total living space to just over thirteen hundred square feet. Not a big place by today's standards, but he'd never needed much room, and Nicole lived the same way.

Marlin said, "I told Bobby all about it. Everybody needs to know how unhinged this guy is."

During that call, Bobby Garza had confirmed that the APD arson investigator agreed that the explosion had been caused by a binary explosive.

"You going to contact George?"

Nicole was bundled up in sweatpants and a thick green sweater. She had her long auburn hair pulled into a ponytail, and she'd scrubbed the makeup off her face when she'd gotten home. Now she was on the end of the couch closest to the fireplace, with her legs tucked under her and a bowl of chili in her lap.

"Phil got a plate number, so maybe, if I can find a phone number or email address. But the problem is, even if he's willing to talk and he describes exactly what happened, how can we prove any of it? It would be George's word against Cross's, and I doubt Cross would talk."

Nicole had faced plenty of situations like this herself. She'd been a deputy prior to becoming the victim services coordinator for the county. She had the skills and temperament for both roles, but she preferred her current career.

She said, "I have to admit, if I were George and I knew everything there was to know about Mason Cross, I'd be inclined to let it go. Cross sounds like a lunatic, and I wouldn't want to worry about him coming after me. How do you stop a guy if you don't know what he's going to do or when he's going to do it?"

Marlin stopped talking for a minute and focused on his own bowl of chili, which Nicole had made from ground venison. Technically, it was "chili with beans," because purists insisted that chili didn't have beans in it. In their view, if you put beans in it, it wasn't chili, it was chili with beans. You couldn't call it chili. Either way, he liked it, no matter what you called it.

When he was done eating, he set his bowl on the coffee table and said, "To me, that's the worst kind of cowardice—getting revenge like that. Lonnie Blair's murder was as cold as it gets, and he stood no chance. But the problem is, if Mason Cross did it, we don't know his motive. At least not yet. If Lonnie had some kind of run-in with him, it seems like Jimmy Lee would've known about it. Somebody would've known."

"Okay, but considering what you know about Cross so far, is it hard to imagine that he might've been angry at Lonnie without Lonnie even knowing it?"

"I could see that."

"Maybe they had a conversation that irritated Cross but didn't bother Lonnie at all. A man like Cross might be prone to see slights or insults where none exist."

"That's true." Marlin took a long swig of beer from the bottle on the table.

"You're still planning to approach Cross about the bullet through Phil's blind?" Nicole asked.

"Yeah, hopefully I can catch him tomorrow. I left him a voicemail today, but he never called back."

"How are you going to approach it?"

"I don't want him to know he's a suspect in the murder, or that I know what happened with George. I'm just gonna play like I'm wondering who shot Phil's blind—just asking around, seeing if anybody knows anything."

"If he has more than two brain cells, he'll figure you're operating under the theory that the person who shot Phil's blind is the same person who blew up Blair. The incidents are too similar, and they were right next door to each other."

"Yup."

"In fact, shooting at Phil's blind might've given him the idea for using a binary explosive. You try to shoot somebody at three hundred yards, even if you're a good shot and use a quality rifle, you stand a real good chance of wounding him, rather than killing him."

"Then there's the possibility he shot Phil's blind but had nothing to do with Blair, in which case he might really want to lie about it, just so he won't be a murder suspect."

"Surely he knows the bomb squad was next door, and then the investigator."

"No doubt. That's why it's better for me to show up, rather than Bobby or one of the deputies. He might see right through it, but it's our best shot."

Marlin heard the heat kick on. The temperature was supposed to drop into the mid-twenties overnight, but the skies were clear and the wind was calm. His favorite kind of cold weather.

He said, "By the way, Phil suggested we all eat at that new place in Dripping Springs sometime soon."

"Which place?"

"I don't remember the name of it. The fancy place."

"Kwizzeen?"

"Yeah, that's it."

"Any special occasion?"

"No, just to get together."

"The four of us?"

Nicole seemed somewhat amused—not by the invitation, but because Marlin was being so deliberately casual about it.

"Yep. Just the four of us."

"It's okay, you know," she said.

"What?"

"The fact that you used to date Lauren. We can socialize with her."

"I know that."

"She's been here a long time, and she's dating your best friend, but we've never even had them over. Why is that?"

"I don't know."

"If you're doing that on my account, you don't need to. I like Lauren. I mean, come on—she's great. I think we could be good friends. But if it makes you uncomfortable..."

"I wouldn't put it that way."

"Then how would you put it?"

"It just feels weird, to be honest."

"What feels weird, specifically? Being around your wife and an old girlfriend at the same time? Or hanging out with your best friend and your old girlfriend, because they're dating?"

"It's so hard to choose just one," Marlin said. "If you and Phil had dated at some point, then we'd really have something."

"It's not too late," Nicole said. "And he's kind of cute. I can see why the ladies fall for him."

"I always figured it was his rakish personality," Marlin said. "And his vast land holdings."

"He's the total package."

"Don't be talking about his package," Marlin said, which drew a guffaw from Nicole.

Then she said, "Are they getting serious, you think?"

"I've got no idea. He hasn't said much."

"Will it bother you if they do?"

"No. It'll just feel..."

"Weird?"

"You know me so well."

She handed her empty bowl to him. His turn to do the dishes.

"Let's do it ," Nicole said. "Just set it up. We'll have dinner at the fancy place and it will be fun, whether you like it or not."

18

Red had resisted buying a cell phone for a long time, and when he'd finally given in a few years back, he'd bought a cheap Korean knockoff, and that was only for work-related calls. He didn't need the damn internet or emails or any bullshit like that. Who the hell needs a map on their phone? If you didn't know where you were going, maybe you should just stay home. He damn sure wasn't taking any stupid selfies with it, or texting stupid messages to friends, or reading any stupid books.

Then he met Mandy. It wasn't like they hit it off at first, because she was kind of a wildcat. A drunk wildcat. A drunk wildcat who didn't mind breaking the law. But he liked his women that way, and after she tried to extort him, then took off across the country, then returned when it was clear she wouldn't be prosecuted, she came to see him and finally gave in to his rustic charms. She wasn't shy about it either. Came on strong.

Then he learned something wonderful about modern women and smartphones. If you were lucky, occasionally a woman like Mandy would send you a photo—the kind of photo that would brighten your day and put a spring in your jeans.

Problem was, his cheap phone didn't do the photos justice, so he caved and bought an iPhone, and Mandy's photos were even better than he'd ever imagined. In color and everything. Worth every penny he'd spent, which was a lot, because the cheapest model had cost more than Red's first truck, back in the day.

Red didn't want to become the kind of brainless zombie who was always looking down at his phone, but his new gadget brought a new set of temptations. Facebook. Instagram. Apps that would let him watch football from any damn location. Amazing. And, of course, now he had the ability to look up information about almost anything, no matter where he was. Red wasn't necessarily the curious type, but occasionally there were things he wanted to know.

Like, say, you're sitting in a beer joint and you get into a disagreement about the year Merle Haggard hit number one with *Big City*. Didn't take more than ten or fifteen seconds to learn it was 1982, just like you said, and now that idiot on the next bar stool owed you a cold one.

Or you're wanting to rebuild the carburetor on your old Ford, but you're not the greatest mechanic. In just a few seconds, you can find a video that walks you through it, step by step, and even tells you which tools you'll need and which new parts to have on hand.

Or maybe you want to find out more information about a scumbag named Drake. You want to know what other shady bullshit he might've pulled in the past. Ten or twenty years ago, that kind of information wasn't easily accessible by the general public. But now it was all right there, in your pocket.

Of course, Red had quickly learned that a lot of stuff you found online wasn't true, and you had to be careful, because he was pretty sure Ryan Reynolds wasn't secretly a Russian defector who'd fled his home country after impregnating one of Vladimir Putin's mistresses, who was both a fashion model and a nuclear physicist. Red had his doubts about all that.

But what about Drake? Drake wasn't famous, so there wouldn't be a bunch of weird lies about him online, right? Red went to the website for the wellness retreat and poked around a bit, finally finding what he wanted on the About Us page. Drake's last name, according to the bio, was von Oswald. Drake von Oswald. What a douchebag name.

Red googled that name, using the trick Billy Don had told him, which was putting it in quotation marks. He got more than a thousand hits. Hell, that was about nine hundred more than Red got when he googled his own name, which he had done once or twice, just for grins.

Red clicked on several of the links and learned that Drake von

Oswald had presented himself over the years as a yogi, a meditation expert, a homeopath, whatever that was, and a spiritual advisor. Sounded like a bunch of horseshit to Red.

Problem was, Red wasn't finding anything useful to make Drake von Oswald's life a living hell. He wanted to find evidence showing that Drake had a history of jerking women around. Right now, despite the fact that Mandy wondered if her drink had been spiked, nobody could prove it, and Mandy still wasn't upset about the photos themselves.

But Red kept digging, lying in bed with Mandy sleeping quietly beside him.

Fifteen minutes later, he was getting sleepy and was about to give up when he found something downright amazing. After he read it once, he still couldn't believe he'd found it, or that it was true. It was a Facebook post written seven years earlier by a woman in California, and surely she had to be on drugs, or maybe she was talking about somebody else, or maybe it was all just a big prank.

I want to warn all of you about a man named Graham Smith. He totally screwed my mother around in ways like you wouldn't believe. This man is pure evil and everybody needs to know about him. What he did was worm his way into my mom's life, trying to date her, and he's like forty years younger than she is. My mom liked him and so she started seeing him, and they were friends at first, and after that—okay, I won't get into all that, but they were a couple. We were all pretty grossed out about it, but this guy had some kind of strange hold on my mom. She said she loved him and that we didn't really understand him. But we knew he was up to something devious. I mean I love my mom and everything, but why would this young good-looking guy want to date a woman who was a senior citizen? She could've been his grandmother!

Anyway, like six months went by and nothing weird happened, so we started to think maybe we were wrong, and then my mom mentioned that Graham had asked to have a power of attorney on some of her financial dealings. Those of you who know my family know that she is comfortable financially and has nothing to worry about in that department. Long story short, she had given Graham POA, and by the time we were able to look into everything he had done, he had sold several of her properties and basically embezzled the money.

The problem was that technically it wasn't a crime since she had given him permission to do all that stuff. He was long gone by then and there was nothing we could do about it. We're just lucky it wasn't worse. He could've taken everything. When I talked to a detective working on the case, he said Graham has done things like this in the past, but nothing quite this big. He said there wasn't much he could do about it, so it's just a hard lesson for all of us.

Update: I've been keeping tabs on Graham for the three years since he pulled all this crap, and I found that he changed his name to Drake von Oswald. Obviously he's trying to start over with a new name, because nowadays a simple online search can tell you the truth about who a person really is. So I'm adding his new name here so that people will find it and know what kind of scumbag they are dealing with.

Update #2: Another year has passed and Graham/ Drake is still free and not charged with any crimes. It's amazing what you get can away with in this country. If nothing else, he deserves to get his ass kicked, although I'm certainly not suggesting anybody do that (wink, wink). I just want him to go to prison before he finds any other victims.

19

Red had to summon every bit of willpower he possessed to let Mandy sleep, instead of waking her with this fresh information.

Instead, he eased out of bed, closed the bedroom door behind him, and followed the narrow hallway to the living room near the far end of the trailer. Red had never heard Billy Don go to bed, which meant he hadn't, because when Billy Don went anywhere inside the trailer, there was no mistaking it. The floors vibrated from one end to the other.

Just as Red suspected, he found Billy Don in his usual spot on the couch, his head tipped backward, fast asleep, now with a black-and-white John Wayne movie playing.

Red continued through the living room to the kitchen, where he grabbed two tallboys out of the fridge. He went back into the living room and bumped one of the cans against Billy Don's arm. He woke up slowly, looked at Red, looked at the beer, then took it and cracked it open and took a drink.

"I found it," Red said, downright giddy at this point.

"I'm sure it wasn't too hard. It was in the fridge."

"Not the beer. I found some dirt on Drake von Oswald. That's his last name—von Oswald. Can you believe it?"

Red went to sit in his recliner.

"What time is it?" Billy Don asked.

"Twelve-fifteen."

"Couldn't sleep?"

"Did you hear me?"

"Yeah, twelve-fifteen."

"About the dirt, genius. I was doing research on Drake von Oswald."

Red was getting pissed that Billy Don didn't seem interested.

"Doing research?"

"Yep."

"What kind of research?"

"You know—looking stuff up on my phone."

Billy Don snorted. "Right. You can barely turn that thing on."

"No, I really was. And you won't believe what I found out."

"You gonna spit it out?"

"I found a Facebook post, and, well…hang on." Red took his phone out. "I took some screen shots, just in case I couldn't find it again."

"*You* took screen shots?"

"It ain't real hard. Don't be acting like I'm some kinda idiot. You're the one who wondered why so many towns are named after their water tower."

"I was kidding about that."

As Red navigated his phone, he said, "Drake used to go by a different name, and when he did, a long time ago, he used to take advantage of old ladies."

"Take advantage how?"

"He'd act like he had the hots for 'em, and once they trusted him, he'd steal their money."

"Get out."

"Ain't kidding."

"How much money?"

"I'm not sure, but I think a lot."

Now he read the entire Facebook post he'd found earlier.

Then Billy Don said, "Why ain't he in prison?"

"Because he did it all legally. Get 'em to sign all the right papers and such. He'd sucker 'em."

"That's about the shittiest thing I ever heard. Stealing from Grandma?"

"Yup."

"Can't believe nobody's beat some sense into him. Or worse."

"Yup."

"What exactly is a power of attorney?" Billy Don asked.

"It's when you can sign documents saying that person can do stuff for you legally," Red said. "Contracts and stuff."

"Why would an old lady sign that for a guy like Drake? Or Graham? Or whatever the hell his name is?"

"People do stupid stuff sometimes," Red said. "Even us, occasionally."

"That reminds me of that one scuzzy guy who did something similar that other time. I can't remember his name. I think it was on TV."

Red didn't even bother to reply to that. Instead he said, "I haven't even met the guy, and I *knew* he was a damn piece of trash."

"So what're you gonna do?" Billy Don asked. "I mean we."

"That's a damn good question. I figure at a minimum, we oughta—"

"Y'all don't have to do anything," Mandy said as she emerged from the hallway, apparently having heard some of their conversation. Her tone suggested that she was a tad irritated.

"Oh," Red said. "You're up."

"Yeah, I'm up. And why are the two of you in here talking about something that don't concern you?"

"I, uh…" Red said.

"I'm just drinking a beer," Billy Don said.

"You were just asking Red what y'all were gonna do," Mandy said.

Billy Don looked down at his lap.

"And you," Mandy said to Red.

"I was just—"

"You was just acting like I need you to save me," Mandy said.

"I didn't mean it that—"

"I can take care of myself," Mandy said.

Red thought, *Apparently not.* But he was smart enough not to say it.

Mandy added, "And if I need any help from you two buffoons, I'll ask for it. We clear on that?"

"Yes, ma'am," Billy Don said.

Red nodded.

Mandy glared at them both for a long moment, then she looked at Red with a much softer expression and said, "Okay, then. You coming back to bed or what?"

Billy Don said, "If he won't, I'd be happy to make sure you—"

"Not funny," Red said as he lifted himself out of the recliner.

20

It was cold and bright the next morning when Marlin found Mason Cross on the metal roof of the small house that now served as the foreman's quarters on the Richters' ranch. Cross stopped what he was doing and watched from his perch as Marlin parked his truck beside a filthy Chevy dually and got out.

"Morning!" Marlin called out.

"Morning," Cross replied, without the slightest hint of friendliness.

He was wearing jeans, work boots, and a stained Carhartt jacket. He had a battery-powered drill in his left hand.

Marlin walked closer. "Let me guess—screws are backing out and water's getting in around 'em."

"That's what usually happens."

"Now the wood is soft under some of them, so you have to drive a new screw a few inches over, then caulk the old hole."

Cross stared at him for a long moment, then said, "You need something?"

"I'm John Marlin, the county game warden," Marlin said.

Cross didn't say anything.

"I left you a voicemail yesterday," Marlin said.

"I heard it."

"I was hoping you might call me back."

"Had other things to do."

"No big deal. I just wanted to introduce myself. I like to know as many landowners and ranch managers as I can. It's just part of the job."

Cross deftly used his deformed right hand to pull a screw from his pocket and then drove it with the drill in his left hand.

"I understand you take care of the hunting lease arrangements," Marlin said. "Get the paperwork signed and so on."

"Who told you that?"

"The Richters. I visited with them last fall, and I left a note on your door at the time."

"I remember."

"Then I came out again yesterday. I was driving by and decided to stop in and say hello. The Richters gave me your phone number."

Cross pulled another screw from his pocket.

Marlin said, "My neck is getting kind of sore from looking up at you. You mind coming down for a minute?"

"Need to get this done today, before the rain comes."

"No rain in the forecast," Marlin said.

"Gonna rain tomorrow."

"You want a hand? I don't mind giving you an hour or two. We could get it knocked out."

"I got it handled."

This guy was a jerk, no doubt about it.

"How many hunters did you have on the place this season?" Marlin asked.

"Four."

"That's all?"

"Yep. Richters didn't want anybody too close to the house, so we don't use the middle or lower pasture."

At least he was answering questions now.

"Not even bow hunters back there?"

"Nope."

"Just rifle?"

"Yep."

"Deer only?"

Cross wiped his nose with the back of his sleeve—more a gesture of impatience than anything else. "They can shoot pigs."

"You got a lot?"

"Some."

"Seems like it's getting worse every year," Marlin said.

Cross drove two more screws while Marlin stood there.

"They take any good bucks this year?" Marlin asked.

"Who?" Cross asked, and his tone suggested that Marlin was bothering him.

"Your hunters," Marlin said. "Who else would I be talking about?"

"I've got no idea. You keep asking questions while I'm trying to work."

"Fair enough. Then one last question. You got a hunting lease license?"

"Of course we do. It's the law."

"I'm going to need to see that."

"Right now?" Cross was making no effort to hide his irritation.

"Yes, sir."

Cross pulled out his wallet, retrieved a folded document, and flung it downward in Marlin's general direction, but it planed and landed several feet away. Marlin picked it up, unfolded it, and inspected the information. Everything was in order.

"This is supposed to be posted somewhere on the premises, not carried in your wallet," Marlin said.

Cross let out a noise of exasperation. "Why are you giving me a hard time?"

"Just wanting a little cooperation," Marlin said. "Goes both ways."

"What exactly do you need?"

"The names of the hunters on the lease."

"Why?"

"One of your neighbors found a bullet hole through his blind back in November."

"Phil Colby," Cross said. "He accused me of doing it. He came close to getting his ass kicked."

"I wouldn't recommend trying that," Marlin said.

"I don't like to be accused of bullshit I didn't do."

"Fair enough. Any idea what happened?"

"The bullet hole? Well, I can tell you're wondering if one of my hunters did it, but I've got no way of knowing that, do I? It would've been a stray shot, and I doubt they'd admit it."

"So you didn't ask any of them about it?"

"Nope. Not planning on it now."

"Got a logbook?" Marlin asked.

Some ranches required hunters to sign in and out, so the owner or foreman would know when hunters were on the premises. It was a safety precaution in case someone failed to return after a hunt.

"Yeah, we keep a log."

"Where do you keep it?"

"Did you see the mailbox just inside the gate?"

"I did."

"That's where it is."

A lot of leases arranged things that way, so the hunters could pull up to the mailbox and access the logbook without getting out. Marlin would be able to tell by the dates whether any of the hunters had been on the ranch on the date the bullet had been fired into Colby's blind.

"I need to take a look at it," he said.

"You got no legal right."

That was true. The logbook wasn't required by the state, and even though game wardens were afforded plenty of latitude to ensure that hunters were following the law, Marlin couldn't see that logbook without a warrant.

"But why wouldn't you want me to see it?" Marlin asked. "I don't get it. If you and your hunters didn't fire that bullet, you've got nothing to worry about."

"I'm done talking. You're wasting my time and I've got work to do."

Marlin stayed where he was, but Mason Cross drove more screws and ignored him. Marlin got into his truck and drove over to the mailbox. Now Mason Cross was watching him again, and it appeared he was yelling something, but Marlin couldn't hear it.

He pulled his phone out and called Alford Richter, who answered on the third ring.

Marlin told Richter he'd just visited with Mason Cross and said, "I'm hoping to get a look at the logbook, but he's not too keen on that. You mind giving me permission?"

"The what?"

"The logbook. Each time one of the hunters comes to the ranch, he signs in and out. It probably also lists the names and phone numbers of the hunters in the front."

"I don't understand why Mason wouldn't want you to see that, but I wouldn't read too much into it," Richter said. "He's just stubborn.

Actually 'contrary' is a better descriptor. That's just his way. Between you and me, I wonder if his injury created some anger that he hasn't been able to resolve."

"You have any problem with me checking the logbook?"

"Not at all, but I thought game wardens could do just about anything without a warrant."

"I can't look at the logbook without permission, and right now, I don't have the names or phone numbers of your hunters."

"Why do you need that?"

"I'd like to ask them if they know anything about the bullet hole in Phil Colby's blind."

"By all means, take a look. We want to cooperate completely."

He thanked Richter, ended the call, and opened the mailbox. Grabbed the logbook and opened it up on his lap. Took a photo of the hunters' names and phone numbers, then thumbed through it to the date that Phil found the bullet hole in his blind. None of the hunters had logged in on that day, or the day before, when Phil and Mason Cross had had their argument. That made it much more likely that Mason Cross was responsible for that bullet hole. Would he have been stupid enough to brag about it later to any of the hunters? Unlikely, but worth checking.

Just as Marlin slipped the logbook back into the mailbox, Mason Cross rapped hard on the passenger side window. "The hell do you think you're doing?" he asked through the glass.

Marlin lowered the window. "Alford gave me the go-ahead," he said. "And you probably need to rein yourself in a little."

"Or what?"

Marlin took a breath.

"Mr. Cross, I already gave you a break on failing to post that lease license. I think that was damn nice of me, but you're still being an ass, and I can't figure out why."

Mason Cross's face in the window was twisted with anger or hate, but he didn't respond. He simply turned and walked away.

Marlin wasn't happy about the interaction, and he wished Cross had been more cooperative. But something was bothering him more. So far, Cross struck Marlin as an angry and unhappy man—one willing to make threats—but was he a killer? What if Cross had had nothing to do with the murder of Lonnie Blair?

21

"Here's an idea," Billy Don said. "Maybe we should call up one of the TV news stations and tell 'em all about Drake von Oswald. Tell 'em what he did out in California, taking advantage of old ladies, and then he changed his name and ran away. They could run a story and embarrass the hell out of him. Make everybody know what kind of lowlife he really is. Those newspeople love doing that kind of thing. If they can ruin somebody's life, it makes their damn day."

"I already thought about doing that," Red lied.

"And?" Billy Don said.

Off the top of his head, Red liked the idea okay, and if he could see it panning out, he'd be happy to take credit for it and say he thought of it first. But if it had flaws, he'd act like he knew it was dumb from the start, and that Billy Don was a step behind him in figuring that out.

So Red thought about it for a minute, and he could see a weak point. "One problem is, he'll just say there was some kind of misunderstanding back then with that old lady, and she *wanted* him to have that money."

"Then they could just ask her. She'd say he was lying, right?"

"She may not even be alive anymore," Red said.

"Oh," Billy Don said. "Yeah."

They were in Red's truck, headed toward Johnson City, planning to run a couple of errands and then grab some lunch, or maybe a late breakfast, depending on what time it was. The rancher out in Round

Mountain hadn't given them the go-ahead yet to clear those three hundred acres, so they had some time on their hands, which was the way Red preferred it. They both still had plenty of cash on hand from that pig-hunting bounty, and the big blackjack score in Vegas, so they could coast for a while.

Now Billy Don brightened up and said, "Hey, they could talk to the daughter that wrote that post on Facebook. She'd tell 'em what was what!"

Red swung into the parking lot at the Lowe's Market, formerly the Super S. He didn't have an answer for Billy Don about that idea yet, so he stalled by pulling up next to one of the gas pumps and saying, "I drive, you pump. Them's the rules. And don't forget to squeegee the windshield."

Marlin had left voicemails for two of the hunters on the Richter ranch when he got a call from a landowner about a buck tangled in a goat fence on Middle Creek Road. He was on his way to that location when one of the hunters, Terrell Cobb, called him back. Marlin knew from the logbook that Cobb and his fellow leaseholders lived in Houston, which meant it was possible none of them had heard about the death of Lonnie Blair.

"Thanks for getting back to me," Marlin said. "How was your season?"

Most hunters expected a game warden to ask a question like that.

"I got a good ten-point," Cobb said. "Big-bodied deer. The antlers weren't bad, either. Other than that, just saw the same old group of does over and over, and some bucks that need a few more years."

"Do the four of y'all each have your own blind, or do you hunt all over?"

"No, we drew straws to pick a place."

"You know that panhandle portion of your lease that runs behind Hidden Hills Ranch? Who hunts that portion?"

"That would be me. I wanted it because there's a little spring-fed creek that runs through there. I figured after the drought last summer, the deer would want a reliable water source."

"Good strategy."

Marlin passed Stoneledge Pass and eased off the gas.

"It worked out nice. I saw a lot more deer than my friends did."

"I believe you can see another blind about three hundred yards south of you, right?"

"Uh, yeah, on Hidden Hills. How did you know?"

Cobb obviously had not heard about Lonnie Blair, and Marlin wasn't ready to reveal everything yet.

"Here's the situation: There was a recent incident involving that blind south of you. I think someone might've fired a shot from your blind at that other blind."

Cobb let out a little noise of surprise.

"You know anything about that?" Marlin asked.

"I can tell you I *never* shoot in that direction. I don't even open the window on the south side of my blind. I only shot one time this season, and that was for that ten-point. He was west of me."

"Did anybody else hunt from your blind this season?"

"Nope. Just me."

"None of the other hunters would've used your blind?"

"Not without asking. We've all been friends since high school, and none of them would hunt my blind without telling me, and they definitely wouldn't shoot across a fence, even accidentally. These guys are all responsible hunters and gun owners. But the weird thing is, now that we're talking about it, there was one time a few weeks ago when it seemed like somebody had been in my blind."

"Why did you think that?"

Marlin was moving along at about five miles per hour. The deer was supposedly stuck in the fence somewhere along this stretch of county road. Maybe it had worked itself free.

"Things had been moved around," Cobb said. "I'm kind of methodical about the way I do things, and I could tell it wasn't the same as when I'd left it."

"What was different?"

"I don't keep a lot of stuff in there—just a chair and a propane heater and a plastic weatherproof tub for my binoculars and a pair of ear guards and some other stuff. I always set the tub on the chair and push the chair into the corner away from the door. But that time, the tub was on the floor and the chair wasn't in the corner."

"Maybe you just forgot," Marlin said.

"No chance of that. I follow a routine, and that's the way I've always done it, and the way I will always do it."

Marlin rounded a curve and saw the deer caught in the fence on the left side of the road. Like many fences around here, this one consisted of two parts—goat fence on the bottom, up to about four feet, topped by a single strand of barbed wire. And like many deer that got caught in a fence when jumping over, one hind hoof had gone under the strand of barbed wire and had become twisted between the barbed wire and the top wire of the goat fence. A crude but effective snare. One hoof high in the air, the rest of the buck flat on the ground. The buck was probably exhausted after a long struggle. Or dead. Marlin eased onto the grassy shoulder on the right.

"Maybe an animal got in there and moved things around," Marlin said. "A raccoon or something."

"I guess that's possible, but it doesn't seem very likely."

"Is that stuff still in the blind?" Marlin asked.

"No, I brought it all home, now that the general season is over. Except for the chair."

"What's the chair made of?"

"Just an old office chair on wheels. Metal frame with a padded seat and backrest."

"Is it *your* chair? You own it?"

"Yeah, I brought it there. I just didn't feel like carrying it down the ladder from the blind. Can you tell me more about the incident? I'm worried that somebody did something really bad or stupid from my blind."

"I can't go into detail right now, but I can tell you it's a homicide investigation," Marlin said.

"Oh, Jesus. That's terrible. Who was killed?"

"A man named Lonnie Blair," Marlin said, because there was no reason to withhold that information. "Did you know him?"

"No, I didn't. And like I said, I *never* shot in that direction. Never. Not once."

"At this point, you're not a suspect in anything," Marlin said. "And I can't imagine you ever will be. I'm just gathering information."

"That's good to know."

"What can you tell me about the Richters and Mason Cross?"

"I never even met the Richters," Cobb said. "But Mason Cross was—to be honest, we all avoided him, because he's not a pleasant guy."

"That's putting it mildly," Marlin said, attempting to provoke Cobb into speaking as freely as he would like. "Anything in particular that he said or did?"

"No, he just seemed angry all the time. Wait, 'angry' isn't the right word. I'd say resentful. Like he was bitter at the world, and he wanted to do something about it. All of my friends and I have already agreed that we aren't going back to the ranch next season, and it was because of Mason. We just don't want to deal with him."

"This is all very helpful," Marlin said. "Might need to talk to your friends, too."

"I'm sure they would all be happy to help. Just give me a call if you need anything else."

Marlin thanked him and hung up, then got out of the truck with a pair of wire cutters and slowly approached the deer, which was on the far side of the fence. Always best to stay on the opposite side from the trapped deer.

Marlin made a clucking noise as he got within ten feet, but the buck remained motionless. Then Marlin saw that the chest rose and fell, rose and fell.

If the deer panicked, he could injure himself further. Marlin edged closer, and closer still, and the buck raised its head.

Marlin took one more step and reached the fence. He extended the wire cutters and quickly snipped the goat fence. That wouldn't impact the integrity of the fence, whereas snipping the barbed wire would've loosened the entire strand, requiring a repair later.

The hoof, now free, fell to the ground. The deer still didn't move.

Marlin saw no injuries, other than a raw spot just above the hoof. Nothing appeared to be broken, but the deer could've been trapped for days.

Marlin backed up several feet and waited.

Still no movement.

Marlin clapped his hands, loud and sharp.

The buck clambered to its hooves and sprinted into the brush, apparently none the worse for wear.

22

As George Besserman drove west on Highway 290 through Dripping Springs, he couldn't help thinking about the poker night he'd attended last month. George wasn't a card player, but a neighbor had encouraged him to join in, so he had.

The poker nights were so successful, they usually had to open two tables, and sometimes three. It was just a fun, friendly evening among the men of Rancho Vista Estates—until the guy who lived over on Desperado Gulch asked George what he did for a living.

Not this again.

George said he worked for a clothing company, and this guy, Hank Paddock, whom George had met only once at the community pool, asked what *kind* of clothing. Hank was smoking a cigar and drinking Scotch neat. While playing poker. Could he be any more of a cliché? Acting like Mr. Vegas. All he needed was one of those card-player visors.

George said his company mostly produced women's clothes, hoping Hank would let it drop after that. He'd think George meant skirts and blouses and other items that most men would find boring.

But no. Hank was the curious sort. "Oh, yeah? What brand is it?" He was slurring his words a bit.

"Where I work?" George said.

"Yeah. What's the company, or the designer? Whatever you call it."

"Sarah's Intimates," George said. "We make a damn nice product."

"Intimates?"

"Yes," George said. "Sarah's Intimates. I'm a shipping manager. Where do you work?"

"At Dell, but hang on," Hank said. "Intimates? What is that exactly?"

Had somebody put Hank up to this? Had George been invited solely so this conversation could take place? Was this a prank of sorts? Setting George up?

"Mostly undergarments," George said.

"Undergarments?" said Barry, who lived on Chuck Wagon Circle. "Right."

"What kind of undergarments?" asked Marty, who lived on Lariat Loop.

"Women's undergarments," George said, refusing to be embarrassed about it. Why should he be? Somebody had to be involved with the manufacture of women's undergarments. Why should it be just women? That made no sense.

"Well, I already knew it was women's stuff," Hank said. "You mean, like, bras and panties? That sort of thing?"

"And a few other items, but yes, that's most of the product line."

Five seconds of awkward silence passed at both tables.

"We gonna order pizza?" somebody asked.

"Are you, uh, gay or something?" Hank asked George, looking confused. "I mean, it's not a big deal if you are..."

"I'm not, but why would you ask that?" George said.

"Well, it just seems kind of weird, is all. A straight man selling panties and stuff."

"I don't sell them. As I said, I'm a shipping manager. But even if I did sell them, why would that be weird?"

"It's just, you know, not the usual thing."

"The usual thing," George said. "What exactly is the usual thing?"

"Ah, give him a break," said Robert, who lived on Barnyard Boulevard. "Hell, I wish I could spend all day fondling panties."

"I don't fondle—"

"Robert, you wouldn't just fondle them, you'd put them on!" said Terry, who lived on Cattleman Cove. Everybody just laughed and laughed at that one.

"I hope you get free samples," said Frank, who lived on Shootout Pass.

George could feel his face getting warm. "I said I'm a shipping manager. That means I don't even—"

"Are these, like, *sexy* bras and panties, with lace and silk and good colors?" asked Peter, who lived on Quick Draw Drive. "Thongs, pushups, garter belts—stuff like that?"

"Or are they the kind my wife wears?" asked Sam, who lived on Six-Gun Alley.

Now everybody was roaring. Well, everybody except George. He tried to play along, smiling, but he knew he wasn't convincing anyone. When the laughter died down, everybody seemed to know that George was offended. That was the worst part of it—George didn't *want* to let it get to him, but he couldn't help it. These clowns were making fun of his career. They'd crossed a line. And they were bigots. Or they were pretending to be, just so they could fit in.

"I didn't mean anything by it," Hank said, still clenching the cigar in his fat face. There was no sincerity in his voice at all. It was just a lame, offhand remark.

A couple of the guys were still giggling, but trying to stifle it. Most of them were staring at the top of the table.

"Not a problem," George said.

"Whose deal is it?" Peter asked.

"Ever try anything on?" Hank asked, as if he were dead serious, and then he burst into a laugh that rattled the chips on the table. A couple of the other guys were laughing so hard their faces were turning red. One of these middle-aged slobs might actually have a heart attack.

George wanted to stand up fast and flip the table over, like in a movie. He wanted to tell all these morons that they didn't know what the hell they were talking about, and that he never even *saw* the products his company produced, and that his job was no different than a shipping manager at a company that produced plumbing supplies or sporting goods or any other damn product.

Instead he said, "The panties are a little snug."

Trying to pretend he was in on the joke and that they weren't laughing at him, because they were all having a good yuk-yuk together.

He hated himself for it.

The incident was humiliating. Emasculating. Frustrating. And George had had enough.

He had decided right then, on poker night, that he wasn't going to put up with that kind of nonsense anymore. No more sneering wiseguys. No more thinly disguised insults. No more mockery. He was going to stand up for himself. No more bullies. That's what it boiled down to. No more bullies—not just about his line of work, but about anything at all. That's the vow he'd made to himself. Don't let jerks get away with being jerks. Call them on it. Make them back down. Make them understand that their behavior was unacceptable.

Then came Mason Cross.

George had never experienced a bigger bully, but what could he have done about it yesterday? The man was probably insane, and he carried a gun. And he'd tried to frame George by dropping that other gun, probably empty, into his lap.

So George had given in, of course, which was totally rational, despite his new vow, and then he'd stopped at that roadside park to regain his composure, and then he'd gone home and tried to forget about the entire bizarre incident.

But he couldn't. He just couldn't. How could you forget something like that?

Sure, Mason Cross had had the upper hand the first time, but there was no reason George couldn't orchestrate a second encounter—one without any unexpected surprises. Well, no surprises for George. Mason Cross, on the other hand, might be very surprised.

Red pushed the cart while Billy Don filled it with some of their regular items—tortilla chips and salsa, Slim Jims, hamburger and hotdog buns, a full case of ranch-style beans. They made a quick pass through the produce section for some apples and oranges and such. Red wasn't all that fond of fruit, but a doctor a few years back told him he was on the verge of scurvy, so he'd made an honest effort to eat a fruit or veggie once or twice a week.

"So what about the daughter?" Billy Don said.

Would the newspeople talk to the daughter of the old lady after all these years? Why would they do that now? Just because Drake opened the wellness center? Maybe, but maybe not.

Red said, "We'd have to tell 'em why we're calling about Drake now. We'd have to tell 'em what he did to Mandy."

"Them pictures?"

"Not just that. Spiking her drink. And we ain't got no evidence of that. Just her sayin' it, and we can't even mention Mandy, because—"

"You're scared of her."

"I'm what?"

"Scared of her."

"Yeah, right."

"You sure as hell are."

"You've lost your damn mind!" Red said. "Besides, you were the one calling her ma'am left and right last night. If anyone's scared of her, it's you."

"Of course I am. I'll admit it. I ain't no idiot. She's a firecracker."

"Well, I'm not."

"Then why are we doing this behind her back?"

"What?"

"Last night she basically told us to mind our own bidness, but here we are, planning something."

"Because we don't want her to be empricated in anything we might do. If she don't know what we're gonna do, they can't blame her for it. We're just protecting her."

Billy Don made a sound like a chicken squawking.

"We're getting sidetracked," Red said.

They were currently in the cookie-and-candy section. If Red wasn't careful, Billy Don would grab half the inventory. He sped up and made it to the end of the aisle with Billy Don snagging nothing more than a family-size package of Nutter Butters.

Red said, "The other problem is, if we contact the newspeople and they're not interested in the story, which seems likely based on everything I already told you, we'd gain nothing from it, but we would've exposed ourselves."

"Wouldn't be the first time I exposed myself."

"What I mean is, they'd know who we are, and then if we did something to Drake, like beat him senseless, and then he calls the cops, the people at the news station might say, 'Hey, a guy just contacted us about that loser the other day. Maybe that guy—the one who called us—beat him up.' See what I'm saying? We would've tipped our hand. They could link us to it. Better if we don't tell anybody what we're gonna do."

"Including Mandy," Billy Don said.

"Damn right, including Mandy," Red said. "Especially Mandy."

"Because you're scared of her," Billy Don said.

23

After freeing the deer, Marlin returned to his truck and sent a text to Bobby and Lauren.

Hunter on the Richter ranch thinks somebody might've been in his blind a few weeks ago. Clear shot from there to Lonnie's blind, but roughly three hundred yards. Hell of a shot. Thinking we should get a warrant for the chair he left in the blind.

A few minutes later, Bobby replied: *How about we meet at 1:00 for a group update?*

Lauren said: *Can we make it 2:00? On my way to an interview and don't know how long it will take.*

They all agreed.

Then Marlin called Phil Colby and said, "Let me ask you something. Is there any chance that bullet hole was there before you and Mason Cross got crossways with each other?"

"Nope. None whatsoever."

Marlin didn't reply right away.

Phil said, "You don't believe me?"

"Sometimes memories get wonky. The other day I couldn't remember the name of our third-grade teacher."

"Mrs. Griffin," Colby said. "Here's how it went: I hunted on whatever day that was—I think it was a Saturday morning—and as I was leaving, that's when Cross waved me over to the fence and asked me to move the blind. You know how that went. I came back the next morning, and the bullet hole was there. You remember that the door is in the back wall of the blind, facing north, toward the Richter place, and the hole was smack in the middle of the door. I literally could not overlook it. That first day, it wasn't there, but the next day, it was."

"Yeah. Okay."

The line was silent for a minute.

"Not getting anywhere with the case?" Phil asked.

"Not sure. Not yet."

"You talk to that guy I ran into at the rest stop?"

"I found a phone number for him online, but I haven't tried it yet."

"What's the holdup?"

"What's the point? He never even met Mason Cross until yesterday, so I don't see how he could help with the Lonnie Blair case."

After a short pause, Phil said, "Yeah, okay. Hey, you wanna grab some lunch in a bit?"

Marlin started to say no out of pure reflex—he wanted to concentrate on the case—but he also needed to eat at some point.

"When and where?" he said.

"Twelve-thirty at Ronnie's?"

"See you then."

Lauren Gilchrist had left three voicemails for Barton Scott since she had reviewed the video with the dance hall manager. Barton Scott hadn't called her back. In the first two voicemails, Lauren had left vague messages that didn't mention why she wanted to talk. In the third, she'd said she was investigating a minor incident at the dance hall a few Saturdays ago, and she was contacting anybody who was there. Make him feel safe, like maybe Lauren thought he was only a witness. Still, no callback.

So she called the vodka distillery on Fitzhugh Road and they said yes, he was there. She hung up and drove out to see him, roughly 20 miles east of Johnson City, in Hays County.

She found him under a pavilion, setting up tables and folding chairs, evidently preparing for an event later that evening. Half a dozen propane heaters were spaced evenly among an equal number of round tables.

Barton Scott was twenty-six years old and had graduated from Sul Ross University three years earlier with a BBA in marketing. Nice-looking kid, Lauren thought. Six feet. Slender. Short black hair. Friendly smile as she approached in uniform.

She introduced herself and he said, "Oh, man, I've been meaning to call you back. Sorry about that. We've been swamped around here."

"No problem. It was a nice drive. You got a minute to talk?"

"Sure thing. Want to sit?"

They each grabbed a nearby chair.

"Nice place," Lauren said. "When did y'all open?"

"Last October. It's been going really well so far. You know, you'd think this area would be oversaturated by now with so many distilleries and breweries and wineries, but it just seems like it's growing even more. Every weekend, we do a record amount of business, and then we beat it the next weekend. Seems like there's no end in sight."

"What do you do here?"

"I'm one of the hospitality managers."

"Sounds like fun."

"Mostly I manage events; parties, company picnics, banquets, that sort of thing."

"Keeps you busy?"

"I'm working sixty hours a week, but they're about to hire an assistant for me, and I can't wait."

"You managed to get to the dance hall two weeks ago this past Saturday night, right?" Lauren asked.

He thought about it, then said, "I did, yeah, but I didn't stay for long. I was pretty beat."

"What time did you get there?"

"You mind, uh, telling me what's going on? You said something happened there that night?"

"A minor incident," Lauren said. "What time did you get there?"

"I'd say it was around ten-thirty."

Close enough. The video showed him arriving at 10:37.

"Were you meeting anyone?"

"My ex-girlfriend, Tracy, and a couple of her friends. Normally Tracy and I would've gone together, but I was working late, so she drove and took her friends. I wasn't even sure I was going to be able to make it, but I did."

"What were you driving?"

"My Jeep."

"So you got there at ten-thirty and then what happened?"

"I went inside and looked for Tracy, but I couldn't find her. Then I found her friends, but they didn't know where she was, either. It gets real crowded in there, so it's not easy to find people unless you wander around the entire hall. So I texted her, but she didn't text back, so I looked for her some more."

Barton appeared slightly nervous, but some people got that way talking to cops, even when they had no reason to be concerned. At some point, Lauren would reveal the reason for the interview, but she wasn't ready to tip her hand just yet. She wanted his full statement on record.

"What did you do after that?" she asked.

"I asked Wanda at the door if she'd seen Tracy, and she thought she'd gone outside earlier, so I went outside, too. Even in the winter, it gets hot inside, especially if you're dancing a lot, and Tracy loves to dance. So I figured maybe she went outside to cool off. But I didn't find her. I found her Tahoe, but she wasn't in it."

"So what did you do?"

So far, Barton's statement was matching the video.

"I sat in my Jeep for a few minutes, hoping she'd text me back, but I was really tired, and I was pretty much ready to go home and crash."

"Did she text you back?" Lauren asked.

Barton frowned. "Are you thinking maybe I saw something, like, related to a crime? You seem focused on me and Tracy, and that confuses me. Did Tracy do something?"

"Not at all. I'm just trying to understand where you were at a given time. Did she text you back?"

"Not that night, no."

"So what did you do then?"

Barton appeared uncomfortable and didn't answer right away. Lauren simply waited.

"I saw Tracy get out of some guy's truck," Barton said. "She went inside, and then he got out and went inside, too."

"Did you get a good look at him?"

"When he opened his truck door I did. From the interior light."

"Did you know him?"

"Never saw him before."

"Any idea why he and Tracy were out there?"

Barton made a cynical sound. "Obviously. They were hooking up."

"What did you do after you saw that?"

"I started to go inside and call her on it, but I changed my mind. It's a good thing, because if I'd seen the guy, I might've lost it." Barton was getting emotional, but trying to hide it. "Did something happen to him? Is that why you're asking me all this stuff?"

Those were perfectly reasonable and logical questions to ask at this point. Even an innocent person might ask them.

"We'll get to that," Lauren said. "If you didn't go back inside, what did you do?"

Barton ran one hand through his hair. Took a deep breath. Ready to break. He wanted to tell the truth, but he was struggling with it.

Lauren waited.

Barton finally said, "I think you already know what I did. It was stupid, but I waited in my Jeep and then followed that guy out of the parking lot."

24

"We could set his vehicle on fire," Billy Don said.

Red gave that idea an unenthusiastic grunt. Kind of predictable. And once the vehicle finished burning, then what? Drake would get paid by his insurance and his life would go back to normal.

"Or call the IRS and say he's cheating on his taxes," Billy Don said.

"Just call 'em up?"

"They've got some kinda hotline."

"Bullshit. For cheaters?"

"No, they do."

Now they were at Odiorne Feed & Ranch Supply, looking at new deer feeders, all lined up in a neat row on the edge of the parking lot, so they could be seen from the highway. Good way to draw people in. Kind of like having a bunch of young ladies in bikinis holding up a sign for a charity car wash. The feeder in Red's backyard was pretty old and used up a lot of batteries, but he wasn't sure if he was ready to toss it just yet. Why ditch something that was still working? Same reason he still had his old truck. And his trailer.

"You're saying the IRS has a hotline so you can narc on your friends and neighbors?" Red said.

"I think so. Fraud. That's what they call it."

"But you don't know for sure."

"No, it's fraud."

"I mean about the hotline."

"I heard about it somewhere."

"What's funny about that is, you hate taxes more than anybody I know."

Billy Don hadn't filed a tax return in years, or possibly ever. How he got away with that, Red wasn't certain. On the other hand, if he ever wanted to collect Social Security, he'd be out of luck.

Billy Don said, "Well, yeah, the reason I stay off their radar is 'cause they can turn your life into a living hell. I had a cousin that tangled with the IRS, and they hassled him so much, he moved to Mexico."

"That's pretty damn extreme," Red said.

"He owed something like eighty grand."

"So what would you tell the IRS about Drake? Just make something up?"

"I'd say he paid me a bunch of cash under the table, and once they start poking around in his financial stuff, I bet they'd find all kinds of things he did wrong."

"Or they might not. They might find nothing. And we'd never know, either, because that's all private kind of stuff. And how long would something like that take? I'm guessing years, because it's the guvermint, and they don't set any speed records."

"If you don't like the idea, just say so."

"I don't like it."

"Okay then."

"In fact, I hate it. I think it's terrible."

"Settle down."

"It's almost like you set out to come up with the worst idea possible."

"I ain't in the mood for your bullshit."

"But I'm enjoying myself."

"Whyn't you put that effort into coming up with something better—if you can."

"I will."

"Do it then."

"You can bet on it."

Red moved on to a different feeder, while Billy Don stayed where he was and pulled his phone from his pocket. Red knew exactly what

Billy Don was doing, but he was tired of the topic.

"This All Seasons model is pretty sweet," Red said, and immediately regretted it. Calling something "sweet" was trendy, and he didn't want to become one of those people. Next thing you know, he'd get all excited about something he read and say, "This!"

"Yep, they got a hotline," Billy Don said. "The IRS."

"Don't care," Red said.

"All you gotta do is call 'em up and...oh, wait. You can't report anybody on the hotline, but you can get a form you use to report 'em."

"That sounds like typical guvermint BS. Why all the goddamn hoops and extra steps?"

"You can print the form or get it mailed to you."

"At which point they know exactly who you are, and it wouldn't surprise me if they wind up looking at *you* for being a tax cheat instead. That's how they get ya."

"But you can also mail it in 'nonymously," Billy Don said.

"We already decided that idea sucks," Red said.

"*You* decided," Billy Don said.

"Which makes it official," Red said.

"You mail it in and then they investigate him," Billy Don said. "They got a whole list of different ways he mighta cheated."

"Yeah, but what if he didn't?" Red asked.

"Oh, come on. Everybody cheats on their taxes. If they do them."

"And a lot of people are really good at it, so they don't get caught."

"I think you're bashing the whole thing just 'cause I thought of it."

"Which is a pretty good rule of thumb," Red said. "If Billy Don comes up with it, try something else instead."

"Let's hear a better idea, smart ass."

"Already got one."

"Which is what?"

"Ain't no sewer lines around the wellness center, so they gotta be on septic, right?"

"Right."

"So we throw a stick of dynamite into the septic system."

Billy Don didn't say anything right away.

Red said, "I can tell you like it. Don't be lying and say you don't."

"It's not bad."

"I made it up just now, right off the top of my head."

Red was pretty sure Billy Don only liked it because it involved dynamite, but that was fine. Red liked it for the same reason. He knew a great deal about septic systems, and he knew it would probably be easy to access. After all, why would anyone feel the need to protect a septic system?

A place like the wellness center probably had at least one very large anaerobic system, which was basically a miniature sewage treatment plant. Expensive as hell, especially in this area, where excavation was so difficult. There would be one large underground concrete tank with at least three or four compartments, and those compartments would be covered by a domed neoprene lid about a foot and a half in diameter. Just remove that lid and drop a stick of dynamite inside. Better yet, drill a small hole in the lid. That would probably take less time than removing the lid. Then run like hell, of course.

"Gotta admit it would be fun," Billy Don said. "We gonna do it?"

"Maybe so."

"We'll blow that sumbitch skyhigh. Think of all the pressure up every pipe. Pieces of toilets will rain down all over the county."

Red didn't know if it would be quite that bad, but it would definitely shut down the wellness retreat for quite a while and people would be talking about it. Then Drake would have to spend a shitload of money to repair it all. Those systems were damn expensive and there were all kinds of inspections you had to pass.

Red said, "I figure we've got that one in our back pocket, and we'll hold on to it and see if we come up with something better."

"But we're still gonna kick his ass, too, right?"

"Oh, hell yeah."

"Good. Before or after the septic thing?'"

"Not sure yet. We'll figure that out."

"I got another idea," Billy Don said.

"What?" Red said, wondering if he really wanted to hear it.

"Lunch at Ronnie's," Billy Don said.

George Besserman parked in the same roadside rest stop where he'd stopped yesterday, when he'd been so unsettled that he knew it wasn't a good idea to drive. He backed into the shadows under a big oak tree, not far from two trucks similarly parked, with nobody in them. George got the sense that people carpooled from here with friends or coworkers. Good. That meant nobody would pay much attention to his Tesla.

He sat quietly for a moment and took a few deep breaths.

As far as his wife knew, he was at the office. As far as his office knew, he was sick at home.

This was a crossroads in his life. He knew that. A fork. Which way would he go? Continue to let people like Mason Cross get away with their unacceptable behavior? Stay quiet instead of speaking up? Let the "alpha males"—which was a bullshit concept, as far as George was concerned—dominate in every setting?

No.

Not anymore.

Hell no.

George hadn't slept last night. Literally not a wink. He'd been consumed by these overwhelming thoughts of taking action.

He'd gotten out of bed at two in the morning to write a note explaining everything. The whats. The whys. The whos. In case he never made it home, which was a possibility. The document was quite long before he was done. He hesitated to use the word "manifesto" because of its negative connotations by association with wackos, but it was certainly a declaration of his independence. He'd emailed the document to himself, which meant nobody would see it unless the police had to conduct a thorough investigation. Which meant he might be dead.

He got out of the Tesla and went around to the trunk. Popped it open. Raised the carpet to reveal the spare tire. Nestled inside the rim was the gun given to George by his brother. It was a Sig Sauer .380 that held eight rounds, including the one in the chamber. George had counted, to be sure.

He quickly and discreetly raised his sweatshirt and slipped the gun into the makeshift holster he had strapped securely above his hipbone. He had fashioned it out of cardboard, duct tape, and a spare belt. After all, he didn't own a holster. Why would he? He had never carried this gun anywhere.

He closed the trunk, locked his car, and walked to Miller Creek

Road. He turned right, away from Highway 281, and began a slow but consistent jog, mindful of the gun that felt heavy under his sweatshirt.

Off to his left was an RV park on the creek, but trees lined the fence and nobody over there would notice him. They certainly wouldn't be able to give a detailed description of him. A middle-aged white guy wearing dark-green sweats. Green baseball cap on his head. Sunglasses. Ear buds.

He passed a couple of houses on the left, but nobody was outside. The traffic noise from the highway faded quickly.

He hadn't jogged in years, and he was winded before he'd covered two hundred yards. Maybe he'd walk briskly instead. Didn't really matter if he jogged or walked. Anybody passing would pay him no mind. Just a guy out getting some exercise. If a vehicle appeared, George would clasp both hands on top of his head, in that familiar pose of an athlete trying to catch his breath.

He'd thought he would be nervous, and maybe he was, a little, but actually he felt an unexpected wave of relief. And why shouldn't he? The biggest bully he'd ever encountered was about to meet the new George. The confident George who no longer put up with jerks.

His plan was simple: Find Mason Cross and pull the gun on him. Show him how it feels. Make him apologize, then leave and never think of Mason Cross again.

George knew it might not go his way, and he was oddly okay with that. His manifesto—oops, his declaration of independence—would explain everything, and surely it would be leaked and end up online, possibly shared thousands or even millions of times. George would bet there were a lot of people just like him—frustrated, angry, fed up. Many of them would—

A black truck was coming toward him. George didn't pay much attention to trucks, and all the different models, and how much cargo they could carry, or anything like that, but this was a big truck with a metal guard on the front to protect the grille.

Uh-oh. It looked familiar.

It rumbled closer and closer, and now George could see that it was filthy. The windshield was so covered with grime, it was astounding the driver could see anything at all.

George stepped onto the grassy shoulder, and as the truck passed, he could see that Mason Cross was behind the wheel.

25

Barton said, "There are cameras inside and outside the dance hall. You notice things like that when you work at a place like this."

He pointed to the rafters of the pavilion behind Lauren, but she didn't look. She didn't need to.

She said, "You've got a camera mounted up there. Nest brand, I think. A black one."

"Yes, ma'am. That was my suggestion, the color, so it wouldn't stand out as much. I helped with the security system around here. I'm sure you've looked at the video from the dance hall, so you saw when I got there and when I left. You saw that I followed that guy out of the parking lot. But I didn't do anything to him. Something happened to him, right?"

"Tell me why you followed him."

"Is he dead?"

"Did you follow him home?"

"I followed him for a couple of miles, and by then, I started to wonder what the hell I was doing. Tracy wasn't worth it if she was gonna treat me that way. Plus I figured the guy wouldn't even have known she had a boyfriend, in which case, it wasn't his fault. Hell, the same thing happened to me once. I hooked up with a girl in Port Aransas and later learned she was engaged to be married that summer. That made me feel pretty gross, to be honest."

"So you stopped following him and went home."

"Yes, and I broke up with Tracy the next day. You can ask her."

"How did you break up with her? In person?"

"No, by text."

"What did you tell her?"

"I said it obviously wasn't going to work out between us, so we should just blow it off."

"You didn't mention seeing her get out of some guy's truck?"

"I wanted to see if she would admit it, but she didn't. After that, I didn't see the point of bringing it up. And, okay, to be honest, there's a girl working here I'm sort of interested in. So I figured it was best if I just let Tracy go."

"Do you still have those texts?"

"On my phone?"

It was a ridiculous question, of course. The kind a nervous person asks.

"Yes," Lauren said.

"Actually, yeah, I do."

"You mind if I see them?"

He slipped his phone from his pocket, accessed the Messages app, and handed it to Lauren. "There's nothing on there I'm concerned about, but it would be nice if you wouldn't poke around in other threads."

Lauren quickly read the relevant texts between Tracy and Barton. Everything was exactly as they'd both described, and it was more civil than Lauren would've expected.

She handed the phone back to him.

"Thanks."

He said, "You gonna tell me what's going on?"

"The man you followed that night is dead," Lauren said.

Barton's eyes widened. "What happened? Did he die that night?"

"No, two days ago," Lauren said. "On Sunday afternoon. I can't share a lot of details, but he was murdered."

"Oh, man. That's terrible, but I promise I had nothing to do with it. I would never do anything like that. How did he die?"

"We're working on that. Did you ever learn his name?"

"No idea. What was it?"

"Lonnie Blair. Ring any bells?"

"I've never met him or even heard of him."

"Tell me what you did this past Sunday. Walk me through it."

"I worked. I'm always working. I usually get here at about eleven and—oh, there was a party that afternoon, so I ended up staying until about eight that night. In fact, I can show you video right now, if you want. On my phone. I have access to all that."

"Sure."

Lauren waited as Barton Scott opened the app and found the right video. He held the phone for her to see, and it was time-stamped.

"That's the camera in the front parking lot. You can see me arriving at ten-fifty seven."

She could see him clearly as he got out of his Jeep and went inside.

He pulled the phone back, swiped the screen a few times, then held it out again. "And here I am leaving that night at eight-oh-nine. There's no way I could've left during the party. Ask anybody that was working that day. And the video shows my Jeep in the lot the entire time. I'll give you as much video footage as you want. Other cameras will show me here all day."

His alibi was solid, but her intuition told her he was holding something back.

Lauren said, "The bottom line is, I don't think you did anything to him, but if you followed him further than you said that night, you need to tell me now. If you go back and change your story later, that'll look really bad."

"I would never kill anybody," he said. "I had nothing to do with that."

"But there's something you aren't telling me, Barton. I need to know what it is."

He rubbed his face with both hands, then said, "I'm afraid you won't believe me."

"Seems like you've been straight up with me so far," Lauren said. "If you tell me the truth, I'll believe you."

He hesitated, then said, "I saw something that night, but it didn't seem important at the time. Now it does."

"What did you see?"

Lauren was hoping Barton had the key to the case.

"You saw that I waited about thirty seconds to follow this guy Lonnie after he drove away from the dance hall, and by the time I got out onto 1623, he had at least a hundred-yard head start, and there was another truck on the side of the road that pulled out in front of me."

"Where on the side of the road?"

Lauren hadn't noticed any other vehicles on video leaving the parking lot just prior to Lonnie or Barton.

"Like a hundred yards from the dance hall. It was parked on the shoulder, like he'd pulled over to make a call or take a leak or who knows? But he pulled onto the road, so he was between me and Lonnie. We were all going east on 1623, and then we turned north on 206, which takes you back to 290. You know that, I'm sure."

"I know the area," Lauren said.

It was the route anybody would take if they lived in Johnson City or Dripping Springs or all the way in Austin. Not unusual for three vehicles leaving the dance hall to all make those turns.

"So we got to 290 and turned right—all three of us—but we hadn't gone far when Lonnie turned left on the road to Sandy. By then I'd cooled off a little and decided I wasn't going to follow him anymore, so I kept going straight and that other truck was still in front of me. But then *that* guy hit his brakes and got into the left lane and did a U-turn in the middle of the highway, real sudden, like he'd missed his turn."

Or he had also been following Lonnie Blair but didn't want to be spotted. If he had turned onto Sandy Road with Lonnie, that would've been conspicuous. Better to make the U and fall in behind Lonnie again a minute or two later, at which point Lonnie would probably think it was a different vehicle. This was likely the truck that had attempted to run Lonnie and Jimmy Lee off the road that night.

"Could you see where he went?"

"I watched in my rearview mirror and he took the same turn to Sandy."

Bingo.

"What did that truck look like?"

"It was a big black dually. A Chevy, I think. It had a grille guard."

"Anything else?"

"The tailgate was really dirty."

"Did you get a look at the driver when he turned around?"

"It was way too dark."

"Any chance you have a dash cam?"

"Sorry, no."

"Did you remember anything about the license plate? Was it a Texas plate?"

"I didn't notice."

"Any bumper stickers or anything else on the back of the truck? Any body damage?"

"Not that I recall. It wasn't the kind of big truck that a lot of guys drive for show, but a real working truck, like a ranch truck. I don't know if any of this is important or not. Maybe it was nothing. Maybe he really did miss his turn. I just thought I should tell you. But it wasn't me. I didn't kill Lonnie. I kept going straight that night and never went anywhere except work the next day."

26

George felt his gut tighten as Mason Cross drove past in his big black dirty truck, but Cross never took his eyes off the pavement ahead. George was insignificant. Just some man on the side of the road who wasn't worthy of a glance.

Lucky.

But now what? What if Cross was leaving for several hours, or even the rest of the day? What if he was going on a trip to look at some cattle, or whatever the hell his day-to-day activities involved? How long did George want to wait?

He kept walking as he tried to decide what to do next. In hindsight, he realized it had been silly to simply expect Mason Cross to be on the ranch when George got there. Surely there were times when he had to run errands or stock up on various supplies. Maybe he had to buy a tool or grab some cattle feed.

Now George was wondering if he should do this some other day. He turned around and began to walk back to his car, but then he changed his mind and turned around again.

A reconnaissance mission would be worthwhile, wouldn't it? He would enter the ranch and explore it. Study the area around the home near the front of the ranch. That had to be where Mason Cross stayed. Besides, what else was George going to do, since he couldn't go home and he couldn't go to work?

After walking nearly a mile, he was getting close to the gated entrance where Cross had threatened George's life. Just a couple hundred yards ahead, on the left.

But George didn't intend to enter at the gate. Instead he veered off the road and into a dense grove of cedar trees that obscured the fence for at least thirty yards. That's why George had worn dark green—to blend in with the cedars. He was proud that he had thought of that.

He got behind the trees, right up against the barbed-wire fence, and squatted low. His heart was racing. He couldn't see the county road now, which meant anybody passing would not be able to see him.

On the ranch side of the fence, the cedar had been cleared, leaving nothing but oak trees, so the terrain was much more open. George could see for several hundred yards, up a rolling hill. Gorgeous place.

George remained crouched by the fence for several minutes, halfway expecting somebody to emerge from somewhere and ask what the hell he was doing.

There was enough room under the lowest strand of barbed wire for George to wriggle under. He knew that if he did it, he would be trespassing, and he couldn't remember the last time he had broken any law more serious than speeding.

Now a vehicle passed on the county road. George could only catch quick glimpses through the cedars. Maroon. Maybe a truck. Then it was gone. Hmm. The man who'd stopped to check on George yesterday at the rest stop drove a maroon truck. Nice guy. Concerned. Tried to help. His name was Phil. Looked like a rancher, the rugged type, and George felt a little self-conscious acting so emotional around a man like that.

Phil had agreed yesterday that Mason Cross was a nutcase. Then George had told him what had happened.

"You know him?" George had asked Phil.

"Yup. Met him this past fall. Not a good experience."

"What happened?"

"Just a little disagreement between neighbors," Phil said. "We share a fenceline."

"But he didn't pull a gun on you."

"No, nothing like that."

"What if he had?"

"I probably wouldn't have reacted well."

"But what would you have done?"

"No telling."

"What should *I* do?"

"Call the sheriff's office. Even if they can't prove Cross threatened you, at least they'll have a talk with him."

"Is that what you would do?"

Phil had hesitated just long enough that he answered without saying anything. No, he wouldn't call the sheriff. That's not the way they handled things out here. A man like Phil would take care of things himself, and even if he failed, he would be able to respect himself for trying.

"Doesn't matter what I would do," Phil finally said, grinning. "I don't always think things through as well as I should."

"I think things through *too* well," George replied, and he realized it was an epiphany. Sometimes he was too cautious. Timid, even. Always weighing the pros and cons of everything. Or risk versus reward. "Sometimes I think I should just go with my gut. Just quit screwing around and act, you know?"

"Not when a man's holding a gun on you," Phil said.

"Ever had that happen to you?"

"Yep. More than once."

"What did you do?"

Phil opened his mouth, about to say something, then changed his mind. "Like I said before, doesn't matter what I'd do."

The message was clear. Phil was plainly a man of action. A man who didn't put up with bullies. The type who would put a dickhead like Mason Cross in his place. The kind of man George was determined to become.

Now—right here, by the fence—was the time to start making that change.

George dropped onto his back and shimmied under the lowest strand of barbed wire, onto the Richter ranch.

Marlin stopped for gas at Lowe's Market, then pulled into a parking spot. He'd be meeting Phil Colby in thirty minutes for lunch. Might as well use the time productively.

He'd bookmarked the Facebook page of Mason Cross's ex-wife, Lacey Fontenot, and now he sent her a message, briefly explaining who he was and what he wanted, and including his phone number. Surprisingly, she called him in five minutes.

"I can't imagine what this is about," Lacey said. "You said you're a game warden in Blanco County, Texas?"

She had a thick Louisiana accent.

"Yes, ma'am, and I'm calling about your ex-husband."

She laughed. "Which one? I've got three to choose from."

He laughed, too. "Sorry I wasn't more specific. I'm talking about Mason Cross."

"Oh, Mason. Is he dead?"

"No, ma'am."

"Huh. I always figured I'd get a call that he was dead, but I guess that dream will have to wait."

"I take it you and Mason aren't on the best of terms," Marlin said.

"Hell, no, and that's one reason I haven't seen him or even talked to him in years. He's a miserable son of a bitch."

"Don't sugarcoat it," Marlin said, laughing again.

"One thing I guarantee is, I'll always speak my mind," she said. "Truth is, Mason is a bitter and angry person, and if it sounds like any of it rubbed off on me, maybe it did. My other two exes were worthless, but all they did was cheat and drink and disappear for days. Half the time, that was like a holiday for me. So Mason is living in Texas now?"

"He is. Working as a foreman on a ranch."

"And he's obviously in trouble for something or you wouldn't be calling."

"I wouldn't put it that way, but his name has come up in an investigation."

"That's close enough. What did he maybe do?"

Considering her enthusiasm, Marlin suspected he would get the same level of cooperation from her regardless of which investigation he mentioned, so he opted to keep the murder of Lonnie Blair out of the conversation, at least for the moment.

"There was an incident involving deadly conduct."

"That sounds like Mason. Is that a felony?"

"Third degree."

"What was the conduct?"

"Firing a bullet through a neighbor's deer blind. Let me repeat that it's just an investigation at this point. I don't know who did it. It could've been a stray shot."

"Yeah, I figure you're required to say that kind of stuff. Was he mad at the neighbor for something?"

"Funny you should ask," Marlin said.

"So that's a yes."

"They had a minor run-in."

"That's all it takes with Mason. What did you need from me? Maybe we can put him in jail together. That would be a treat."

"Just some questions at first."

"Go for it."

"How long were y'all married?"

"Seven years. I was eighteen and he was twenty, which was dumb enough, even if we'd been a good match. Actually, it wasn't too godawful for the first couple of years, but then, well, you probably know about the accident."

"I noticed that he'd lost some fingers, and I heard it happened in the military, but that's all I know."

"Yeah, he was in the Army, which is perfect for a guy like him. He enlisted right after high school, and he was planning to make a career out of it. This was right when things were heating up in Afghanistan, and the idea of going over there to kill some of those folks thrilled him. That's all he talked about. But then—"

She stopped talking abruptly. Marlin gave her some time.

"It chokes me up to talk about it, regardless of what a shit he was," she said. "I don't even know all the facts, because you know how the military is about that kind of thing, but I know most of it. They were doing some kind of demolition training exercise and something went wrong. Mason lost those fingers, and his arm was broken, but he was lucky to live. Sad thing is, a soldier next to him didn't make it. It was all an accident, of course, but the investigation determined that Mason was to blame."

27

"He didn't handle it well, and I can understand that. His service record had been flawless before that, but afterwards, he got into all kinds of trouble—mouthing off to superiors, getting into fights, missing curfews—and they eventually gave him an OTH discharge."

Other than honorable. There were worse discharges to receive, but even an OTH discharge was considered severe. It drastically limited the recipient's benefits and prevented future enrollment in the armed forces.

"How long between the accident and the discharge?" Marlin asked.

"About four months. Look, I know I sound like a cold-hearted bitch, so let me say it was terrible what happened. Part of Mason's frustration came from not having the full use of his hand. You'd expect just about anybody to have some major mood swings when something like that happens. So I get it. I really do. If Mason had been a sweet, loving, wonderful man beforehand, well, I could blame everything on the accident. But that wasn't the case. It simply made him a bigger asshole. In fact, it was worse than that. It was like something broke inside his head, and it was all he could do to keep a lid on himself."

"Did the Army provide any kind of therapy?"

"Oh, you bet. He was diagnosed with PTSD, but he said that was all bullshit. He wasn't what you'd call a cooperative patient, so that treatment never went anywhere."

"How long were you married after the discharge?"

"Four more years, if you can believe it. I hung in there, hoping he'd change, or at least learn how to cope, and also because the idea of leaving made me feel guilty. I mean, who bails on a guy in that position? Me, apparently, because that's what I did eventually. Looking back, I should've done it a lot sooner. Is any of this helpful?"

"Very much so. Can I ask what made you so unhappy in the marriage—before the accident?"

"I was too young to understand what a real man was supposed to be, but it sure wasn't Mason. He didn't have an ounce of compassion or empathy in him. Or love. If he ever loved me, he didn't know how to show it."

"Did he have any close friends? Anyone he'd tell his troubles to?"

"Not a single one, which is just sad. Not that he'd tell them anything."

"Earlier you made it sound like he could hold a grudge."

"Oh, God yes. You could look at him wrong and he'd remember it a year later. If someone ever said something to him that was out of line, or if they somehow did him wrong, and he didn't do something about it, he'd consider that a sign of weakness, and he figured others would, too. It would just eat him up until he confronted that person or somehow retaliated."

"Think he'd be capable of harming someone?"

"Without a doubt."

"I'm not talking about a heat-of-the-moment kind of thing, but a cold, calculated act of revenge later on."

"Why? Did he think somebody was inside that deer blind when he shot it?"

"No, but there were a couple of other things that happened."

"What were they?"

First, Marlin told her about the deer blind that burned to the ground in Webb County after the hunter had crossed the fence illegally to retrieve a deer.

"I hate to keep saying this, but that sounds like Mason, too. Reason is, we're pretty sure he started a fire at my brother's house."

"Tell me about that."

"When I finally decided to leave Mason, I didn't sit him down and tell him, I just left, and my brother helped me. Believe me, that was the best way to do it, to avoid an ugly scene. I stayed with my brother for a couple of weeks, and one night, while we were sleeping, the shed behind his house caught fire. Luckily, it didn't spread to the house, but it was arson, no question, because they left a gas can behind. The cops figured he did that on purpose, to make sure we knew it wasn't some kind of accident."

Marlin remembered that the same thing had happened in Webb county; the arsonist had left the gas can on the scene, apparently to make his intentions clear.

"Did they question Mason about your brother's shed?"

"He wouldn't talk, and since nobody saw anything, there wasn't much we could do about it."

"I don't suppose you can describe the gas can," Marlin said. What were the odds the two gas cans were similar? Had Mason hauled one of those cans all the way to Webb County when he'd moved there from Louisiana?

"Just a red gas can. Sorry."

"There's one other thing that happened," Marlin said, and he told her in detail about the killing of Lonnie Blair.

"Good lord. That's one twisted way to kill somebody," she said. "And again…"

"It sounds like Mason?"

"It really does. He'd think that was a brilliant tactical way to do it. And he's a hell of a shot. What did this poor guy Lonnie do to him?"

"We haven't been able to figure that out. Maybe nothing."

"No argument or nothing?"

"Not that we can find. Not yet. And that's why I'm leaning toward the possibility that somebody else killed him."

"You might be right, but don't be surprised if you find out Mason had some kind of problem with him."

"When was the last time you talked to Mason?" Marlin asked.

"Oh, years and years. I talked to him on the phone one time after I left, and that was it. I hear news about him now and then through his cousins, mostly on Facebook."

"Such as."

She laughed. "One of them said Mason was falling in love and we should all wish him well. Maybe he could get a fresh start. Wish him well? Hell, I was tempted to figure out who the woman was and warn her."

"When was this?"

"Last fall, I think. I don't think it was in the summer."

Depending on when exactly the cousin had posted it, Mason might've still been in Webb County or up here in Blanco County.

"Any chance you could find that post and send me a screen shot?"

"Oh, sure, and it had a photo with it."

This was getting better.

"I'd love to see it."

"If you wanna hang on for a few minutes, I'll go to my computer."

Better to wait than to hang up and hope she followed through. So he said, "You bet. I'll wait."

The line went quiet for a minute, and then Marlin heard the sound of her sitting in a chair, followed by her tapping on a keyboard.

Another minute passed in silence. She was presumably scrolling back through her cousin's posts.

Then she said, "Here it is. What's your phone number?"

Marlin gave it to her. The screen shot—which included the photo and the accompanying text—arrived seconds later.

The post the cousin had written said, "Cuz Mason has his eye on this pretty gal. Wish him luck."

The photo showed Mason standing next to Carissa Richter.

George used his phone to navigate toward the first structure on the ranch, which he could see as soon as he topped a rise. A house. Not a modern house, but one that was maybe fifty or sixty years old, or maybe more. Small, like they used to build them. Maybe one thousand square feet. Mason Cross's house.

There was a well-worn dirt parking area in front of the house, but there were no vehicles to be seen, unless you counted a tractor or backhoe or some kind of big yellow contraption parked about twenty yards to the right of the house. Mason probably used that to maintain the roads on the ranch.

George stood beside a thick-trunked oak tree and waited. For what? He knew there was no other structure for half a mile. A large home had been built to the rear of the property a few years ago, according to the property tax information George had accessed earlier. The ranch owners, Alford and Carissa Richter, lived in it.

George wondered what kind of people the Richters were. Reasonable? Friendly? Would they be appalled if they knew how Mason Cross had treated George? Maybe he should call them. Feel them out. Tell them what had happened and see how they responded. Would they fire Mason Cross? That would be a suitable outcome, as far as George was concerned. Send the man packing. Maybe then he would understand the consequences of his actions.

Lame. What a wimpy way to address the situation. Not in keeping with his vow to turn over a new leaf.

George began to walk toward the house, slowly but deliberately, moving from the cover of one oak tree to another.

It was a beautiful day to be trespassing. Temperature in the lower fifties, but the air was crisp and dry. No wind. Lots of sunshine.

George continued walking, and when he got within thirty yards of the house, he began looking for security cameras. He didn't see any hanging from the eaves. He got even closer, and now he approached the steps to the front porch. The doorbell wasn't a security camera, either. No surprise. This was a ranch, completely surrounded by fence, and with a gated entrance. Any type of prowler or burglar would have to be insane to approach such a place. Country people owned guns, as George had already learned.

Now George was twenty feet from the front door.

"Hellloooo?" he called out, even louder than he meant to.

No reply. Still, George's heart was banging wildly. His palms and underarms were moist.

"Anybody home?"

Of course not. He already knew that.

He walked closer, then slowly mounted the three wooden steps and stood perfectly still in front of the door.

He suddenly realized he was fortunate there were no dogs around. You'd expect a lot of dogs on a ranch, but he saw no evidence that any dogs lived here. No doghouse. No water or food bowls. No scratches on the door.

He stared at the doorknob for the longest moment. Just a locking knob, with no deadbolt lock above it. Not very secure. Anybody—even George—could kick the door in. And nobody would hear.

But what if it wasn't locked?

What the hell was he doing? Was he really considering going inside? That would almost certainly be a felony, right?

Damn it, stop looking for an excuse to back out. This was a new beginning, remember?

He reached out and gripped the doorknob. Turned it. The damn door opened. He swung it wide but didn't step inside. Not yet.

He could see a small entryway that opened into a living room. It was sparsely furnished and unremarkable. Beige carpet. A gray upholstered sofa and matching chair. Medium-sized TV resting on an entertainment center. All the curtains were drawn. A small lamp on an end table illuminated the room. To the left was a darkened hallway that probably led to a couple of bedrooms and a bathroom. The kitchen was to the rear of the house, behind the living room.

George took a breath, trying to settle his nerves.

All was calm and quiet.

28

Marlin walked into Ronnie's and the first people he saw were Alford and Carissa Richter, seated at the table closest to the door. His first thought was that they were out of place in a barbecue joint, and then he felt guilty for making class judgments. They were eating plates of barbecue just like everybody else.

His second thought was about the photo Lacey Fontenot had sent. He'd had no idea what to make of that, but if he'd had to guess, he'd have said that Mason Cross was carrying an unrequited torch for Carissa, and maybe his cousin was teasing him about it. So what?

Alford saw Marlin and gave him a wave. Marlin didn't see Phil anywhere yet, so he walked over to the Richters' table and said hello.

"This is more like it," Alford said.

"Pardon?" Marlin said.

"I'd much rather see you in these circumstances." He lowered his voice. "Making any progress on the case?"

He and Carissa were both looking at Marlin expectantly.

"Still working on it," Marlin said.

He could see Phil pulling up outside in the maroon Ford F-250 he'd bought the previous summer.

"Alford told me you spoke with Mason this morning," Carissa said. "I hope he wasn't too ugly."

Marlin said, "Nothing I couldn't handle."

"Were you able to reach the hunters on our place?" Alford asked.

"I'm embarrassed to admit I've never met them—or even talked to them. Mason handles all that."

"Speak of the devil," Carissa said, pointing through the windows to the highway.

A large black Chevy was rolling south on 281. The same dually Marlin had seen that morning parked outside Mason's house.

"He comes into town for lunch every day," Alford said. "Dinner, too. He literally keeps no food in his house. None whatsoever. Not even canned food. Not a bag of chips or a frozen dinner. Nothing. Can you imagine that?"

"A couple of months ago, his refrigerator stopped working, so he put it in the back of his truck to haul off," Carissa said. "When we asked him about it, he said it wasn't a big deal, because he only used it for beer and soft drinks. We bought him another fridge, a really nice one, but he didn't seem to care either way. We could've gotten him one of those small dorm-room fridges and he would've been fine with it."

"I think he's the top customer at Fat Boy Burgers," Alford said. "I bet that's where he was just now."

"They do make a tasty burger," Carissa said.

"And the catfish plate is excellent," Alford said.

Phil entered the restaurant, saw Marlin chatting with the Richters, and walked over. Alford Richter kept his seat but shook Phil's hand.

"I've been learning more about the encounter you had with Mason last fall," Alford said. "I want to apologize for that. I meant to call before now and talk to you about it."

"I appreciate that," Phil said. "We had a little disagreement, but it's water under the bridge now."

"If he shot that hole in your deer blind, I wouldn't hesitate for a minute to fire him, but I just can't see him doing that. Of course, I've been wrong before."

"I'd say you're probably wrong this time, too," Phil said with his typical directness.

"Oh," Alford said. "I'll admit he's a hothead."

"Why don't we eat?" Marlin said to Phil.

The door to the restaurant opened again and in walked Red O'Brien and Billy Don Craddock. They both stopped when they saw Marlin, and O'Brien muttered something, and Craddock said something back. Probably wondering if they should go somewhere else for lunch.

Ultimately, though, they went to the counter to place their orders.

"You really think he did it?" Alford said to Phil.

"From what I've seen and heard, your boy Mason has an anger-management problem," Phil said.

"Maybe so, and if he committed a crime, obviously that needs to be addressed," Alford said. "On the other hand, I'd hate to punish him for something he didn't do. Innocent until proven guilty and all that."

"Then there's the murder of Lonnie Blair," Phil said.

Marlin nearly winced.

Alford frowned. "What about it? Are you suggesting Mason had something to do with that?"

"You haven't wondered about that yourself?" Phil said.

"It's never crossed my mind," Alford said. "What motive would Mason have? I don't think the two men even knew each other." He looked at Marlin for confirmation one way or the other.

"How's the brisket today?" Marlin said.

"Very tasty," Carissa said. "I'm afraid I ate too much."

"It's been good seeing y'all," Phil said.

"We were just about to take off anyway," Alford said. "Good visiting with you both."

By the time Marlin and Phil reached the counter, there was one man ahead of them. O'Brien and Craddock had already ordered and made their way to a table in the back.

"Just can't help yourself, huh?" Marlin said quietly to Phil. "I can't believe you said that."

"No impulse control," Phil said. "No social skills. Plus I just don't give a—"

"Settle down," Marlin said.

A few minutes later, they had their food and took a table beside the windows at the front of the room. They ate in silence for several moments.

"Was he right about that?" Phil asked.

"Who about what?"

"Alford saying Mason had no motive to kill Lonnie Blair. You haven't dug anything up?"

"Can't we just have a little barbecue and talk about something else?"

"Oh, sure. Yeah. No problem. Sorry about that."

"I question your sincerity."

Before Phil could offer a sarcastic rebuttal, Red O'Brien and Billy Don Craddock stopped at their table on the way out of the restaurant.

"Gentlemen," Marlin said.

Even though he'd cited the two rednecks on several occasions for poaching violations, Blanco County was a small community and he tried to keep a civil relationship with everyone who lived there. Besides, despite their shortcomings and character flaws, several years back, the men had saved Marlin and a young boy when they were being held at gunpoint by a murderer. Hard to forget something like that.

"That's some weird stuff about Lonnie Blair," O'Brien said.

"We're not talking about that right now," Phil said. "He just wants to have lunch and talk about something else."

"Well, okay," O'Brien said. "Then I guess we made it through another season without you writing us up for something."

"You've outwitted me once again," Marlin said.

"Don't take it too hard," O'Brien said. "We're a couple of tricky sons of bitches."

"Some of that is accurate," Phil said.

Craddock said, "Who was that pretty lady y'all were talking to earlier? I've seen her somewhere."

"A neighbor of mine," Phil said.

"On Miller Creek Road?" Craddock said.

"That's where I live," Phil said.

He wasn't quite as patient with the two men, partly because that was just Phil's nature, and because Phil had had plenty of negative encounters with both of them.

"Guess I've seen her around town," Craddock said.

Nobody replied.

"She's a looker, for sure," Craddock said, now basically talking to himself. "She looks like an actress or something. Or a lady you'd see working in one of those big office towers in downtown Austin. There's always a lot of pretty gals walking around down there."

"And you're one of the guys who gives 'em the creeps by staring at 'em," O'Brien said.

"You think they don't want us looking at 'em?" Craddock asked. "The ladies downtown, I mean. I think they like it."

"Got a sister?" Phil asked him.

"Huh?"

"Imagine if some three-hundred-pound cedar chopper ogled her as she was walking down the street, minding her own business. Think she'd like it?"

"Probably not."

"There you go."

"But if I was some young handsome dude, she might," Craddock said, and that seemed to trigger something else in his head, because he added, "Wait, now I 'member where I saw her. She was walking out of the Super S with Lonnie Blair."

Colby looked at Marlin and grinned.

"Wait a second," Marlin said to Craddock. "Come outside with me."

29

George stepped inside Mason Cross's house, and it might've been the greatest adrenaline rush he'd ever experienced in his life—even greater than that time he'd run from the cops. Well, technically, maybe he hadn't *run* from them, possibly because that cop hadn't come after him. George didn't know for sure, because he'd been going eight miles per hour over the speed limit, and a cop had passed by, and George decided on a crazy whim to take a quick right into a quiet neighborhood. What a thrill that was! Even though he wasn't sure whether the cop had ever turned around or not, that didn't make it any less exciting.

And now this.

George stood quietly for several minutes just soaking it in. The door was open behind him, and he could feel a slight breeze at his back.

This was breaking and entering, right? Not just trespassing anymore. Didn't matter if the door was unlocked. Or maybe it was burglary. George wasn't sure, and did it really matter?

He wasn't just nervous, he was exhilarated. Electrified. He realized that simply being here—in Mason Cross's private domain—was a little bit of payback in and of itself. He was *intruding* on Cross's space—*violating* his inner sanctum—and it was delicious. George was suddenly aware that despite his thundering heartbeat, he was grinning from ear to ear.

"Fuck you, Mason Cross," he said quite suddenly, and plenty loudly, and he startled himself. Then he laughed. "Fuck you. Fuck you hard and repeatedly."

The home was quiet.

"Fuck you!" he yelled at full volume. "You're gonna pay for—"

An abrupt gonging sound from the rear of the house made him jump, and he turned fast for the door, but before he could run, he realized it was a goddamn grandfather clock. The first chime spooked him and he panicked, but he figured it out before the second chime. Who the hell had a grandfather clock nowadays? Now it was chiming three, and four, and so on, all the way up to twelve. Damn thing wasn't even keeping proper time. It was well past noon. George waited it out, and when it was finally done, he exhaled a long breath.

"Fuck you and your stupid clock!" he yelled, and he laughed again, and he knew he was on the verge of totally losing it.

Calm down. Keep it under control.

He closed the door behind him, just in case the owners of the ranch drove past and glanced over at their foreman's house. Then he stepped forward slowly. Now he was on the left side of the living room, a few feet from the couch. He didn't see anything of interest in here. A couple of magazines rested on the coffee table, but they looked like hunting and agricultural publications. That's what ol' Mason read at night for fun? What a loser.

He stepped over to the mouth of the hallway and could see four doorways, two on the left and two on the right. All of the doors were open. George padded quietly on the carpet and stopped at the first door on the right. This was the master bedroom. Also sparsely furnished. A bed, unmade. A nightstand. A dresser. No other furniture. Mason's sad little bedroom.

George was tempted to explore it, but this room was at the rear of the house and he was worried he wouldn't hear any vehicles approaching the front of the house. If Mason came back, George wanted as much warning as he could get, because—

Wait a damn second. He was doing it again. Being a chickenshit. A coward, to be honest. The only way he was ever going to get past his instincts was to do the opposite. If his impulse was to turn around and leave, well, what was the opposite? That's what he should do.

He marched into the bedroom and began to look through Mason's dresser drawers. Socks and underwear in the top drawer. T-shirts in the second drawer. Jeans and work pants in the third drawer. And then—*whoa!*—at least half a dozen handguns and cartons of ammunition in the bottom drawer. Jesus. Who needed that many guns? For what purpose?

George could see the same semi-automatic handgun Mason had dropped into his lap yesterday morning. He stared at it for a long time—maybe a full minute. Just a tool, but it looked almost evil. He knew that didn't make sense, but he couldn't help it. It brought back bad memories.

George counted eight guns in total—five revolvers and three semi-automatics. Of the eight, six were black and two were nickel-plated. Some were in holsters, while others were loose, all piled together. A jumble. George figured these were all cheap guns that were already scratched and scuffed, so what did it matter how they were stored?

Judging by the ammo boxes he could see, the eight guns were all nine millimeter, .357, or .380. And there were several extra clips, too. Or were they called magazines? Or were those the same thing?

"I don't give a flying fuck what they're called," George said.

It would be just like Mason to correct somebody on that. You're talking to him and you call it a clip, but he says no, it's a magazine, and there's a level of contempt in his voice while he says it. How could you be so ignorant? Don't you know anything about guns?

George looked into the closet and saw a dozen hanging shirts—most of them work shirts, but a couple that were dress shirts Mason probably wore into town on a Saturday night. Leaning in a back corner of the closet was an assault rifle. Mason would probably gripe about that, too: *It's not an assault rifle. That's just a phrase the media uses to scare people.* The rifle had one of those long curved clips. Banana clip. That's what they called them. Wasn't it really a magazine?

"Who the hell cares?" George said out loud.

Next to the rifle was a cardboard box about the size of a microwave oven. George looked inside and saw extra clips for the rifle—at least fifteen or twenty of them, all loaded. Was this nut expecting an armed revolution or something?

He exited the closet and poked around in the bedroom some more, but there was nothing of interest. A credit card bill on the nightstand, but there wasn't anything unexpected there. Lots of small charges to a place listed as FATBOY—almost every day.

George crossed the hall and went into one of the smaller bedrooms.

That's where he found something he didn't understand.

"Go ahead and tell me what you saw, and feel free to give me as many details as possible," Marlin said.

"Like I said, I saw 'em coming out of the Super S together," Billy Don Craddock said. "That's about it."

"Meaning the Lowe's Market?" Marlin said.

"Right. Lowe's Market. I still call it Super S."

"What day was this?"

"Maybe a month or two ago. That's probably why it took me so long to remember."

"What time of day was it?"

Marlin and Craddock were standing beside Marlin's truck. Just the two of them. Phil and Red O'Brien were still inside.

"Probably either morning or afternoon. I remember it was light out."

"Where were you at the time?"

"Sitting in the truck, waiting for Red."

"He was in the grocery store?"

"In the hardware side of it," Craddock said. "We needed a new hose bib, because one kept dripping. You know, they make little kits to rebuild those bibs, but they cost more than a whole new bib. Make sense of that. Why would anybody buy the kit?"

Marlin had asked for as many details as possible, and that's what Craddock was giving him.

"Where were they when you first saw them?"

"I never saw the hose bibs. I didn't go inside."

"I mean Lonnie and the woman. Did you see them exit the store together? Or were they already walking across the lot?"

"I can't remember for sure, but I think they walked out together. Then they stopped for a minute and kept talking, the way people do when they have to split up because their vehicles are in different directions."

"Can you describe their demeanor?"

"Probably, if I knew what that was."

"How were they acting?"

"Oh, yeah, I'd say ol' Lonnie was doing his regular thing—hitting on her big time."

"I didn't know you knew Lonnie very well," Marlin said.

"We weren't buddies or anything, but I'd see him around, mostly in the beer joints."

"You didn't know the woman he was talking to?"

"In the beer joints?" Billy Don asked.

"No, in the parking lot of Lowe's Market. The woman I was talking to earlier in the restaurant."

"No idea who that was, but she's good-looking enough to remember. Who is she?"

"I'll get to that. How sure are you that the woman in Ronnie's just now was the same woman in the parking lot with Lonnie?"

"Hunnert percent."

"Did they seem like they'd just met, or like they knew each other already?"

"He seemed to like her a lot, so I guess they'd just met."

"How close were they to your truck?"

"It was Red's truck, and they was maybe thirty feet."

"Could you hear anything they were saying?"

"No, but I could hear her laughing every now and then. Whatever Lonnie was selling, she was buying it."

"Meaning she was enjoying the conversation?"

"Yes, sir. It was a hookup waiting to happen."

"How long did they stand there talking?"

"I'd say three or four minutes."

"Then what happened?"

"He went and got into his truck, and she got into some little foreign car, and they both drove away."

Marlin wasn't sure what to make of all this. Carissa Richter had said she didn't know Lonnie Blair. It was possible she'd talked to him at the Lowe's Market and had no idea who he was, then or even now. She might not have even gotten his name—just some good-looking stranger flirting with her in the parking lot. Probably a fairly regular occurrence for Carissa Richter. And for Lonnie.

But Marlin wasn't buying it. Maybe it was time to talk to her again.

He had plenty of time. He wasn't meeting with Bobby and Lauren until two.

30

This bedroom had no furniture in it. Mason obviously used it for storage.

The grandfather clock—a fine-looking antique—stood in one corner, looking out of place. Next to it were maybe twenty cardboard boxes, stacked in columns of three and four. They had obviously been sitting there since Mason had moved in, filled with junk he didn't really need.

To the right of the boxes, near the corner but several feet from any wall, was a tall metal safe with "Winchester" printed across the door. A gun safe. Really more of a rifle safe. George could picture Mason moving it in here with some kind of heavy-duty dolly, and he wouldn't have tried to work it neatly into a corner, because the damn thing probably weighed half a ton, or close to it. Just put it near a corner and be done with it.

Why hadn't Mason stored all those handguns in there? Probably because they were cheap guns that weren't worth much, and what were the odds they would ever get stolen from this house anyway? Or maybe he wanted them closer, near his bed, in case he needed one in the middle of the night. Or maybe he didn't want to hassle with opening the safe every time he needed a handgun. Or maybe it was already filled with so many guns and rifles, there wasn't any more room. For that matter, why hadn't he stored the assault rifle in there? Maybe he wanted quick access to it.

George went to the small closet, opened the door, and peered inside. The closet was surprisingly dark, but he could see it was empty. No clothes hanging on the rod. No boxes or other containers on the floor.

He started to close the door, but he glanced at the upper shelf, and he realized it wasn't empty after all. He saw an object up there. The closet had a bulb with a pull-string, so he yanked it, but nothing happened. Bulb was burned out or missing. So he used the flashlight on his phone.

Resting on the shelf was a red five-gallon bucket with black text on it.

**BOOM TOWN
BRAND EXPLODING TARGETS
BULK MIX— 50 POUNDS**

Technically, the rest stop at Miller Creek Road and US Highway 281 hadn't been an official rest stop for several years. Marlin couldn't remember the exact timeline, but he thought the rest stop—and several others in the county—had been eliminated after the 2008 recession due to budget cutbacks. The only real difference at the rest stop was that two picnic tables and two garbage cans had been removed. Otherwise, motorists still treated it as a rest stop, stopping to stretch their legs or make a quick phone call or even take a nap. Others parked their vehicles there to carpool with friends or coworkers to other destinations. It wasn't unusual at all to see three or four vehicles backed into the shade of several oak trees that grew just to the west of the long strip of pavement.

As Marlin drove south on the highway and prepared to turn right on Miller Creek Road, he saw three trucks and one red Tesla coupe parked nose-out at the rest stop.

Wait a sec. Hadn't Phil said that George Besserman drove a red Tesla? It wasn't like Blanco County was crawling with Teslas.

Marlin took a right, and then another right into the former rest area. He stopped in front of the Tesla. Nobody inside. Nobody in the trucks, either, which meant no witnesses to tell Marlin who had been driving the Tesla or how long it had been parked there.

Marlin checked his notes and saw that the plate matched the number Phil had given him yesterday. He got out of his truck and approached the car. Looked into the windows. Nothing unusual.

Okay, what now? What did this mean? Why was George Besserman parked here? Where was he now? He lived in Austin, so why was he in Blanco County again on a weekday? Marlin couldn't think of a reasonable explanation. On the other hand, he could think of a foolhardy explanation.

He got back into this truck and dialed the number he'd found online for George. Three rings and then to voicemail.

"George, my name is John Marlin and I'm a game warden in Blanco County. I sure would like to talk to you as soon as possible. Why don't you call me back as soon as you can, okay?"

Marlin hung up and waited for a few minutes. No return call.

He turned around and went back to Miller Creek Road, where he drove west, toward the Richter ranch.

George stared at the five-gallon bucket for a long moment, and then his phone rang in his hand and startled him so badly, he let out an odd yip.

He looked at the screen to see who was calling. He didn't recognize the number. He dismissed the call, and a minute later, he saw that he had a voicemail. He listened to it. Why was a game warden calling him? It made no sense. George wasn't a hunter. He silenced his phone and put it back in his pocket.

Back to the bucket. An exploding target? Seriously? What kind of inbred redneck entertainment was that?

He read the rest of the text on the label and learned that the tub was filled with two separate components, in bulk quantities, that you mixed together. It was perfectly safe before then. The instructions said you could mix just a little, in the proper proportions, or mix the entire bucket. There were multiple warnings and cautions and lots of fine print. What did a man like Mason Cross use this for? Surely he didn't shoot it for the entertainment value? That's probably what most people did, but George couldn't see Mason Cross doing that.

Whatever. Did it matter?

He closed the door to the closet and went into the hallway. Proceeded to the next doorway on his right. This was the bathroom. Surprisingly clean. Across the hallway was a third bedroom. Very small. Completely empty. But he couldn't resist inspecting the closet. Nothing in there.

He followed the hallway back into the living room, crossed into the kitchen, and flipped the light switch.

The pattern held, meaning there was almost nothing in here. Nothing on the counters except a coffee maker and a bottle of Wild Turkey. No toaster. No microwave oven. No canisters to hold flour or sugar. None of the little knickknacks or odds and ends that usually end up on kitchen counters.

George crossed the linoleum floor and opened the refrigerator door. Amazing. Nothing in there except beer, soft drinks, and tonic water. Not one edible item.

He opened the freezer and saw a bottle of gin, resting on its side, and ice in a tray from the icemaker. Nothing else.

He went to the pantry and swung the door open with a soft squeal of the uppermost hinge. More empty shelves. No food whatsoever—canned, boxed, bagged, or otherwise. Talk about taking the bachelor lifestyle to the extreme. Who doesn't keep any food at all in the house? Not even a snack?

George closed the pantry door, and that's when he heard a vehicle pulling up outside.

31

For at least five full seconds, George froze in a panic. Then his instincts finally kicked in and he hurried to the small bedroom with the rifle safe. He opened the closet door, stepped inside, and closed it behind him.

His heart was pounding so hard, he worried it might simply give out. He would drop dead and his resolve to be a more assertive man would end as quickly as it began.

He hadn't expected Mason to return so quickly, if that was him outside. Maybe it was one of the owners. Or a visitor. Or a repairman of some kind. Maybe, if George was lucky, the person wouldn't enter the house.

He heard a vehicle door closing. Just one, fortunately. Just one person.

Then he heard the front door open and close. Oh, God. It had to be Mason. Would he notice anything unusual? George had put everything back the way he'd found it. Right?

He realized right then that he'd made a mistake. A huge one. He had left the light on in the kitchen. He was sure of it. When he'd hurried out of there, he hadn't flipped the light off. Would Mason notice?

George could hear movement—boots on the floor—and then he heard the sound of a man urinating in a toilet. Then the sound of a flush. Then running water as the man washed his hands. Proper hygiene. Amazing.

Boots on the floor again, and then everything abruptly went quiet.

Mason had stopped right where he was standing, because he had noticed the light in the kitchen. That's what explained the silence. Had to be. He was standing there, puzzled, and maybe suspicious. Trying to remember if he'd left the light on. Listening for any movement.

Ten full seconds passed.

Then George heard Mason step into the kitchen. Then more silence. Then the slow squeal of the pantry door hinge. Mason was checking to see if anybody was in there. Surely he hadn't brought anything home that would need to be stored in the pantry, so he was opening the door for a different reason, and the only logical explanation was that he was checking for an intruder.

George realized his right hand was resting on the grip of the gun that was still in his homemade holster. Sweaty. Slick. Why wasn't he carrying out his plan? He should simply sneak out of the closet, find Mason, point the gun at him, and demand an apology. That's why George was here, after all. But he couldn't do it. Not now that Mason suspected that someone was inside his house. The element of surprise was gone.

George pulled the gun from the holster. This was insane. It had all been a terrible idea. Why had he come here? What had he been thinking? He had never done anything this foolish. He might have to kill a man—or be killed.

Where was Mason right now? Still at the pantry? Or had he walked very softly to some other part of the house?

George couldn't stand like this, unmoving, for much longer. How much time had passed? His knees were already aching. His back was tight. He could feel beads of sweat running from his armpits, even though it was no more than seventy degrees inside the house.

A floorboard squeaked just outside the closet door.

Oh, God.

Mason was on the other side of that door. George could *sense* him.

Red stopped at the Valero convenience store for a pack of Red Man, because nothing was more satisfying after a big plate of barbecue than a wad of chew. He figured while he was there, he might as well grab a cold six-pack of Keystone tallboys, so he did.

He paid at the register, and when he turned around, he was standing face to face with Drake von Oswald. Red looked at him. Drake looked back—and he smiled.

"Blessings," he said.

"What?" Red asked.

"Blessings."

"I'm not sure what that means, just that word all by itself."

"You have a wonderful day," Drake said, obviously waiting for Red to move out of the way, so he could approach the counter with the items in his hands. Nobody was waiting behind him. Red had to decide in an instant whether he should take advantage of this chance encounter, and if so, how?

"I recognize you," Red said.

"Oh. Have we met?"

Drake was holding a bottle of water. What kind of moron pays for water when it's free right out of the tap?

Red said, "I got a postcard about some kinda wellness place, and it had a hot lady on it, and when I went to the website, I saw some more pictures—mostly of her, but I saw you in one of them."

"Oh, you did?"

"Yep."

"And you remember me from that?"

Was he implying something? "Well, I damn sure remember that lady, and you were there with her, so…"

"Well, I'm glad to know the campaign is working. Are you considering becoming a member of the retreat?"

Now Drake was studying Red—sizing him up. His eyes seemed to say, *This man is interested in wellness? Really?*

Red was tempted to say he had no interest in hanging out with a bunch of suckers and rubes, especially if he had to pay to do it, but instead he said, "Thinking about it. Seems like I need to make some changes in my life. Break some bad habits. Maybe try to get in shape."

That was exactly the kind of thing a scammer like Drake would want to hear. In fact, Drake looked at the beer and chewing tobacco in Red's hand and nodded knowingly.

"Coming to that conclusion is the biggest hurdle in the road to a new life. I commend you for your honesty."

I commend you for being full of shit.

"I appreciate that," Red said. "I don't get commended very often."

Drake didn't reply.

"The membership prices are a little high, but I've got some money socked away," Red said.

"You should stop in for a tour," Drake said. "In fact..." He pulled out his wallet, removed a business card, and handed it to Red. "If you call that private number, you'll reach Anastasia, my assistant. Just tell her you're calling for a tour. She'll set it up at your convenience."

"That's damn nice of you," Red said. "Would you be the one showing me around?"

"Anastasia would, and she's lovely, but if I get a chance to say hello, I certainly will. It's very busy around there right now—we're growing every day—but it pulls me in a lot of different directions. A good problem to have, for sure."

This guy was a smooth-talking son of a gun, and Red could see why Mandy might've let him talk her into taking her clothes off.

"By the way, who's that lady?"

"Which one?"

"On the postcard," Red said. "She's finer than frog hair."

Drake said, "Well, she's a client at the retreat who was kind enough to let us feature her in some marketing materials."

"Smoking hot," Red said, partly because he was proud of dating a woman like that, and partly because he wanted to see how Drake would respond.

"She's a lovely woman, indeed," Drake said. "An actual client at the retreat."

What was his deal? Did he describe every woman as "lovely"?

"How'd you get her to take her clothes off like that?" Red asked. "I mean, did she just volunteer or what? Because most of the ladies I know wouldn't just strip down in front of a camera like that, even for money. You must be a silver-tongued devil."

"Most of our clientele understand that rejecting social norms can be liberating," Drake said.

"I guess I need to tell my girlfriend to try that sometime," Red said. "Instead of just getting her drunk."

Red laughed like it was a joke, but he was waiting to see if Drake would admit that liquor was involved.

"I'm sure she would appreciate a more holistic approach to her sexuality," Drake said.

So he dodged the issue. Pretty slick, especially since it was a bunch of gibberish.

"If I keep talking to you, I'm gonna have to buy a dictionary," Red said, laughing again. "Did she know from the start that it was gonna be a photo without any clothes?"

"You sure ask a lot of specific questions," Drake said, and nothing more.

Red said, "She from around here? I ask because most of the girls from around here are kinda conservative."

"I believe she is."

"From here or conservative?"

"I believe she's from around here."

"Like born and raised?"

"I'm not sure about that."

"What's her name?"

Drake grinned. "I can certainly understand your interest, but I can't violate her privacy."

"Yeah, that's cool," Red said. "I get it. I could be some kind of stalker type. I'm sure I'll run into her at some point. Small town."

"That's the attitude," Drake said. "Think positive. I *can* tell you she is unattached."

"To what?" Red asked.

"I mean she's single, and she isn't seeing anyone."

What the hell was this guy talking about?

"How do you know that?" Red asked.

"She told me," Drake said. "We were talking during the shoot and it came up. She said it was hard to meet a decent man in a town this size, and most of the good ones were married."

Red didn't say anything.

"You okay?" Drake said. "You look a little...queasy."

32

George couldn't control his breathing. He was making noise. He couldn't help it. So loud. And his heart was pounding in his ears.

He was about to die. He knew that. He was trapped in this closet and there was no way out. He didn't know what he should—

"Okay!" he suddenly yelled, without even thinking about it. It just burst out of his mouth. "I'm in here! Don't shoot!"

It was an enormous relief to break the tension. This wasn't the way he wanted it to end, but it was better than dying. Wasn't it? But nothing happened.

"I'm sorry I came inside!" George said. "I was angry, but that's no excuse."

He heard a slight shifting on the floorboards outside the closet.

"I'll just leave, okay? You'll never see me again. That's a promise!"

George realized he was trying to reason with an insane person. Not smart. But what was the alternative? Then he had an idea.

"I'm going to turn myself in right now," George said. "I'm calling 911 to—"

The closet door swung open quickly, and there was Mason Cross with the assault rifle, and he fired first. George was sure of it, and that would be important later.

Mason fired and then George fired, and it was so incredibly loud in that little closet, George wasn't sure he would ever hear again.

And then Mason was gone. He yelped in surprise, or perhaps pain, and then he was gone, staggering headlong out of the room.

Had that really just happened?

George looked down at his own torso. His chest. His stomach. Where had the bullet hit him? He hadn't even felt it. But he saw no blood. He used his free hand to lift his sweatshirt and double-check. Nothing. Not a scratch. How was that possible? Mason had been no more than five feet away.

He turned around and looked at the wall behind him. One small bullet hole. Amazing.

What about Mason? Was he hit, or had George also missed completely?

Where was Mason right now? The house was eerily quiet.

Drake was a damn liar. Red had to remember that. He was a scammer and a con artist and a lowlife. He stole money from old ladies. Doesn't get much sleazier than that.

"I'm fine," Red said. "Ate a hardboiled egg earlier and it tasted kinda funky. I'll be all right."

"Maybe you'll see her at the retreat at some point," Drake said, winking. "More incentive to come for that tour."

So there it was. He was lying about Mandy to get Red to become a client at the retreat. Using her as bait—first on the postcard, and now this. That explained it, right?

Red did his best to look kind of skeevy. "I hear there's a naked area. Says on the postcard."

Drake shifted impatiently from one foot to the other. Red noticed he was wearing sandals. Not the hippie kind, but more like the kind a rich bastard would wear when he was trying to look like a wacky genius who doesn't follow the rules. No business suit for this guy.

"We do have a clothing optional module at the moment. Something we're testing out. If it's popular, we'll keep it."

Red was glad no other customers had come into the store.

"Does that lady go in there? The one from the postcard? I'm just curious, is all."

Drake laughed. "She really caught your eye, didn't she? I'm afraid that's something else I can't really discuss. It's a very discreet and mature environment, where consenting adults can free themselves from the modern constraints of an uptight culture."

More gibberish, Red thought.

"Sounds pretty great," Red said. "Constraints suck."

"It's been a pleasure visiting with you," Drake said. "I'm sorry, I didn't catch your name."

"Arch Stanton," Red said.

Drake stuck out his hand and they shook. "Arch, it's great to meet you, and I'm sure I'll see you again soon. You give Anastasia a call at your convenience."

He edged his way around Red to the counter to pay for his water. Guys like Drake always wanted to be the one who ended a conversation.

Red went outside and got into the truck, and Billy Don said, "How many sticks of dynamite you think we oughta use?"

"What?"

"For the septic system. How many sticks of dynamite?"

"Forget about that for a second. I just ran into Drake."

"Where?"

"Well, I just came out of the Valero, so piece it together."

Billy Don looked toward the store. "Is that him coming out right now?"

"Yep."

"Looks even more like a douchebag in person."

"Yep."

"Those pants look like pajamas," Billy Don said.

"Women's pajamas."

"And what's up with that shirt?"

"More like a blouse," Red said.

"That's exactly right. A goddamn blouse."

"I suckered him into a free tour," Red said.

"Of what?"

"The retreat."

"How'd you manage that?"

"I pretended to be interested in improving myself."

Drake walked around to the side of the store and got into a fancy sports car, but he just sat there, talking on his phone. Red sat for a moment without firing up his truck's engine, trying to decide how much he wanted to tell Billy Don.

"Gimme a beer," Billy Don said.

"He said something kinda weird," Red said.

"Drake did?"

"Yep. I think he was jerking my chain."

"What'd he say?"

"He said Mandy told him she wasn't seeing anybody. That she didn't have a boyfriend."

"That ain't good."

"But that's 'cause I was acting all interested in her—like I didn't know her, but I wanted to meet her. So I think he said that to get me to join his dumb club."

Billy Don opened a beer and guzzled about half. "Just ask her if she said it." Then he let out a belch that filled the cab of the truck with a yeasty funk.

"I don't even see why I should bother," Red said. "The guy's playing me."

"Yeah. Or..."

Billy Don guzzled the other half of his beer.

"Or what?" Red asked.

"Or she's fixin' to cut you loose like a bad habit."

"That's stupid. That's not even the right saying."

"Then what's the right saying?"

"Drop you like a bad habit."

"Then that's what she's fixin' to do."

Red was feeling kind of queasy again, and even worse, now he'd lost his appetite. What if it was true about Mandy?

"I told him my name was Arch Stanton," Red said, which made him feel a little better, but not much.

Billy Don grinned. "Really?"

"Yep."

"Did he know where it came from?"

"Didn't seem to."

"That's funny."

Maybe it was, but Red wasn't laughing. He was so sick of this guy, and he'd only just met him. He was also sick of trying to figure out how to make him pay for what he'd done to Mandy. Maybe he'd been making it too complicated. Maybe the simplest plans were the best.

Red started his truck, but instead of driving away, he pulled to the side of the store and parked beside Drake's car, shielding it from the view of anyone driving past on the highway. And since there were no windows on the side of the store, the clerk and any customers inside wouldn't be able to see anything either.

"Gonna take care of bidness," Red said, but Billy Don was focused on his phone again, not paying any attention.

Red got out of his truck and walked over to Drake's car. Red could see now that it was a Corvette, but it wasn't as nice as it had looked from a distance. The paint was faded and chipped in a few places, and there was a pretty big ding in the front fender.

Red stopped beside the driver's door. Drake was talking and didn't look at him. Red rapped on the window. Now Drake looked, and he lowered the glass.

"Yes, may I help you?" he said, as if Red were a perfect stranger and they hadn't just spoken for five minutes inside the store.

"I know who you really are, you lying sack of shit," Red said.

George wasn't safe in the closet, so he dashed into the bedroom and hid behind the rifle safe. But this was only a temporary solution. Should he open the window and jump out? What if Cross was in the hallway right now, waiting? What if he peeked around the doorway, saw George at the window, and shot him square in the back?

George was trapped. Until he knew where Mason Cross was and whether he was injured, George was trapped.

His ears were ringing, but he could hear. And right now, he heard nothing. No moaning or screaming. No cussing. Did that mean he'd missed Mason entirely? Or was Mason dead? Or was he wounded, but keeping quiet, because he was one tough son of a bitch?

George had no idea what to do, so in the spirit of no longer being a wimp, he did the opposite of what he wanted to do. It took some effort, but he did it.

"Mason!" he shouted. "You got what's coming to you! What do you think of that?"

Then George laughed as if it were the greatest moment of his life.

Nothing happened. No reply. No sound of movement in the house at all.

"You destroyed my son's car!" George yelled. "And pulled a gun on me. Think I'm gonna let you get away with that, you enormous asshole?"

It felt amazing, to be honest—to talk to someone that way. Somebody who deserved it.

Then George did something even more outrageous and impulsive. He aimed the gun at the ceiling and fired another shot. He didn't flinch as badly this time.

"Come on back here, Mason! Pull a gun on me now!"

Nothing happened for a long moment. Then Mason fired a dozen shots through the bedroom wall in the span of maybe five seconds. Large chunks of sheetrock flew, and dust filled the air. George felt and heard several rounds smack solidly into the other side of the rifle safe. Mason must've been using the assault rifle George had seen in the closet of the master bedroom.

Finally, the shooting stopped.

George didn't move—except for his trembling hands. He took his finger off the trigger of the gun, because he didn't want to shoot it accidentally.

"Mason," George called out, possibly sounding not quite as forceful as before. "Nobody has to die today. That includes you."

He thought that was a good line—like something Bruce Willis might say in a movie.

Mason didn't reply. George didn't want to die. He knew that much. He'd been stupid to come here and risk his life, all because of a ruined car engine.

George said, "Just apologize for what you did and I'll leave."

Mason responded by unleashing another long barrage of shots through the wall.

33

"Pardon me?" Drake replied, but he didn't mean he hadn't heard what Red had said. It was more along the lines of *How dare you speak to me that way?*

"I know what you did to all those little old ladies," Red said. "You're about as low as it gets."

It was obvious from the pause that followed and the expression on Drake's face that he had no idea what to do. Finally he told the person on the phone he had to go. Then he got out of his Corvette and closed the door.

"I think you must be confused about something," Drake said. "I'll do my best to correct the record."

"You conned a bunch of old ladies," Red said.

"I did?"

"Yep."

"Which ladies? When? Where?"

"Don't play dumb," Red said.

"But I really have no idea what you're talking about."

"That's how you've always gotten by," Red said. "By lying. *Graham.*"

"That used to be my name, yes, but I don't know why you keep mentioning some old ladies. Please enlighten me. Truly."

"You took their money, got caught, and then decided maybe you'd better move on down the road. You ran away, like some kind of coward.

So you came to Texas."

"I did that? You know this for a fact?"

"Damn right."

"Where are you getting this information? It's false, I assure you." The dude was a hell of an actor.

"The name Marge Slubb doesn't ring a bell?" Red asked.

"Marge Slubb," he said, seeming to carefully consider it. "I've never heard that name in my life."

"Right."

"I'm telling you I don't know the woman. It's the truth. I don't know what else to tell you."

"You tricked her into signing a POA, and then you sold some of her properties and kept the money for yourself."

"I'm baffled, really. That's all there is to it. I can't even imagine why—oh, wait a minute."

"What?"

"I bet I know what happened. I bet it was a different Graham Smith."

"Are you kidding me? Don't try that bullshit."

"Think about it. I'll admit that Graham isn't the most common first name you'll ever hear, but Smith as a last name? You take any unique first name and pair it with Smith, there's bound to be quite a few. Especially in a state the size of California. Forty million people live there. You should Google it and see how many Graham Smiths you find."

"But how many of those Graham Smiths are now named Drake van Oswald?" Red asked. "The woman's daughter specifically said you changed your name."

"I can explain that, too."

"I'm sure you can."

"This woman, the daughter, probably found me online and thought I was the right Graham Smith, because why else would I change my name?"

"Well, why did you?"

"Because my father was a terrible person and that was his name, too. I didn't want to be associated with it."

For a moment, Red didn't know how to reply. He realized he'd never actually seen a photo of the Graham Smith in question. What if the woman who'd posted on Facebook about Graham Smith had truly gotten two Graham Smiths mixed up? How come Red had never considered that possibility? He suddenly felt pretty stupid. He was about to give up and go back to his truck when he realized Drake had slipped up.

Red grinned. "You're pretty slick."

"How do you mean?"

"You blew it. Guys like you always do."

Red let that remark hang in the air for a minute, because he was enjoying the fact that he'd outsmarted this huckster.

"Care to explain?" Drake finally said.

"I never said Marge Slubb lived in California."

Boom. There it was.

"What?" Drake said.

"You said 'Especially in a state the size of California,' but I never said anything about California. So how would you know that's where she lived?"

Now Drake was truly speechless. He'd been busted. The smooth-talking con artist had nothing to say.

"Not so clever now, are ya?" Red said.

"You're delusional," Drake said. "You need to go away."

"And that's not even the worst thing you did," Red said, because now it was time to make Drake admit what he did to Mandy. "You did something *waaayyy* worse than that. And so far, you've gotten away with it."

Drake let out a big sigh. Then he stepped forward and stood less than one foot from Red.

"You need to get the fuck out of my face," he said, now using a much different voice.

"Oh, yeah? Or what?"

"I'll have to put an end to this harassment."

"Just admit what you did and I'll leave you alone."

"I didn't do anything. You are making false accusations. Your best choice would be to walk away and never speak my name again."

Red grinned. "Which name? The old one or the new one?"

"Either."

"Graham Smith," Red said. "Drake von Oswald. There, I used 'em both."

"You're a disagreeable little man, aren't you?"

"I ain't so little," Red said. He could see a vein bulging in Drake's neck.

"Last chance," Drake said.

Red said, "First thing I'm gonna do is call the sheriff and tell him you—"

Drake suddenly punched Red in the face—a quick, hard jab that stung his nose.

George was about to dial 911—what other choice did he have?— when he heard a groan somewhere in the small house. So he waited.

Ten seconds later, another groan. Genuine. Mason Cross was in pain.

"You need an ambulance?" he called out.

"You're a...dead man," Mason said, and he sounded grievously wounded.

George took out his phone again and started recording video.

"You shot first," he said.

Another long moan.

"I was giving up," George said. "I said I was going to leave. Why did you shoot at me?"

"You're in my fucking house!" Mason yelled, and he moaned even louder. Then he said, "I need help. I'm bleeding."

Okay, hold on. Think about it. Was it all a bluff? Was he trying to draw George out, just so he could shoot him? Pretty devious. He had tried the same type of thing at the ranch gate yesterday.

"Where are you hit?" George asked.

"Ribs," Mason said. "Low. Right side."

"Is it a hole or did it graze you?" George asked.

Five seconds went by before Mason said, "Hole. Out the other side."

Jesus. George was no expert in anatomy or biology, so he wasn't sure what the bullet might've hit. Liver? Kidney? Lung? Intestines? Several of the above? If Mason had really been hit.

"Are you standing or sitting?"

"On the fucking floor."

"Where's your rifle?"

"Need a doctor."

"You're gonna shoot me," George said.

George heard a thumping sound—a heavy object hitting the carpeted floor.

"Tossed it," Mason said. "It's empty anyway."

George didn't believe him.

"You should call 911," George said.

He moved out from behind the rifle safe and stepped toward the window.

Mason said, "Don't have my phone. Need you to stop the bleeding."

He sounded faint. Like he was getting weak.

"Want me to call 911? Are you bleeding that bad?"

"Right now," Mason said.

"Right now what? Call or give you help?"

"Help," Mason said.

George reached for the window lock, a small brass lever, and eased it open. Now he should be able to raise the window, and get outside with Mason being none the wiser. Take off running behind the house and never come back. Cross his fingers that Mason would die without the chance to tell anyone who shot him.

George lifted upward on the window and—it wouldn't budge. He looked closely and realized it had been painted shut. Sloppy work had glued the window to the frame.

Great. Now what? Break the window? Mason would hear it and know what George was doing. George could run, but he stood no chance of getting away from a man like Mason Cross on open ground.

George moved back to his spot behind the rifle safe. He felt certain Mason was faking. Trying to outwit him.

"Come in here and I'll help you," George said.

No answer.

"Can you make it in here?"

Nothing.

"If you want any help, you'd better answer," George said.

Silence.

"Since you aren't answering, I guess you don't need my help anymore," George said. "You're dead or close to it, so there's no reason for me to come check on you."

The bastard still didn't answer. Maybe he really was dead. George stopped recording video on his phone.

So what could he do now? If he stepped out of the bedroom, he might get shot. If he broke the window and ran, he might get shot. If he called 911 and Mason was dead, George would almost certainly wind up charged with murder.

He was trapped. Doomed. Screwed. He didn't have a single—

Wait a second. Hold on. Maybe there was a way out of this mess.

He moved very slowly, making as little noise as possible, and went into the closet.

Then he reached up and wrestled the five-gallon bucket of Boom Town off the shelf.

By the time Marlin reached the gated entrance of the Richter ranch, he still had not heard from George Besserman. Marlin had the passcode for the keypad, but he was hesitant to enter. If he were checking a deer camp or investigating a possible hunting infraction, he could legally drive right in, but this was something different.

He dialed Alford's number—and got no answer.

Yesterday morning, Alford had said, "Let me give you the gate code. Come on out anytime."

Marlin decided that was good enough. He punched in the code and the gate swung open.

Marlin drove onto the ranch, all but certain he was letting his imagination get away from him. There had to be an innocent reason why George Besserman had parked at the rest stop. Once Marlin confirmed that Mason Cross was fine and that Besserman was not on the ranch, he would proceed to the Richters' house and discreetly question Carissa about her relationship with Lonnie. Maybe she truly had no idea that the man in the Lowe's Market parking lot had been Lonnie Blair.

He crested a small rise and saw the foreman's home ahead, on the right, perhaps a hundred yards away. Mason Cross's black Chevy truck was parked out front. Nobody was outside. Nothing seemed out of place. Cross was probably inside, finished with his hamburger by now, and maybe taking a quick nap.

Marlin eased along the caliche driveway with his windows down, so he could hear well. The only sound right now was small rocks crunching under his tires.

34

Red was so surprised, he didn't react for a moment, other than to stumble one step backward from the impact. But he stayed on his feet. His nose throbbed a little, but when he wiped it with the back of his hand, there wasn't any blood.

"That might've been the dumbest thing you've ever done," Red said.

"I'm not a violent man, but that's what you get for making baseless accusations."

Red shook his arms loosely at his sides, limbering up. This was going to be fun.

"When's the last time you had your ass kicked?" he asked.

"Just get back in your truck and I'll forget this ever happened," Drake said.

"Oh, you're gonna remember," Red said.

"You aren't making a wise choice," Drake said. "I am trained in self defense. Besides, I'm younger, larger, taller, and in better shape."

"Red won't let that stop him," Billy Don said from behind Red somewhere. He had finally noticed what was happening and gotten out of the truck.

Drake said, "Hang on. Two against one is hardly a fair—"

"I'm just here to watch," Billy Don said. "And to take a picture of your body when it's over."

Red appreciated the vote of confidence, but that remark didn't seem to shake Drake at all.

"Well, let's get this over with," Drake said.

Red had never been a skilled fighter. He was more of a brawler, and he knew from his experiences that most people didn't like getting punched in the face. That's why most fights didn't last long. Once somebody took a shot to the teeth or the jaw, most of them weren't interested in going any further. They didn't want to wind up with a fat lip or a black eye or worse. Drake was a pretty boy and would fall into that category for sure. Red, on the other hand, wasn't concerned enough about his appearance to let a few bruises or cuts bother him. He would gladly take two or three punches in order to land a single decent blow to Drake's smug face.

Red raised his fists and got into a standard boxer's stance. Drake, on the other hand, was trying to look like he knew karate or some shit like that. Had to be for show. He didn't know what he was doing.

"Take your best shot," Red said.

"You're the one insisting on this nonsense," Drake said.

"You started it by popping me in the nose," Red said, edging closer. "Didn't hurt, but I could press charges."

"Then why don't you?"

"I'd rather beat your sorry ass."

"When will this beating begin, pray tell?"

"You talk like a sissy," Red said.

"Bor-ring!" Billy Don said in a singsong voice. Now he had his phone out and he was shooting video.

Red moved left, and when Drake shifted to face him, Red moved right. This was the way pro fighters did it. Lots of jockeying for position. Circling each other. Looking for an opening. Waiting for the right moment. Then you strike. Fast. Hard. Like a warrior. Eventually.

"We're gonna be here all day," Billy Don said.

"I've got all day," Red said.

"One of y'all get it started," Billy Don said.

Drake said, "I don't even even understand what—"

Red moved forward quickly and stomped Drake's foot hard with the heel of his Red Wing boot.

"Son of a bitch!" Drake said, hopping.

Red swung a looping right at Drake's face. He missed badly, but it caused Drake to back away.

"I didn't know you were going to cheat!" Drake said, limping on the stomped foot.

"That's not cheating," Red said.

"You kicked me."

"That was a stomp, not a kick. What are you, stupid?"

"Well, it wasn't fair."

"Oh, we have rules now? Did you have rules when you ripped off all those old ladies?"

"Why do you continue with those lies?"

"Make me stop, tough guy," Red said.

"I didn't rip anybody off," Drake said. "You're confused or delusional. Maybe both."

"You knew Marge Slubb lived in California," Red said.

"That's because you said so, you moron."

"I said it after you said it. Besides, I'd rather be a moron than a thievin' pervert."

"I guess you got your wish," Drake said.

"Good lord," Billy Don said. "Is this a dadgum playground? You gonna fight or play pattycake?"

Red moved forward again and tried to throw a left jab at Drake's mouth, but Drake pushed it aside easily with his right hand. Red tried another one, with the same result. On the third try, Drake deflected it, then snapped another quick jab that connected squarely with Red's nose. This time, blood began to trickle. Maybe Drake really did have some training.

"This is an embarrassment," Drake said. "We're grown men."

"Some of us more than others," Red said, although he wasn't sure what that meant. It sounded good, though.

"Get in there and pop him," Billy Don said.

Red's arms were already getting tired, which wasn't a good sign. He faked a lunge at Drake, who flinched at the sudden movement.

"What a wimp," Red said, laughing.

Red faked another lunge, and Drake flinched again.

"That's funny and all, but it ain't getting much done," Billy Don said.

"Maybe not," Red said, "but at least we know—"

And he lunged for real this time. He rushed at Drake with his head down and his arms wide, wrapping around Drake's torso and driving him off his feet and to the pavement, where Drake let out a loud, "Oooph!"

There, they both struggled to get the upper hand. Red was on top, but Drake managed to smack Red a couple of times across the face with an open palm. Red was trying to grab both of Drake's wrists and stop him from flailing around, but it wasn't working.

Red saw an opening and landed a solid punch to Drake's mouth. As Red suspected, that changed everything.

"Enough!" Drake said.

"Hell if it is," Red said.

He threw an even harder punch, but Drake moved his head to the right and Red's fist hit the pavement. His right hand exploded with a sharp pain.

Drake used the opportunity to roll to his right, attempting to get out from under Red. But Red was able to grab Drake's left wrist and pull his arm behind his back. Drake let out a yelp.

"Quit squirming," Red said.

"You're breaking my arm!"

"I will if you don't quit squirming."

"Okay! Stop pulling!"

Red eased up just a bit. His right hand was starting to swell.

"Now we're gonna have us a little talk," Red said.

"Get off of me," Drake said.

"You're a weasel, you know that?" Red said. "A poor excuse for a man. But now it's time for you to 'fess up to everything you've done."

"But I didn't do—ahhh! Stop pulling!"

"That's the way it's gonna work," Red said. "Every time you lie or deny what you did, I'm gonna pull your arm a little further back each time."

"You're a sadist."

"I guess so. Now tell us what you did."

"If you think I did something wrong, call the police."

Red pulled Drake's arm back. Drake responded by screaming.

"I warned you," Red said. "Didn't I?"

Drake nodded vigorously.

"Now admit what you did."

"Okay."

"Right now, I mean."

"I accepted money from Marge Slubb," Drake said.

"And?"

"And several other women."

"You *accepted* it?"

"Yes."

"Come on, Drake. There's a better word for what you did."

"I stole it. I stole the money."

"That's right. You stole money from little old ladies. You should say that yourself. You'll feel better."

"I stole money from little old ladies."

"Good. You're a con man."

"That's right. It's true. I'm a con man."

Red looked at Billy Don's phone and grinned for the camera. "Now we're getting somewhere."

"Let me up," Drake said.

"We're just getting started," Red said. "Now tell us about the other thing."

"What other thing? Ooowwww!"

"You know what other thing," Red said.

The victory would be so much sweeter if Red could force Drake to state exactly what he had done to Mandy. Make him describe it in detail. Make him feel ashamed for doing it, if he was even capable of that. Besides, what if Drake had done more than Red suspected? What if it went beyond spiking Mandy's drink? What if Mandy didn't remember everything, as Billy Don had suggested? If Red simply said, "Admit you spiked Mandy's drink," Drake might readily agree to that, because it left out the worst part.

"I really don't," Drake said. "I swear."

"Sure you do, and you're gonna say it loud, for all of us to hear. Otherwise, I'll break your arm off and beat you with it," Red said.

Billy Don had a good chuckle about that one.

"I don't know what you want me to say," Drake said.

"The truth," Red said. "And you'd better hurry, because I'm losing my patience."

Tell me what you did to Mandy, Red thought. *What drug did you use? Had you done it before? Tell me!*

Just thinking about what happened made Red angry, so Red tugged on Drake's arm some more.

"Oh, son of a bitch, that hurts," Drake said, his face turning bright red. Even in the cool temperature, sweat was beading on his forehead.

"Then start talking," Red said.

"If you post that video, I'll sue you," Drake said.

Red pulled Drake's arm so far back, he was surprised Drake didn't pass out. He did, however, scream with such anguish that Red almost felt bad for him. Almost.

"Don't worry about the video," Red said. "In fact, Billy Don, turn your phone off so the man can talk."

Billy Don gave Red a look that said *Are you serious?*

Red winked at him.

Billy Don lowered his phone, but he still had it aimed in their direction.

"Now talk," Red said.

Drake was reluctant, but he said, "He made me do it."

Who was Drake talking about? Was there somebody else involved in Mandy's photoshoot?

"Who did?"

"Alford Richter," Drake said.

Red didn't know who that was.

"Keep talking," he said.

"He found out about Marge Slubb and the other ladies, too, and he used it against me. He threatened to sue me because I never disclosed any of that before signing the partnership agreement. Unless I gave him an alibi."

Now Red was completely baffled. What did this have to do with Mandy?

"An alibi for what?"

"For Sunday, when Lonnie Blair died."

What the hell? Red was caught off guard by Drake's comment, but he managed to avoid showing his surprise.

"Keep talking," Red said to Drake.

"I agreed to tell the cops that Alford was with me when Lonnie Blair was killed," Drake said. "How did you find out about that? I don't understand. Do you know Alford?"

"I'm the one asking questions," Red said, because it was the perfect answer. Cops used it on him all the time. "Why did Alford need an alibi? Did he kill Lonnie?"

"I have no idea. He said he didn't."

"Did he have a reason to?"

"You don't know?"

"I got a pretty good idea, but I wanna hear it from you."

"But I don't even know why you're—"

"Tell me!" Red said.

"Okay. Okay. It was because Lonnie was sleeping with Carissa."

"Ha!" Billy Don said from behind Red. "D'you hear that? I was right."

35

George put the bucket of Boom Town on the floor and popped the lid. He saw five large transparent bags filled with a white granular substance that looked like Styrofoam, and a matching number of small silver packets that contained the second component, the catalyst. There was even a set of earplugs. How nice of them. Was that for the gunshot or the resulting explosion? You were supposed to be at least one hundred yards away when you shot the target, so if the ear plugs were for the explosion, damn, it must be loud.

Mix one big bag and one small bag? That would make a ten-pound target.

Why not use all of it and make a fifty-pound target? Go big or go home. The new George. Grab life by the balls. Be bold.

He stopped and listened for a long moment. Had he heard something? He'd been so focused on the Boom Town and what he might do with it, that he hadn't been paying as much attention to any sounds coming from other parts of the house.

"Mason?"

No reply.

"This is your last chance. If you really need a doctor, speak up."

Nothing.

He hadn't heard anything. If he had, it was simply the creaking of an old house. But he waited a full five minutes. Not one sound.

George dumped all of the bags onto the floor. Then he tore open a large bag and dumped it into the bucket. Followed that with a small bag of catalyst, which was a black material. Then he put the lid back on the bucket and gently shook and rotated it, turning it this way and that, including inverting it completely.

He opened the lid and looked inside. The contents were now gray.

He repeated the same process four more times.

Now he had a fifty-pound target, but what was he going to do with it?

Create a diversion. That's the only idea he had. Create a diversion by setting it off, and immediately jump out the window and run. And hope that Mason, if he was alive, would be too disoriented to understand what was happening.

Okay, then. A plan.

How intense would the explosion be? Deadly? Possibly, even if he used the rifle safe as protective cover. On the other hand, George figured an explosive without any sort of incorporated shrapnel or other projectile might simply create a loud noise and a lot of smoke. Was he stupid to assume that? Probably, but that's what the new George would do.

Still, it would be best not to detonate it right here in this room. He looked through the open doorway to the master bedroom across the hallway. If the bucket was in there, George could still hit it from here.

George wished the floor in the bedroom and hallway was hardwood instead of carpeted. He couldn't simply slide the bucket across the hallway. Instead, he would have to roll it on its side. No big deal. It was round and would roll just fine.

George stepped out from behind the rifle safe with the heavy bucket swinging from his right hand and slowly approached the bedroom door, stepping as lightly as possible. He bent down and rested one knee on the carpet. Placed the bucket on its side. Took aim. Then gave it a firm push. The bucket rolled smoothly and in a straight line across the hallway and directly into the master bedroom.

Then it veered right and rolled out of sight.

George simply stared for a long moment, amazed at his bad luck. Why had the bucket taken a right turn? A rough spot in the carpet? The contents inside the container had shifted? Did it really matter?

Acting on impulse, without thinking, he suddenly dashed across the hallway.

Red thought about some of the times he'd been questioned by John Marlin, Bobby Garza or his deputies, or any number of other cops, game wardens, park rangers, security guards, bouncers, stadium ushers, or tour guides over the years. They always asked a ton of questions, to fill in as many details as possible. Pain in the ass, sure, but he figured it made sense.

"How did Alford find out about Lonnie and Carissa?"

"She had been acting differently—happier—so he followed her one day when she went riding."

"Where'd she go?"

"Behind the neighboring ranch. She tied up, then hopped the fence and walked over to Lonnie's deer blind."

Sweet deal for Lonnie, Red thought.

"How long ago was this?" he asked.

"Maybe a month. He made her end it."

"But you don't think he killed Lonnie?"

"As I said, I have no idea. He said he didn't, but he needed an alibi to keep the cops off his back."

"Did you believe him?" Red asked. "Never mind. I don't know why I'm asking. You're a liar through and through."

"How did you figure all this out? How did you know I lied for Alford?"

"You got conned, asshole."

"What?" Drake said.

"I never knew any of this. I suckered you. How does it feel?"

Drake opened his mouth, but nothing came out.

Red said, "Now I'm gonna ask you one more question. All the other questions were nothing compared to this one. You lie and I'll cut your balls off. You hear what I'm saying?"

Drake nodded.

"On the other hand, if you tell the truth, no matter what it is, I'll let you go. You foller?"

Drake nodded again.

"What did you put in Mandy's drink?" Red asked.

To George, it felt as if he were in the hallway for an agonizingly long period. Several seconds, at least. But in reality, he knew it couldn't have been more than a quarter-second.

He made it across.

There were no shots.

No sounds at all.

The bucket was a few feet from the bed. George picked it up and placed it against the rear wall of the room, where it would be easily visible from behind the rifle safe across the hallway.

Then he prepared to dart back to the other bedroom. He was tempted to take a quick peek down the hallway first, but that would be stupid. Overconfident. Mason could be waiting, with the rifle raised.

Not a chance of that, George thought. Not at this point, after so much silence. If Mason wasn't dead, he was so committed to his bluff that he hadn't moved. The house was so still and quiet that George would be able to hear the slightest creak of a floorboard. So it would be safe to return to the bedroom, as long as he did it quickly.

Still, he waited a full minute. Nothing. Time to go.

George dashed out of the master bedroom and a shot immediately broke the silence.

36

Red drove with his left hand on the steering wheel because his right hand was aching, but he was pretty sure it wasn't broken. He could open and close it without any problems.

Meanwhile, he was still processing everything he'd just heard from Drake.

"Problem is, I'm not sure we can believe any of it," Red said.

Billy Don didn't answer.

"I mean, we know he's a bona fide liar. He told all kinds of crazy stories to make all them old ladies believe him. Maybe he's trying to do the same thing to us. Maybe he's just trying to make it so confusing and weird, I won't know what to believe."

"Maybe so," Billy Don said, and then he let out a long belch.

"Maybe he figured out I was there about Mandy, so he made all that up to sidetrack the conversation."

"You got a Tums?" Billy Don asked. "My stomach don't feel so good all of a sudden."

"Hell, you ate four pounds of sausage. What did you expect?"

Billy Don didn't say anything.

Red said, "I guess I could tell the law, but what if it's all bullshit? We'd look like idiots."

"When has that ever stopped us?" Billy Don said.

They happened to be passing the Bill Elsbury Law Enforcement Center—the sheriff's office—at that very moment.

Red kept driving south on 281, leaving Johnson City, and pondering the situation.

In Red's experience, cops hardly ever believed anything he said, partly because he didn't always tell the truth. Besides, what would stop Drake from saying he made it all up? He could say he did it because Red was torturing him, which was basically true. Red could get into trouble for that, and why risk it?

Okay, then. Decision made. Red kept driving. He wasn't going to worry about it. Wasn't even going to think about it anymore. Just let it go. Not his problem. He was glad he was no longer thinking about it. The cops would figure it all out.

"This ain't good," Billy Don said. "I ain't gonna make it home."

"Damn it," Red said.

"What? I just need a toilet. Go back to the Valero."

"I can't do it," Red said, hitting the brakes.

"Can't do what?" Billy Don said.

"Why am I always such a good guy?" Red asked as he eased into the center lane and made a U-turn. "Why do I always have to do the right thing?"

"Hell, if it's that big a deal, just pull over and I'll hop the fence."

Red continued back into town and took a left into the law enforcement center.

"Uh, this wouldn't be my first choice, but I ain't picky," Billy Don said.

Red pulled into a parking spot, and Billy Don was out the passenger side before the truck even stopped rolling.

Red killed the engine, got out, and began to walk toward the double doors into the office. Then he saw Lauren Gilchrist, the chief deputy, pulling into a marked spot near the front.

Hell, that was perfect timing, wasn't it? Red figured if he was going to share what he'd just heard, he might as well tell it to one of the prettiest women in the county.

Just as George Besserman dashed across the hallway the first time, Marlin was approaching the T intersection in front of the foreman's house. He almost turned right to approach the house, but he chose to coast to a quiet stop forty yards from the house instead. Just a minor precaution, so nobody in the house would hear him coming.

He killed the engine and simply listened for a long moment. Nothing to hear.

Based on what Phil had said about George Besserman, it was outlandish to think he might take matters into his own hands. He was too timid to even report Mason's threat to the sheriff's office. A guy like that wouldn't suddenly turn vigilante. Would he?

Marlin radioed the dispatcher and said he was going to be out at the foreman's residence on the Richter ranch for a few minutes. Then he stepped from his truck and gently pushed the door closed. Slowly walked the forty yards to the house. Mounted the three steps to the porch and listened again.

Had his right hand resting on his .357 and raised his left hand to knock. But didn't.

Because he smelled spent gunpowder. Faint, but unmistakable. A gun or rifle had been fired here recently, as in within the past few minutes. Maybe several times.

Time to back away and reassess. Call Mason. Call the Richters.

It was the smart move—but Marlin never got the chance. Before he lowered his left hand, a shot thundered inside the house.

Marlin reacted instantly on pure instinct. He dove to his left, over the low porch railing, and hit the ground beside the house. There, he pressed against the concrete foundation as tightly as he could.

Less than two seconds passed before a torrent of gunfire erupted—a steady stream from a semi-automatic weapon. Marlin didn't count, but there must've been at least ten shots. Sounded like a rifle. Possibly an AR-15 or something similar.

Marlin flipped onto his back, so he could see the front door, and drew his .357 with his right hand. Then he used his left hand to key the microphone clipped high on his shirt and request immediate help.

When Lauren Gilchrist exited her SUV, Red O'Brien called to her as he walked across the parking lot. After he reached her, he said, "You got a minute? I just found out something really weird about Lonnie Blair and a guy named Alford Richter."

"What did you find out?"

"Well, this all started when that dude who runs the wellness center conned a bunch of old ladies in California. This was eight or ten years ago, or maybe more. He had a different name then. His real name. Graham Smith. There was one lady who gave him a hundred thousand bucks. Anyway, so then he moved over here, and he opened the wellness center—which is also a big con, if you ask me. Ever done any research on detox diets?"

Lauren was still contemplating what she had learned from Barton Scott, and she was anxious to meet with Bobby and John, so her patience was limited.

"What did you learn about Lonnie Blair and Alford Richter?" Lauren asked.

She had spoken to Red O'Brien before, so she knew that his ability to clearly relay information was limited. He tended to jump all over the place, so his comments might seem disjointed and perhaps even a bit delusional.

"Okay, what happened was, you might've seen that postcard with that nice-looking babe on it. That gal is Mandy, my girlfriend. You might know her, or you might not, but the point is, when I saw that card, I just about flipped, 'cause she's basically naked on it, and it made me wonder whether she was cool with that from the start, or whether she got talked into it, possibly with a little bit of liquid encouragement— if you know what I mean."

"What did you learn about Lonnie Blair and Alford Richter?" Lauren asked.

"I'm almost there," Red said. "Promise. So Mandy said there was some drinking at the photoshoot, and that loosened her up quite a bit, but she also wondered if maybe this Drake asshole—pardon my language—slipped something into her screwdriver, because she felt a little different than she normally does when she drinks vodka. Long story short, I decided to ask Drake about it, and in the course of our conversation just a few minutes ago, he got a little confused about what I was asking, and he just flat-out confessed that he gave Alford Richter an alibi for Sunday afternoon when Lonnie Blair was killed."

Lauren saw no evidence that O'Brien was intoxicated or pulling a lame prank. "He said that?" she asked.

"Yep, but the only problem is, this guy Drake is a lying sumbitch, so it might be a total load of bullshit. Pardon my language. Also, I was, uh, kind of encouraging him to talk by, uh, twisting his arm a little bit."

"Figuratively or literally?" Lauren asked.

"Whichever one means I was really twisting it. I figured I should let somebody know."

Lauren was just about to ask O'Brien to come inside the sheriff's office and tell his tale from the beginning, and ask for the video from Craddock, but right then the radio on her hip crackled to life and she heard John's voice.

Shots fired at Mason Cross's house. John needed backup.

37

George made it back into the bedroom, behind the rifle safe, and maybe two seconds passed before Mason unleashed another withering volley of shots through the wall. When the shooting finally stopped, George realized he'd been hit. He'd seen that happen in plenty of movies—someone not knowing he'd been shot—but he'd always figured that was silly and unrealistic. How could you get hit by a bullet and not know it?

But now he felt a burn across his left shoulder blade, and he realized the back of his shirt was becoming saturated with blood. It must've been that single shot when he'd been crossing the hallway.

He reached back with his right hand to assess the wound, and as far as he could tell, there was no bullet hole, but instead he felt a furrow maybe four or five inches long. If that bullet had hit him in, say, the left bicep, it likely would have then passed through his arm and entered his chest cavity. He'd probably be dead by now. It had been that close. Was it weird that he was oddly excited by it all?

Now he was shielded by the rifle safe, but he had a clear view of the Boom Town bucket in the master bedroom across the hall. No reason to wait. He extended the handgun, took careful aim, and fired a shot. To his surprise, he actually hit the bucket.

Absolutely nothing happened.

Well, some of the mixture began to slowly leak out, but there was no explosion. What the hell? He shot at it again and scored another direct hit.

Zilch.

No boom.

Son of a bitch. What was going wrong?

He took aim a third time, but before he could fire, Mason responded with another hail of gunfire. George thought he might truly understand, for the first time, what it felt like to be in a war.

Oddly, in the middle of all this shooting, George remembered that the label said the bullet had to be traveling at least 2,000 feet per second. Well, crap. Maybe his little gun didn't fire bullets that fast.

Now what?

One last idea. A Hail Mary.

He fired a shot into the ceiling, and Mason responded exactly as George hoped he would—by firing another volley through the wall. George was hoping he would fire until the magazine was empty.

As soon as the shooting stopped, George took three quick steps and launched himself through the window, shattering the glass, and noticing before he hit the ground that a marked truck of some kind was parked about forty yards away.

The moment after Marlin released his microphone, he heard another shot, but that one sounded like a handgun, and that shot was closer, perhaps fired in the room just above the spot where Marlin was lying prone on the ground. Then another shot from the same gun.

That was answered by eight more shots from the assault rifle.

Then a pause.

Two people in a gunfight. Mason Cross and George Besserman? Besserman had come to confront Cross?

Marlin wasn't the target. Staying low and out of the line of fire was the smartest choice. No reason to sprint for his truck. A guy like Mason Cross might see him through a window and shoot purely from reflex.

Likewise, Marlin saw no value in making his presence known. He doubted any shout from him would end the firefight. He decided he should text Bobby and Lauren to update them on—

Just then the window directly above Marlin shattered.

He swung his .357 upward, ready to fire if necessary. A man in dark-green sweats fell to the ground just a few feet away, but he immediately scrambled to his feet and took off running. Marlin didn't get a good look, but he was confident the man wasn't Mason Cross. Had to be Besserman.

As far as Marlin could tell, Besserman wasn't armed, but there was a horizontal streak of blood across his back.

Marlin lay still as Besserman ran toward Marlin's truck, the only cover in sight.

A moment passed.

And another.

Then shots exploded from inside the house. Plumes of dust erupted all around the running man, and suddenly he pulled up lame on his right leg. Had he been hit?

He quickly veered left and dove behind the truck.

Silence for ten full seconds.

Then more rapid gunfire. The person inside the house fired at least twenty rounds into the passenger side of Marlin's truck, from one end to the other. Even at this distance, Marlin could hear the radiator hissing as hot fluid escaped. All of the airbags deployed in one large burst. Both tires on this side of the truck went flat.

"Mason Cross!" Marlin yelled. "State game warden!"

No reply. Possibly reloading.

"Mason Cross! Put your weapon down!"

Still no reply, but Marlin thought he might've detected movement inside the house. Just a subtle shifting of weight on the floorboards. Maybe it was nothing. Or maybe Cross was on the move, hoping to figure out where Marlin was.

"Deputies are coming!" Marlin yelled. "Exit the front door with your hands up!"

Marlin then immediately crawled army-style along the foundation of the house and rounded the left front corner. Now he was on the west side of the house and his best guess was that Mason Cross was in one of the rooms on the east side. Or had been.

Marlin pulled his phone and quickly typed a group text to Bobby, Lauren, and Darrell Bridges, the dispatcher. He wrote as quickly as he could, spelling and punctuation be damned.

One subject ran from house and now using my truck as cover

possibly geogre besserman unarmed and might be wounded, one
subject still inside likely Mason cross, I am on western perimeter of
house against foundation

Then he added another text.

Cross armed with rifle and firing on my truck

As if to punctuate that point, Mason Cross opened fire on the truck
again, and Marlin did his best to count the shots. It seemed to be an
unending barrage, but in reality, Marlin counted more than twenty
rounds.

Marlin sent a third text.

High capacity mags

Marlin guessed that, purely based on odds, at least one deputy
would've been patrolling within two or three miles of this location and
would arrive soon.

Marlin texted again.

Careful coming over the rise after the gate, you'll be exposed

Lauren Gilchrist, riding south with Bobby Garza, read each of
Marlin's texts aloud.

"There's more I need to tell you, but I'm thinking we should wait
until we get to the ranch," she said.

The speedometer was currently reading 105. Fortunately, traffic
was light and visibility was good on these long stretches of Highway
281.

"What is it?" Bobby asked.

She quickly summarized the story Red O'Brien had told. Then she
said, "I'm not saying it's accurate, but if Mason Cross had nothing to
do with the murder of Lonnie Blair, and if this guy George Besserman
is out of the house now, why is Cross still firing his weapon?"

"I think he's just flat-out nuts," Bobby said. "He might've always
fantasized about a day like this. Going out in a blaze of glory—or that's
the way he'd see it."

"Got a plan?" Lauren asked.

"Not yet. Need to see the lay of the land."

A SWAT team was already on the way from Austin, but what

could she and Bobby do in the meantime to get Marlin out of jeopardy? Besserman might need rescuing, too, or he might be a threat. Maybe he'd come out to the Richter ranch to kill Mason Cross and things hadn't gone according to his plan.

Several other deputies were responding from locations around the county, and Garza had already instructed them not to enter the ranch. He'd asked two of them to block the roadway a good distance from the ranch in either direction. The rest of them would meet at the gate and devise a response. EMS units were also en route.

Lauren sent a text to Marlin: *Five minutes out.*

From his position on the ground at the corner, Marlin could see his truck, the front porch, and the window George Besserman had used to exit the house.

Marlin didn't want to give his new location away by calling out to George Besserman, so he watched for movement on the far side of the truck, in the space between the chassis and the ground. He saw nothing.

Had Besserman been hit when he was running for the truck? What about earlier, when he'd been inside the house? How about Mason? Was he wounded?

Marlin checked his phone and saw a text from Lauren.

Five minutes out.

Marlin saw a slight movement near the front driver's side tire of his truck. Just a quick flash of green. Besserman's sweatpants or sweatshirt. So he wasn't dead.

Problem was, Marlin couldn't protect Besserman from here. Mason Cross could continue to fire on him and Marlin couldn't do anything about it—not from his location on the side of the house. Fortunately, Marlin had parked his truck parallel to the house, so the engine compartment and two front wheels might provide adequate cover, as long as Besserman stayed put. But what condition was he in?

Marlin pulled his phone out and dialed Besserman's number. Surprisingly, he answered.

"He got me," Besserman said. "Twice."

"Where?" Marlin whispered.

"First time across the back, but it's not bad. Then he got me in the thigh just now."

"How bad is it bleeding?"

"Slow, but I can't stop it. There are two holes. I tried to stop it with my hands, but it kept bleeding anyway."

Marlin was keeping an eye on the nearest window. Mason Cross would have to open the window and stick his head out to see Marlin.

"How much blood have you lost?" Marlin asked.

"I don't know. My sweats are getting soaked."

Marlin was amazed that Besserman sounded so collected. It took a lot of courage to remain calm under these circumstances. But how long could he go without medical care?

"Are you wearing a belt?"

"No."

"Put your phone on speaker and keep trying to stop the bleeding with your hands," Marlin said.

A moment later, Besserman said, "Okay. Can you hear me?"

"I can," Marlin said. "Wrap both hands around your thigh and squeeze as tight as you can."

Marlin waited.

Besserman said, "It's helping a little."

"But still bleeding?"

"Yeah."

Marlin thought about the first-aid kit in his truck. He couldn't ask Besserman to move from his position to retrieve it, and he would lose even more blood in the process.

"Are you armed?" Marlin asked.

"Not anymore. I left my gun inside, I think."

"It's Mason Cross inside, right?"

"Yeah."

"Anybody else?"

"No, just him. That man's insane."

"Do you know if he's wounded?"

"He pretended to be earlier, but I don't know."

"That window you jumped out of…is that a bedroom?"

"Yeah, it is."

Besserman quickly described the layout of the house to him. Very simple—and helpful.

Marlin wanted to ask Besserman why he was here and how the gunfight had started, but those questions would have to wait.

"Okay, hang on," Marlin said. "Let me think about this. Don't move. Stay behind the engine compartment."

Now Marlin heard the faint sound of a siren. Help was nearly here, but that didn't mean Besserman would be receiving medical attention anytime soon.

Marlin had to do something quickly.

38

The tires squealed as Bobby Garza took a hard right on Miller Creek Road. Lauren had an uneasy feeling they weren't going to make it in time.

Less than six minutes had elapsed since John had radioed for help, but it seemed like an hour. She checked her phone, hoping to see a new message from John, but the screen was blank.

Was George Besserman wounded, and if so, how badly? If his life was in danger, John would act. No question about it. He would risk his own life to save Besserman.

She heard other officers on the radio. Ernie Turpin had just arrived at the gate to the Richter ranch. Callie Young was approaching from the south part of the county and was now just a few minutes away.

But that didn't mean anyone could help John and George Besserman immediately. It would take time to assess the situation and devise a plan. They might even need to wait for a SWAT team to arrive from Austin. Both men could be dead by then.

Marlin was used to coming up with solutions under pressure, but in this instance, he saw very few options.

He couldn't move Besserman to a new location.

He couldn't reach Besserman to provide treatment. Not right now, anyway.

He couldn't wait for reinforcements to extract them both.

He had to stop Mason from focusing on Besserman. Distract him. And if possible, neutralize him.

Marlin army-crawled along the foundation all the way to the northwest corner of the house—the rear corner on the left side. He rounded that corner and continued along the back side of the house, toward a patio, then stopped beside a window, which, like the others, was covered by a curtain. No help there.

The patio was made of bricks, many of which had broken loose around the perimeter over the years. Marlin grabbed one and hefted it in his left hand. Perfect.

He took a deep breath and prepared himself. Pulled his .357 again and gripped it in his right hand. From a squatting position, he flung the brick through the window. Then he quickly grabbed another brick in his left hand and retreated to the northwest corner.

Less than three seconds passed before Marlin heard several quick shots from inside the house again. Mason Cross was firing at the window Marlin had just broken—firing randomly through the curtains, hoping to hit human flesh.

Marlin pointed his .357 at the ground ten feet behind the house and fired two shots. As soon as he heard Cross shoot again, Marlin hurried along the side of the house, rounded the corner to the front, and approached the broken window Besserman had used for his escape. The curtains were parted and Marlin would be able to see inside the house, but for now he stood to the left of the window, flush against the exterior wall.

Then he heaved the second brick up and over the house—but just far enough to land on the roof above the master bedroom in the rear of the house. The instant the brick landed, Marlin stepped in front of the open window, his .357 extended ahead of him, ready to fire.

There was nobody inside the bedroom. Nobody in the small portion of the hallway he could see. Nobody in the master bedroom across the hallway.

But he saw blood on the carpeted floor of the small bedroom, and the trail led into the hallway and turned left. That meant it had to be Cross's. Besserman had been hit running from the master bedroom, across the hallway, and into this bedroom. He wouldn't have left a trail like the one Marlin saw.

Cross had left that trail when Marlin had thrown the brick through the window less than a minute earlier. And he had not returned into the hallway. He was still in the back corner of the house, most likely wondering what to do next.

If the second brick had done its job, right now Cross was thinking Marlin had somehow gotten onto the roof. Didn't matter how. A ladder, a tree, whatever. The point was distraction. Confusion.

Marlin waited.

Sweat was running into his eyes. His mouth was dry.

The sirens had all gone quiet. Bobby and Lauren and several other deputies were gathered at the gate by now, deciding what to do. What *could* they do? Most likely a SWAT team was already on the way.

Marlin saw movement inside the house. Just a small…something. A shadow?

More movement. A black object floating in mid-air. No, not floating. It was the muzzle brake at the end of a rifle barrel. Just an inch or two showing through the bedroom doorway, coming from the left. Mason Cross was just outside the bedroom door, in the hallway, moving ever so slowly toward the center of the house.

Several more inches of barrel showed, including the front sight post of the rifle. An AR-15 or similar.

More movement forward.

A left hand wrapped around the underside of the barrel.

Now Marlin saw the magazine curving downward, and the trigger, and Cross's disfigured right hand grasping the pistol grip.

Marlin remained still and silent, ready to shoot.

Then Mason Cross stepped forward, totally visible in the hallway now, looking to his left, away from Marlin. The brick on the roof had worked. He had no idea where Marlin was.

Just as Marlin began to squeeze his trigger, Cross wheeled clockwise, leading with the rifle barrel, and Marlin's handgun bucked in his hand.

Cross flinched and Marlin fired a second shot.

And a third.

Cross staggered and his rifle tipped upward, firing into the ceiling.

Marlin fired a fourth time.

Cross crumpled to his knees. The AR-15 slowly slipped from his hands and landed on the carpet. Cross's arms were straight down by his sides.

He tried to say something, but it was unintelligible.

Then he fell forward onto the floor.

Marlin watched for a long moment. Mason Cross remained still. Marlin knew that time was urgent for George Besserman, but he couldn't leave Mason Cross unattended—not without confirming he was dead or disarming him.

He kept his gun pointed at Cross but used his left hand to thumb his microphone.

"Seventy-five-oh-eight to county. One subject down inside the house. Got him at gunpoint. I need backup at my location and medical at my truck for the wounded civilian."

That was the best solution—keep an eye on Cross while an EMS unit came for Besserman. At the same time, at least two deputies would approach on foot and help Marlin deal with Mason Cross.

Mason Cross opened his eyes and realized he was disappointed to be alive. Not just now. It had been that way for a long time.

He felt his fingertips cooling. And his hands. But the barrel of the AR-15 was warm.

He was facing his bedroom and his eyes came to rest on a red-and-black five-gallon bucket against the rear wall. He knew what that was. He smiled, or thought he smiled.

Boom Town?

What was this guy George doing with a bucket of Boom Town? Trying to blow him up? Hadn't that hunter Lonnie Blair been blown up?

Mason understood he'd never know the answers. Did it matter? Not really.

He sensed the game warden behind him still, in the window, watching. He'd heard him on the radio, requesting medical staff. For George Besserman, sure, but not for Mason. He wasn't having any of that. It was going to end here. He didn't have long.

He was able to move his right hand a small amount, and the rifle with it. Get it pointed in the general direction of the bucket. The game warden would be watching. Would he recognize the bucket, too? Would he understand the danger and shoot Mason again?

Did that matter, either?

Marlin was watching Mason Cross closely, but something in the background was catching his attention. Across the hallway, in the other bedroom, against the rear wall, was a red-and-black five-gallon bucket.

Now Marlin realized Mason Cross had just moved the rifle a few inches.

"Cross, do not move!" Marlin yelled.

Was it Boom Town? What else could it be? Was this all an elaborate trap set by Cross?

Marlin had to make a snap decision.

Shoot Cross again or run? Had to be one or the other. There was no middle ground.

Just as Cross moved the rifle a few more inches, Marlin turned and ran.

He'd covered no more than twenty yards when the world behind him erupted and he was knocked off his feet.

39

A full 24 hours later, Lauren Gilchrist entered an interview room in the sheriff's office. Carissa Richter was waiting inside. She was a beautiful woman. Intelligent. Wealthy. Educated. Connected. But in this room, none of that mattered. What mattered was the truth. The facts. The evidence.

"Want a Coke or anything?" Lauren asked, still standing inside the doorway. "Coffee?"

"No, thanks."

This interview would be critical, in part because yesterday afternoon, Drake von Oswald had refused to speak, other than to say he'd made up his confession to Red O'Brien because O'Brien had been physically abusing him. Today, it appeared von Oswald had left town and wasn't coming back. He had every right to do that, and Lauren doubted they would ever see him voluntarily again. Right now they couldn't charge him with anything. Maybe that would change.

Surprisingly, Alford Richter had agreed to an interview, and he was currently speaking to Bobby Garza in another room. But Lauren suspected that Alford wouldn't talk for long. As soon as the questions got tough and it became obvious he was a suspect, he would feign being indignant and shut it down. First, he would try to learn what the sheriff knew without giving away anything new.

Lauren closed the door and took a seat across the table from Carissa.

"Crazy day yesterday," Lauren said. "We're still trying to piece it all together. I'm hoping you can help with that."

"I'll do my best. How's the game warden?"

Lauren would withhold that knowledge for now. Of course, Carissa already knew that Mason Cross had not survived. The medical examiner had concluded that the blast killed Cross, but that he likely would've died shortly thereafter from two gunshot wounds to the torso. It would be difficult, if not impossible, to determine whether George Besserman or John Marlin had hit him. Or maybe they both had.

The damage to the house was extensive, including a post-explosion fire that had certainly destroyed a lot of evidence. George Besserman had undergone surgery and was in serious condition, but the doctors expected him to survive. He had not been interviewed at length yet.

"I'll get to that," Lauren replied. "But let's talk for a few minutes first. Do you know a man named Red O'Brien?"

"I don't believe so."

"Billy Don Craddock?"

"Those names aren't familiar."

"How about Mandy Hammerschmitt?"

"I don't know her."

"They're all local residents. Yesterday Mr. O'Brien had a conversation with Drake von Oswald, your business partner, about the postcard mailer he sent out, which features Mandy Hammerschmitt on it. Have you seen it?"

"I don't believe so. I'm not very involved with the retreat. In fact, that's all Alford's thing."

"The postcard is kind of risqué," Lauren said. "That concerned Red O'Brien a little bit, since Mandy is his girlfriend. When she told him Drake had served her a couple of strong drinks at the photoshoot, Red decided to have a chat with Drake."

"What does any of this have to do with Lonnie Blair?" Carissa asked.

Lauren nodded, because that was an understandable question.

"During the course of the conversation, Drake became confused about what Red was asking him, and he revealed that he wasn't meeting with your husband when Lonnie Blair was killed. Do you have any idea why Drake might've lied about that?"

Carissa Richter appeared visibly shaken.

"I have some suspicions. I didn't know he was lying, I can tell you that much."

"What *can* you tell me?"

"Maybe I should talk to my attorney first."

"That's up to you," Lauren said. "You're free to end this interview at any time. Just keep in mind that we only want the truth. If you didn't have anything to do with the murder—"

"I didn't."

"Then let's talk. This is your chance to clear yourself and set the record straight. Don't you want to do that?"

Carissa nodded.

"What are your suspicions?" Lauren asked.

Carissa took a deep breath. "I'm concerned…that Alford might've killed Lonnie."

Alford Richter was nervous, despite his attempts to appear cool and collected. Bobby Garza could tell. Alford couldn't maintain eye contact for long. Or sit still. His mouth was dry, but his palms weren't. He had wiped them on his pants a minute ago, thinking Garza hadn't noticed.

"Right now, my chief deputy, Lauren Gilchrist, is interviewing your wife about the murder of Lonnie Blair," Garza said. "I'm not sure what she's saying, but I have a pretty good idea."

"I can't imagine she knows anything helpful," Alford said. "I asked her about it myself several times in the past two days and she told me she knew as little as I did."

"Does it concern you that she's talking to Lauren?"

"Of course not. I don't know why you would ask that. Well, not unless you think Carissa did it. I can understand why you might be leaning in that direction, but it seems apparent at this point that it was Mason. Why else would he go out the way he did yesterday? Why would a man behave that way?"

"You'd be surprised," Garza said. "Some people live their whole life waiting for a situation like that. A shootout. A blaze of glory.

There's no logic or reason behind it. He'd had some problems before—the kind that made him a good candidate for a set-up."

"So you think somebody framed him?"

"We're still sorting it all out. You can help us with that."

"I'll try."

"It appears Drake von Oswald has decided to depart Blanco County."

"You're kidding. He left?"

"Any idea why he might do that?"

"Well, I realized after we became partners that he was a little flaky, unfortunately. That's understating it. He was basically a con man."

"When did you last talk to him?"

"It was Sunday, when we had a meeting at the retreat."

"What was that meeting about?"

"Just going over membership figures and projected revenue. That kind of thing."

"Were things going well?"

"So far, very much so. I guess that's all over now."

"Do you know a man named Red O'Brien?"

"I don't believe I do. I meet a lot of people."

"Yesterday, Drake told Red O'Brien a wild tale. Any idea what that might've been?"

"I don't understand why you keep wanting me to guess about these things. I don't know this man Red, so I can't tell you what Drake might've told him, especially since Drake was a skilled liar. You want me to tell you what I discovered about him?"

"Not right now. Let's talk about what he told Red O'Brien."

"That could've been anything, and whatever it was, I doubt it was true."

"Drake said he wasn't really with you at the wellness retreat when Lonnie Blair died," Garza said.

"I need to tell you something, and you're probably gonna get mad, but I want you to hear me out," Red said as soon as Mandy came through the door.

He figured he might as well get it over with. He hadn't seen her since he'd had the showdown at the convenience store with Drake, and he'd been trying to decide how much he would tell her. To tell her the good, he had to tell her the bad, too. Tricky position.

"What would I get mad about?" Mandy asked. "What did you do?"

"Will you promise not to get mad?"

"I'll do my best."

"There's some good news, too," Red said. "Just remember that. Bottom line, it's good news."

"What did you do?"

"I had a talk with Drake."

He stopped there for a minute to see how she would react.

"I figured you would, because you're so damn stubborn. Once you get something in your head, you can't let it go. You're pigheaded."

"Thank you."

"It wasn't a compliment."

"Pigs got big, strong heads. Besides, you tellin' me you don't sometimes do the same thing?"

"Yeah, okay, maybe I do, and it might be why we get along so good, but now you're stalling. Just tell me what happened."

She seemed only moderately peeved. He could work with this. He also noticed, when she took her jacket off, that she was wearing a tight top with a low neckline, which was usually a sign of good things to come. He was glad Billy Don had run into Austin for something.

"Actually, there's two pieces of good news," Red said. "First one is I mighta helped solved a murder."

"What're you talking about?"

So they sat down at the kitchen table and he began to tell her about Drake's history as a con artist cheating old ladies, back when he was called Graham Smith. Mandy couldn't help but be curious about it all, so she asked a lot of questions, including "Why didn't you tell me about all this when you found out?"

"Because you didn't want me butting in," Red said. "Remember on Monday night when you caught me and Billy Don talking about all this in the living room? I'd just found out about Drake and the old ladies, but you were pretty damn clear about not wanting any help from me. You called us buffoons."

"Because you are."

"You said you could take care of yourself."

"Because I can."

"I know. I'm just explaining why I didn't tell you. Hell, for all I knew, you'd heard everything we said. I guess you heard less than I thought. Anyway, you shouldn't be mad at me, you should be mad at Drake. He's the problem, not me."

That diversion seemed to work. "I always knew he was a lying son of a bitch," Mandy said.

Red wasn't sure that was entirely true, but he knew better than to point it out. Instead he said, "Yeah, and that's why I'm glad I got the chance to kick his ass, and that's when he told me all about the murder. See, I was trying to get him to admit whether he spiked your drink or not, but he got confused and told me about giving an alibi to the man who killed Lonnie Blair."

Mandy's eyes went wide. "You're crazy. You're lying."

"Even better, Billy Don got it on video. Most of it."

"Then let's see it."

"I don't know. You sure change your mind a lot. One minute you're telling me to mind my own business, the next you're—"

"If you don't play that video right now, I swear to God I'll—"

"Okay," Red said. "Jeez. Just hang on."

He took his phone out, but first he had to explain about the conversation he'd had with Drake inside the convenience store. Red left out the part about Drake saying that Mandy said she wasn't seeing anybody. Red didn't see any reason to muddy the waters with that obvious lie. Then he had to describe the way he'd approached Drake's car outside, and all of the little bits that had happened before Billy Don started recording, which included Drake mentioning that Marge Slubb lived in California, and Red catching him in that slip-up. Then Drake popped Red in the nose and the fight was on.

"That's when Billy Don finally got out of the truck and started recording," Red said, and he hit the play button.

40

Marlin was feeling pretty good, all things considered.

His left arm was in a cast, fractured in two spots, and he'd needed six stitches for a gash high on his forehead. He was generally sore all over, both from crawling along the ground and the blast that had knocked him off his feet.

But on the plus side, he was pretty sure he had never lost consciousness, and the ER doctor had determined that Marlin had no concussion, which seemed to surprise her. She had even relented and let him go home last night, rather than staying for observation.

His decision to run from Mason Cross's house had probably saved him. If he had taken the time to aim his .357 and squeeze off another shot—not just a shot, but an *accurate* shot under extreme pressure—there was no guarantee it would've stopped Mason Cross from firing his AR-15.

Regardless, it would've taken some serious injuries to stop him from watching the interview that was taking place right now. As usual, Bobby was doing a masterful job. He had an instinct for questioning. He knew when to press and when to pull back. He was patient and thorough. For that matter, Lauren had all the same qualities, and she was currently interviewing Carissa Richter.

Marlin wondered what Carissa was saying. Was she admitting she'd been sleeping with Lonnie Blair? Had she known that Alford wasn't really at a meeting with Drake—assuming Drake had told the truth to Red O'Brien? Was Carissa even talking at all? Marlin figured if she wasn't, Lauren would've already joined Marlin in here to watch Bobby interview Alford.

"Drake said he wasn't really with you at the wellness retreat when Lonnie Blair died."

Bobby had just spilled it all. How would Alford react?

Marlin kept listening to the interview as he quickly checked his phone. He was expecting a critical call or text from Henry Jameson, the forensic technician for Blanco County. Still nothing, but surely he would hear from Henry any minute.

"You're concerned your husband might've killed Lonnie Blair?" Lauren said.

"Yes."

"What makes you think that?"

"I was—our marriage has been in rough shape for a while. Several years. I'm sure we've both contemplated divorce. I'm not proud of it, but I was seeing Lonnie Blair. You probably already know that."

"We do, but hearing it from you tells me you're shooting straight with me. When did you start seeing Lonnie?"

"About two months ago."

"How did it start?"

"He flirted with me at the Lowe's Market and gave me his phone number. I told him I was married, but that didn't stop him."

Also didn't stop you from accepting his number, Lauren thought.

"Then what happened?" Lauren asked.

"He had told me that he hunted on the ranch next to ours, so the next time I went for a ride, I texted him and said 'Don't shoot me!' I don't know why I did that, but I did. Just lonely, I guess. So then he texted back and said he'd meet me at the fence to say hello. It went from there. I walked back to his deer blind with him. He's very…charismatic. I mean he was."

"How many times did that happen?"

"Probably five or six over the course of three or four weeks."

"But then it stopped?"

"Yes."

"Why?"

Carissa looked down the table. "Alford found out. So I told Lonnie we had to stop."

"Did you tell him Alford knew?"

"No, Alford didn't want me to tell anybody he knew, because he would look weak if he didn't confront Lonnie. He just wanted me to end it. Alford had an affair about four years ago, so he wasn't in a position to judge me too harshly."

"When you heard what happened to Lonnie, did you wonder if Alford had done it?"

"I would've, yes, except that he was supposedly with Drake at the wellness center. Plus, based on what I knew about Lonnie, I figured there were probably a lot of angry husbands and boyfriends who might've done it."

"Why would Alford have killed Lonnie the way he did?"

"I think he was trying to frame Mason. Right from the start, Alford didn't like him and wanted to let him go. He said Mason was disrespectful and possibly even dangerous. He also didn't like the way Mason seemed to respond to me."

"Which was how?"

"It became obvious pretty quickly that Mason was smitten with me. A harmless crush, as far as I was concerned, but Alford didn't like it one bit."

Lauren remembered that Mason's ex-wife had told John about a photo of Mason and Carissa on Facebook. Mason's cousin had posted it and seemed to insinuate that Mason was interested in Carissa. Mason probably never knew the photo was online.

"Is Alford the jealous type?"

"He could be. Sometimes."

Lauren still wasn't ready to dismiss Mason as a suspect.

"A couple of weeks ago, Lonnie was on the way home from a dance hall and somebody in a large black truck tried to run him off the road. A couple of days after that, Lonnie found a bullet hole in his trailer."

"Was anybody injured?" Carissa asked.

"Fortunately, no."

"You think Mason did that?"

"I'd say there's a strong chance."

Carissa contemplated that information for a moment. Then she said, "I think Mason might've seen Lonnie helping me back over the fence one time, but he pretended he didn't see it. He was out working in that area and I didn't expect him there."

"And he was smart enough to put two and two together," Lauren said.

"Yes."

"And maybe it made him jealous," Lauren said.

"Maybe."

"Jealous enough to harass Lonnie," Lauren said.

"Possibly."

Lauren was about to point out that this information only strengthened the case against Mason, and perhaps he had been jealous enough to kill Lonnie, but right then she received a text from John Marlin. She read it and smiled. Then she read it a second time. Finally. The break they all needed. Rock-solid evidence that pointed directly to the killer.

Lauren pushed back her chair and said, "Mrs. Richter, I appreciate your time. I might need to ask you some more questions later."

Carissa Richter seemed surprised by the abrupt end to the interview, but she said, "Just so you know, I'm leaving Alford. I don't intend to ever speak to him again. As soon as I walk out that door, I'm leaving town. You have my number, but I don't intend to come back here for anything short of a court order."

Lauren was standing now. "I wish you all the best. I really do."

Red watched Mandy's face as she watched the video of him and Drake at the convenience store. He could tell she was amused by what she was seeing, despite her saying she didn't want him getting involved. She even laughed when Red stomped Drake's foot.

"That's not cheating, by the way," Red said. "That's not a kick."

A few seconds later, Red rushed Drake and drove him to the ground, and then Red ended up punching the pavement, which hurt like hell, but then he got Drake's arm behind his back, and that's when the confession came tumbling out. Two confessions, actually. First, he confessed to stealing the money from the old ladies. Then he confessed to giving Alford Richter an alibi.

Drake explained why Alford wanted to kill Lonnie Blair, and how Alford had found out about Lonnie and Alford's wife getting it on inside the deer blind.

"No way he's making all that up," Mandy said, plainly caught up in all the drama.

On the video, Drake said, "How did you find out about any of this? How did you know I lied for Alford?"

And Red said, "Because you got conned, asshole."

"What?" Drake said.

"I suckered you," Red said, laughing. "How does it feel?"

Drake opened his mouth, but nothing came out.

Red stopped the video there.

Alford Richter furrowed his brow. "I have no idea why he would say that. We had a meeting. When I came home, I heard there was an explosion at the ranch next door."

Garza simply stared at him.

Richter added, "I realized after I partnered with him in the wellness retreat that I was sloppy with my due diligence. I hired a private investigator to do some research on Drake and wasn't happy with what we found. Maybe I'm telling you things you already know, but there have been some serious allegations against him in the past. He's a con artist and a pathological liar. I've been speaking with my attorney about dissolving the partnership, but it's a bit complicated."

Garza didn't respond for a long moment. Then he said, "Drake said Carissa had been cheating on you with Lonnie Blair."

Richter grimaced. "I'd rather not get into that."

"If it isn't true, now's the time to tell me."

Ten seconds passed. And ten more.

"Yes, it's true," Richter said. "Unfortunate, but true."

"How did you find out?"

He let out a rueful laugh. "Her mood had changed. She was happier, wearing nicer clothes. But not for me. And she was riding her horses more, so I followed her one day. She went over to his blind and stayed there for half an hour."

"What did you do about it?"

"I waited for her to get back and I confronted her. She readily admitted it. Then I made her end it. I wasn't happy about it, but I put her in a similar position a few years ago, so perhaps I had it coming."

"You cheated on her?"

"I did, yes."

"Were you angry at Lonnie Blair?"

"I didn't even know the man. I blamed Carissa, not him. I certainly didn't kill him. I still wonder about Mason, especially given what happened yesterday. I would be willing to bet Mason had some kind of disagreement with Lonnie Blair and killed him as a result. Surely that possibility has occurred to you."

"It has, sure."

"He was not a well man, obviously. And the explosion at his house? What caused that?"

"Do you have any guesses?"

"Damn it, why would I guess? I don't understand your insistence on me guessing about things. What's the point? I feel like you are intentionally ignoring your most obvious suspect."

"Meaning Mason."

"Of course Mason!" Richter took a deep breath and tried to calm down. "All I'm saying is that Mason had a violent past, and this murder seems to follow that same pattern."

Just then, Garza's phone vibrated with an incoming text from John Marlin. Garza read it and had to refrain from showing his overwhelming pleasure.

Time to switch gears.

Garza carefully contemplated how he should approach Alford Richter now. The proper order of questioning would be critical. He was tempted to take a break to hear what Carissa Richter had said to Lauren, but he was concerned that Alford Richter would leave the interview and never come back. Now was the time to slam the door closed.

"You know a man named Terrell Cobb?" Bobby Garza asked.

41

Red said, "Sure felt good to kick his ass. He's not so tough. Most of those pretty boys fold right away."

Mandy gently lifted his right hand. "Does it hurt?"

"Yeah, some, but it's okay."

"You think any of that's true about the murder?" Mandy asked. "He's such a liar, it's hard to know what's real and what isn't."

"I guess if Alford Richter gets arrested, we'll know it was true. You'd think the cops would keep me updated on the case, seeing as how I mighta given them the critical piece of evidence, but I haven't heard a word since last night. They could be a little more grateful."

Late yesterday evening, Ernie Turpin had called Red and asked for the video of Drake confessing. Billy Don pointed out that the file was too large to email or text, so he used something called Dropbox to share it with Ernie, and then he somehow managed to get it loaded from Dropbox onto Red's phone. Ernie had informed Red that they might need to take possession of Billy Don's phone later—something about the chain of custody for evidence—but Red hadn't passed that news on to Billy Don yet, because Billy Don would have a conniption when he heard that.

Red was aware that the video showed him committing assault, but Drake had popped him in the nose first, and Red had a witness to that, so surely he was on solid legal ground. Red had asked Ernie about all the rumors swirling around—an explosion on the Richter Ranch, and maybe Mason Cross was dead, and John Marlin was somehow involved—but Ernie wouldn't say a damn thing about it.

"I guess Drake committed a crime, lying to the cops like that," Mandy said now. "But if he changes his mind and tells the truth, they'll probably let him off."

"He deserves some time in prison," Red said.

"Hell yeah, he does."

Red was doing his best to focus on his story, but he kept getting a peek of a cherry-red bra under Mandy's top. It was distracting as hell. He was pretty sure he hadn't seen this one before.

"You want a drink?" Red asked. He knew it was tacky to ask her that question after the whole Drake incident, but what was he supposed to do? Never offer her a drink again?

"Maybe in a minute," Mandy said. "What's the other bit of good news?"

Red said, "Well, I think it's good news, and I hope you will, too."

He held his phone up and hit play again.

On the video, Red said to Drake, "Now I'm gonna ask you one more question. All the other questions were nothing compared to this one. You lie and I'll cut your balls off. You hear what I'm saying?"

Drake nodded.

"On the other hand, if you tell the truth, no matter what it is, I'll let you go. You foller?"

Drake nodded again.

"What did you put in Mandy's drink?" Red asked.

"What?"

"When you took those pictures and talked her into stripping, what did you put in her drink?"

"I don't even—what are you talking about?"

Red leaned in close. "I'll cut 'em off. Right here. Right now. With a rusty knife. You think I'm lying?"

"Absolutely not. I know you will."

"Then tell me what you put in her drink."

"But you said you want the truth," Drake said.

"That's right."

"I didn't put anything in her drink. I swear. I just gave her some vodka. That's all. Then we did the shoot. I even showed her the photos afterward and made sure she was okay with them. She seemed pleased."

"That's true," Mandy said to Red. "He did. Sure, I was buzzed, but he asked. I remember that."

On the video, Red said, "Maybe it's time for you to stop taking pictures of pretty women."

"I agree," Drake said quickly.

"And stop conning old ladies," Red said.

"It'll never happen again."

"In fact, don't con anybody at all," Red said.

"I won't. You have my word."

Red finally let his arm go, and after taking a moment to recover from the ordeal, Drake got into his car and drove away. The video ended there.

"Terrell Cobb," Alford Richter said. "I don't think so."

"He's one of the hunters on your ranch."

"Oh, well, as I told the game warden several times, Mason took care of all the lease arrangements."

"So you don't know Mr. Cobb?"

"Correct. I don't know him."

"You never had any interaction with him as he came and went from the ranch?"

"Not that I remember."

"When was the last time you climbed into one of the tower blinds on your ranch?"

Hesitation. Just a split second. But enough. Obviously Alford knew where Garza was going with this, and he had to decide if it was a bluff or not, while at the same time maintaining a demeanor of innocence. No stuttering or stammering. An innocent person wouldn't need to weigh his answers before giving them.

"I've never been inside any of those blinds," Alford said.

"You have no doubt about that?" Garza said.

"None whatsoever."

Perfect.

"It won't look good if you change your story later," Garza said.

"Why would I do that?"

"You'd be surprised what people do inside this room," Garza said. "Sometimes they get desperate or scared or confused."

"I can imagine that you try to trick people into admitting where they've been or what they've done, especially when you have no way to prove it. Maybe it works sometimes, but in this case, you're wasting your time. I have never been inside those blinds. End of story."

"Okay, good," Garza said briskly. "Yesterday, John Marlin talked to Terrell Cobb and he—Cobb—said the last time he was out at the ranch, which was two weeks before Lonnie Blair was killed, it appeared somebody had been inside his blind. Do you have any comment on that?"

"Maybe it was Mason," Alford said.

"Do you know which blind I'm talking about? The one on the panhandle portion of your ranch. It faces south, toward Hidden Hills Ranch."

"Doesn't matter which blind it was, since I've never been inside any of them."

"That's good, because we think it's possible the killer fired the shot that killed Lonnie Blair from that blind."

"This is just nuts," Richter said. "You people really have no idea what you are doing, do you? Frankly, I'm embarrassed for you."

Garza ignored the jab and said, "Here's the clincher, though. We found your fingerprints on the chair inside Terrell Cobb's blind."

Garza let that sink in for ten long seconds.

"You don't look well, Mr. Richter."

"I'm fine, I assure you. Are you saying you searched that blind without a warrant?"

"Not at all. The warrant is posted on the door to the blind, as per our legal requirement."

"How did you get onto my ranch?"

"Hopped the fence from Hidden Hills Ranch. Perfectly legal, since we had a warrant."

"That's outrageous."

Garza said, "You just told me you'd never been inside that blind. You said you'd never met Terrell Cobb. Never interacted with him as he came and went from the ranch. So there's no logical reason why your fingerprints would be on that chair."

Marlin was riveted. This was better drama than anything on TV.

First thing that morning, Marlin had worked with Bobby Garza to secure a search warrant for Terrell Cobb's deer blind and the chair inside. The judge had signed it just before ten o'clock, and Henry Jameson, the forensic technician, had processed the blind shortly thereafter. He'd carefully removed and transported the office chair back to his lab, with the hopes he could collect fingerprints.

And he had.

Henry found two sets of prints, one of which belonged to Cobb. Henry had been able to visually compare the other set to Alford Richter's prints, which were in AFIS from a pre-employment criminal background check several years earlier. It was a match.

Richter had touched the chair inside the blind. But why? How could an intelligent man commit such a stupid mistake? Garza had a theory.

"Here's where I think you slipped up," Garza said. "I'm betting you visited that blind twice. The first time—about two weeks ago—was simply to see if you could make the shot from there. You weren't even sure you were going to follow through with it. It was just a wild idea. So the thought of wearing gloves never even occurred to you. Now, the second time, this past Sunday—you did wear gloves. But those older fingerprints were still there on the chair."

Garza stopped talking and the room was silent for a full minute. Alford Richter's body language said he was defeated. He said nothing.

"We believe you attached a bucket of Boom Town to the outside of Lonnie Blair's blind. The way that blind is situated, nobody would've ever seen a bucket hanging on the north side of it—not unless you were three hundred yards away, on your ranch, looking through a rifle scope."

Richter shook his head but kept silent.

"You also hid a bucket of Boom Town in Mason's house, on a dark shelf in a closet he probably never used. You wanted to point the finger at him, but I don't think you really cared if it worked, as long as it stopped us from suspecting you. Problem was, we never had probable cause to search his house."

Richter didn't say a word.

"You have to be eighteen to buy Boom Town, and you wouldn't have bought it online—too much of a paper trail—so you probably drove to Austin or San Antonio and got it at Cabela's or Academy. You would've paid cash, but you'll be on video. Later today we'll be getting warrants for the location data on your cell phone and the search history on your computer and anything else we can think of. Might take a while for us to piece it all together, but we'll get there. I promise."

Garza waited for Richter to respond. Ten seconds passed.

Garza said, "You got anything to say? Want to give your side of the story?"

Ten more seconds passed.

"I want my attorney," Alford Richter said.

Red looked at Mandy. She was looking back at him and shaking her head.

"I can't believe you got him to admit all that," she said.

"But it's good news, right? That he didn't spike your drink?"

"I guess, but I feel a little silly for thinking he did."

"So it would've been better if he *had* spiked it?"

"No, I'm not saying that. It's just that I started worrying so much about what really happened that day, I let my imagination run away with me. But I'm glad to know he didn't, because that means I didn't forget anything. I didn't have enough vodka to forget stuff. So nothing happened that we don't know about."

"And it means I didn't have to put him in the hospital. I would've, you know."

"Yeah, I know."

She rose from her chair. He thought maybe she was going to fix a drink now, what with all this talk about that sort of thing, but she stayed where she was.

She said, "I want you to know that despite all my bitching, I do appreciate you looking out for me. In fact, last night I spent a lot of time thinking about all of this mess. I realized you were only trying to help, because we're a team. You've got my back and I've got yours. And sometimes I might need some help, even though I might not want to admit it."

"Or, uh, I might need some help, too, because it goes both ways," Red said, knowing she would want to hear that.

"Exactly," Mandy said, and she began to unbutton her blouse. "You shore up my weaknesses and I shore up yours."

"Shore will," Red said, grinning, but his eyes were focused on her hands.

Two buttons. Three. Four.

"But you have to know when to back off," Mandy said. "Let me handle things myself."

"I can learn," Red said.

She stopped unbuttoning for a moment.

"Can you?" she asked.

"Definitely," Red said. He could hardly sit still.

"I'm not so sure."

"I really can."

"Okay. Guess I'll take your word for it."

She finished with the last button, then slipped her blouse off and laid it over the back of the nearest chair. It was definitely a new bra.

"Holy moly," Red said.

"You like it?"

"Good God, yes."

He reached out to touch her, but she gently swatted his hand. *Not yet.*

"I'm gonna make a deal with you."

She unbuttoned her jeans.

"What kinda deal?"

"Right now, we're going to have a little fun, and after that, we're never going to talk about the postcard again. Ever. Not one word."

She lowered the zipper of her jeans.

Red said, "Deal. Absolutely. Sign me up."

"Yes, but that means you can't even—"

"I won't."

"You can't even refer to the postcard in a vague kind of way. You can't mention the wellness retreat. Nothing about Drake von—"

"Drake who?" Red said.

"Very good," Mandy said.

She slid her jeans down her hips and kicked them off, leaving them on the floor. She was wearing matching cherry-red panties.

She said, "You should know that if you break the deal, you'll never see me again in anything except a burlap sack."

"You'd still look good. But I won't."

"Okay, then," she said.

She gave him a follow-me finger wag and walked out of the kitchen, down the hallway, toward his bedroom. This was going to be great.

As he trailed behind her, his eyes fell on the tag of her new bra. *Sarah's Intimates.*

He'd never heard of that brand, but they made a damn nice product.

42

Three days later, at seven in the evening, Nicole Marlin pulled her SUV into a spot in front of Kwizzeen, the new restaurant everyone had been buzzing about in Dripping Springs. Phil Colby had texted that they would be a few minutes late.

She began to open her door, but Marlin said, "You mind if we just sit out here for a minute? It's kind of nice with the windows down."

"Sure," Nicole said.

The night was crisp, clear, and still, with a half-moon high above.

"How you feeling?" Nicole asked.

"About tonight? I'm sure it'll be great."

"I meant your arm."

"I know. I was just kidding."

Marlin had had some discomfort as the bones had begun to stitch themselves back together. The doctor had said the pain might increase for the first week or so, then begin to decrease.

"The agony would kill a lesser man," he said. "For me, it's not a problem."

"Of course not."

"In fact, I didn't even take any pills today."

"What? Why not?"

"I wanted to drink a cold beer or two, and that doesn't go well with the meds. I'd probably fall asleep on the table. The good news is, all I have right now is a dull throbbing. It's really not that bad. Better than a few days ago."

Nicole nodded. "I feel like I've said this a lot in the past few years, but I'm glad you're okay."

Marlin knew that Nicole worried about him on the job, but he wasn't quite ready for retirement. Sure, it crossed his mind now and then. He'd put in his time, and he would receive full benefits. It had been a long and rewarding career. He'd had the best of both worlds—working as a game warden, and helping the sheriff's office with the types of cases most game wardens never experienced.

A homicide by an exploding target? How insane was that?

Marlin was pleased with the way things were shaping up at the district attorney's office.

Alford Richter, speaking through his lawyer, had agreed to confess if the death penalty was taken off the table. The details of the deal were still being ironed out, but he would do life without parole, as he should.

Drake von Oswald, formerly known as Graham Smith, was probably going to skate away clean. Nobody had been able to find him yet, but it would be difficult to charge him for lying to investigators, and the prosecutors didn't see much value in pursuing it. Best case, they might be able to saddle him with a few years of probation. The wellness center was currently sitting empty, with the doors locked.

Carissa Richter had indeed left town—all the way to some small village in New Hampshire. A new beginning. She had done nothing wrong—at least not from a legal standpoint—and since she had already given her statement, the sheriff's office probably wouldn't need to bother her again.

George Besserman, who'd been discharged from the hospital yesterday, had cooperated fully. He'd admitted he'd gone to Mason Cross's house to extract an apology out of him, possibly at gunpoint. Technically, he'd committed burglary of a habitation, criminal mischief, and aggravated assault, and he would likely end up with a long term of probation after a plea deal. It helped that he had recorded some video in which Mason Cross seemed to acknowledge shooting at Besserman first, despite Besserman's apparent willingness to give up. He had explained how he'd found a bucket of Boom Town in a closet and tried to use it as a diversion to allow him to make an escape. He had also agreed to get some therapy to handle his anger more appropriately when he encountered bullies in the future.

Lauren had gotten location data on Mason Cross's phone and determined that he'd been in the area the night someone in a black Chevy truck had tried to run Lonnie Blair off the road. He'd also been in the area two days later, which was roughly the time someone had fired a bullet through Blair's trailer. Maybe that explained why Cross had refused to lay down his weapon for Marlin four days earlier; he knew he would be facing punishment eventually for those crimes, and his resentment of authority was so great, he couldn't bear the idea of surrendering. Or maybe he was just an angry, violent asshole.

"Where are you?" Nicole said.

"What?"

"You were lost in thought."

"Yeah, I was."

"Still thinking about the case?"

"No," Marlin lied. "I was thinking we need a vacation."

"Were you really?"

"As far as you know."

"Funny."

"But we should really go somewhere."

"Like where?"

"Oh, I don't know. Paris? Madrid? Lubbock?"

"Those first two sound pretty good."

"A Caribbean cruise?"

"That works, too."

"We could hike the Andes."

"Keep going."

"Fiji. Australia. South Africa."

"You'd better stop before I take you seriously."

"Nicole, I'm not kidding. You pick the place and let's go. I mean it."

"That sounds great. I'll start making a list."

"Do it."

"We haven't gone anywhere in a long time."

"I know. Hey, I just had an idea. You know what we should do?"

"What?" Nicole asked.

"Tell me if you'd rather not."

"I have to hear the idea first."

He paused for a moment for dramatic effect.

"We should invite Phil and Lauren to go with us."

Her eyes widened. "Seriously?"

"Absolutely."

"I love it," she said.

"You sure?"

"If they want to."

"Who wouldn't want to go on vacation with two great people like us?" he asked.

Headlight beams swung across the interior of Nicole's SUV as Phil and Lauren pulled into the lot.

Nicole leaned toward Marlin and gave him a long kiss.

"I'm glad you're okay," she said.

"You already said that."

"I know. Because it's true."

"I appreciate that. By the way, I think I'm going to need a favor tonight."

"What is it?"

"You might need to cut up my steak for me."

"Anything," Nicole said. "Anything."

GONE THE NEXT

1

The woman he was watching this time was in her early thirties. Thirty-five at the oldest. White. Well dressed. Upper middle class. Reasonably attractive. Probably drove a nice car, like a Lexus or a BMW. She was shopping at Nordstrom in Barton Creek Square mall. Her daughter — Alexis, if he'd overheard the name correctly — appeared to be about seven years old. Brown hair, like her mother's. The same cute nose. They were in the women's clothing department, looking at swimsuits. Alexis was bored. Fidgety. Ready to go to McDonald's, like Mom had promised. Amazing what you can hear if you keep your ears open.

He was across the aisle, in the men's department, looking at Hawaiian shirts. They were all ugly, and he had no intention of buying one. He stood on the far side of the rack and held up a green shirt with palm trees on it. But he was really looking past it, at the woman, who had several one-piece swimsuits draped over her arm. Not bikinis, though she still had the figure for it. Maybe she had stretch marks, or the beginnings of a belly.

He replaced the green shirt and grabbed a blue one covered with coconuts. Just browsing, like a regular shopper might do.

Mom was walking over to a changing room now. Alexis followed, walking stiff-legged, maybe pretending she was a monster. A zombie. Amusing herself.

He moved closer, to a table piled high with neatly folded cargo shorts. He pretended to look for a pair in his size. But he was watching in his peripheral vision.

"Wait right here," Mom said. She didn't look around. She was oblivious to his presence. He might as well have been a mannequin.

Alexis said something in reply, but he couldn't make it out.

"There isn't room, Lexy. I'll just be a minute."

And she shut the door, leaving Alexis all by herself.

~ ~ ~

When he first began his research, he'd been surprised by what he'd found. He had expected the average parent to be watchful. Wary. Downright suspicious. That's how he would be if he had a child. A little girl. He'd guard her like a priceless treasure. Every minute of the day. But his assumptions were wrong. Parents were sloppy. Careless. Just plain stupid.

He knew that now, because he'd watched hundreds of them. And their children. In restaurants. In shopping centers. Supermarkets. Playgrounds and parks. For three months he'd watched. Reconnaissance missions, like this one right now, with Alexis and her mom. Preparing. What he'd observed was encouraging. It wouldn't be as difficult as he'd assumed. When the time came.

But he had to use his head. Plan it out. Use what he'd learned. Doing it in a public place, especially a retail establishment, would be risky, because there were video surveillance systems everywhere nowadays. Some places, like this mall, even had security guards. Daycare centers were often fenced, and the front doors were locked. Schools were always on the lookout for strangers who —

"You need help with anything?"

He jumped, ever so slightly.

A salesgirl had come up behind him. Wanting to be helpful. Calling attention to him. Ruining the moment.

That was a good lesson to remember. Just because he was watching, that didn't mean he wasn't being watched, too.

2

The first time I ever heard the name Tracy Turner — on a hot, cloudless Tuesday in June — I was tailing an obese, pyorrheic degenerate named Wally Crouch. I was fairly certain about the "degenerate" part, because Crouch had visited two adult bookstores and three strip clubs since noon. Not that there's anything wrong with a little mature entertainment, but there's a point when it goes from bawdy boys-will-be-boys recreation to creepy pathological fixation. The pyorrhea was pure conjecture on my part, based solely on the number of Twinkie wrappers Crouch had tossed out the window during his travels.

Crouch was a driver for UPS and, according to my biggest client, he was also a fraud who was riding the workers' comp gravy train. In the course of a routine delivery seven weeks prior, Crouch had allegedly injured his lower back. A ruptured disk, the doctor said. Limited mobility and a twelve- to sixteen-week recovery period. In the meantime, Crouch couldn't lift more than ten pounds without searing pain shooting up his spinal cord. But this particular quack had a checkered past filled with questionable diagnoses and reprimands from the medical board. My job was fairly simple, at least on paper: Follow Crouch discreetly until he proved himself a liar. Catch it on video. Testify, if necessary. Earn a nice paycheck. Continue to finance my sumptuous, razor's-edge lifestyle.

~ ~ ~

You'd think Crouch, having a choice in the matter, would've avoided rush-hour traffic and had a few more beers instead, but he left Sugar's Uptown Cabaret at ten after five and squeezed his way onto the interstate heading south. I followed in my seven-year-old Dodge Caravan. Beige. Try to find a vehicle less likely to catch someone's eye. The windows are deeply tinted and a scanner antenna is mounted on the roof, which are the only clues that the driver isn't a soccer mom toting her brats to practice.

Anyone whose vehicle doubles as a second home recognizes the value of a decent sound system. I'd installed a Blaupunkt, with Bose speakers front and rear. Total system set me back about two grand. Seems like overkill for talk radio, but that's what I was listening to when I heard the familiar alarm signal of the Emergency Alert System. I'd never known the system to be used for anything other than weather warnings, but not this time. It was an Amber Alert. A local girl had gone missing from her affluent West Austin neighborhood. Tracy Turner: six years old, blond hair, green eyes, three feet tall, forty-five pounds, wearing denim shorts and a pink shirt. My palms went sweaty just thinking about it. Then I heard she might be in the company of Howard Turner — her non-custodial father, a resident of Los Angeles — and I breathed a small sigh of relief. Listeners, they said, should keep an eye out for a green Honda with California plates.

Easy to read between the lines. Tracy's parents were divorced, and dad had decided he wanted to spend more time with his daughter, despite how the courts had ruled. Sad, but much better than a random abduction.

The announcer was repeating the message when my cell phone rang. I turned the radio volume down, answered, and my client — a senior claims adjuster at a big insurance company — said, "You nail him yet?"

"Christ, Heidi, it's only the third day."

"I thought you were good."

"That's a vicious rumor."

"Yeah, and I think you started it yourself. I'm starting to think you get by on your looks alone."

"That remark borders on sexual harassment, and you know how I feel about that."

"You're all for it."

"Exactly. Anyway, relax, okay? I'm on him twenty-four seven." Crouch had taken the Manor Road exit, and now he turned into his apartment complex, so I drove past, calling it a day. I didn't like lying to Heidi, but I had a meeting with a man named Harvey Blaylock in thirty minutes.

"Well, you'd better get something soon, because I've got another one waiting," Heidi said.

I didn't say anything, because a jerk in an F-150 was edging over into my lane.

"Roy?" she said.

"Yeah."

"I have another one for you."

"Have scientists come up with that device yet?"

"What device?"

"The one that allows you to be in two places at the same time."

"You really crack you up."

"Let me get this one squared away, then we'll talk, okay?"

"The quicker the better. Where are you? Has Crouch even left the house?"

"Oh, yeah. Been wandering all afternoon."

"Where to?"

"Uh, let's just say he seems to have an inordinate appreciation for the female form."

"Which means?"

"He's been visiting gentlemen's clubs."

A pause. "You mean tittie bars?"

"That's such a crass term. Oh, by the way, the Yellow Rose is looking for dancers. In case you decide to — "

She hung up on me.

~ ~ ~

I had the phone in my hands, so I went ahead and called my best friend Mia Madison, who works at an establishment I used to do business with on occasion. She tends bar at a tavern on North Lamar.

Boiling it down to one sentence, Mia is smart, funny, optimistic, and easy on the eyes. Expanding on the last part, because it's relevant, Mia stands about five ten and has long red hair that she likes to wear in a ponytail. Prominent cheekbones, with dimples beneath. The toned legs of a runner, though she doesn't run, but must walk ten miles a day during an eight-hour shift. When Mia gets dolled up — what she calls "bringing it" — she goes from being an attractive woman you'd certainly notice to a world-class head turner.

On one occasion, she revealed that she has a tattoo. Wouldn't show it to me, but she said — joking, I'm sure — that if I could guess what it was, and where it was, she'd let me have a look. Nearly a year later, I still hadn't given up.

"Is it Muttley?" I asked when she answered.

"Muttley? Who the hell is Muttley?"

"You know, that cartoon dog with the sarcastic laugh."

"You mean Scooby Doo?"

"No, the other one. Hangs with Dick Dastardly."

"I have no idea what you're talking about."

"Before your time, I guess. Are you at work?"

"Not till six. Just got out of the shower. I'm drying off."

"Need any help?"

"I think I can handle it," she said.

"Okay, next question. Want to earn a hundred bucks the easy way?" I said.

"Love to," she said. "When and where?"

3

Harvey Blaylock was maybe sixty, medium height, with neatly trimmed gray hair, black-framed glasses, a white short-sleeved shirt, and tan gabardine slacks. He looked like the kind of man who, if things had taken a slightly different turn, might've wound up as a forklift salesman, or, best case, a high-school principal in a small agrarian town.

In reality, however, Harvey Blaylock was a man who held tremendous sway over my future, near- and long-term. I intended to remain respectful and deferential.

Blaylock's necktie — green, with bucking horses printed on it — rested on his paunch as he leaned back in his chair, scanning the contents of a manila folder. I knew it was my file, because it said ROY W. BALLARD on the outside, typed neatly on a rectangular label. I'm quick to notice things like that.

Five minutes went by. His office smelled like cigarettes and Old Spice. Rays of sun slanted in through horizontal blinds on the windows facing west. As far as I could tell, we were the only people left in the building.

"I really appreciate you staying late for this," I said. "Would've been tough for me to make it earlier."

He grunted and continued reading, one hand drumming slowly on his metal desk. The digital clock on the wall above him read 6:03. On the bookshelf, tucked among a row of wire-bound notebooks, was a framed photo of a young boy holding up a small fish on a line.

"Boy, was I surprised to hear that Joyce retired," I said. "She seemed too young for that. So spry and youthful." Joyce being Blaylock's predecessor. My previous probation officer. A true bitch on wheels. Condescending. Domineering. No sense of humor. "I'll have to send her a card," I said, hoping it didn't sound sarcastic.

Blaylock didn't answer.

I was starting to wonder if he had a reading disability. I'm no angel — I wouldn't have been in this predicament if I were — but my file couldn't have been more than half a dozen pages long. I was surprised that a man in his position, with several hundred probationers in his charge, would spend more than thirty seconds on each.

Finally, Blaylock, still looking at the file, said, "Roy Wilson Ballard. Thirty-six years old. Divorced. Says you used to work as a news cameraman." He had a thick piney-woods accent. Pure east Texas. He peered up at me, without moving his head. Apparently, it was my turn to talk.

"Yes, sir. Until about three years ago."

"When you got fired."

"My boss and I had a personality conflict," I said, wondering how detailed my file was.

"Ernie Crenshaw."

"That's him."

"You broke his nose with a microphone stand."

Fairly detailed, apparently.

"Well, yeah, he, uh — "

"You got an attitude problem, Ballard?"

"No, sir."

"Temper?"

I started to lie, but decided against it. "Occasionally."

"That what happened in this instance? Temper got the best of you?"

"He was rude to one of the reporters. He called her a name."

"What name was that?"

"I'd rather not repeat it."

"I'm asking you to."

"Okay, then. He called her Doris. Her real name is Anne."

His expression remained frozen. Tough crowd.

I said, "Okay. He called her a cunt."

Blaylock's expression still didn't change. "To her face?"

"Behind her back. He was a coward. And she didn't deserve it. This guy was a world-class jerk. Little weasel."

"You heard him say it?"

"I was the one he was talking to. It set me off."

"So you busted his nose."

"I did, sir, yes."

Perhaps it was my imagination, but I thought Harvey Blaylock gave a nearly imperceptible nod of approval. He looked back at the file. "Now you're self-employed. A legal videographer. What is that exactly?"

"Well, uh, that means I record depositions, wills, scenes of accidents. Things like that. But proof of insurance fraud is my specialty. The majority of my business. Turns out I'm really good at it."

"Describe it for me."

"Sir?"

"Give me a typical day."

I recited my standard courtroom answer. "Basically, I keep a subject under surveillance and hope to videotape him engaging in an activity that's beyond his alleged physical limitations." Then I added, "Maybe lifting weights, or dancing. Playing golf. Doing the hokey-pokey."

No smile.

"Not a nine-to-five routine, then."

"No, sir. More like five to nine."

Blaylock mulled that over for a few seconds. "So you're out there, working long hours, sometimes through the night, and you start taking pills to keep up with the pace. That how it went?"

Until you've been there, you have no idea how powerless and naked you feel when someone like Harvey Blaylock is authorized to dig through your personal failings with a salad fork.

"That sums it up pretty well," I said.

"Did it work?"

"What, the pills?"

He nodded.

"Well, yeah. But coffee works pretty well, too."

"You were also drinking. That's why you got pulled over in the first place, and how they ended up finding the pills on you. You got a drinking problem?"

I thought of an old joke. *Yeah, I got a drinking problem. Can't pay my bar tab.* "I hope not," I said, which is about as honest as it gets. "At one point maybe I did, but I don't know for sure. Probably not. But that's what you'd expect someone with a drinking problem to say, right?"

"Had a drink since your court date?"

"No, sir. I'm not allowed to. Even though the Breathalyzer said I was legal."

"Not even one drink?"

"Not a drop. Joyce, gave me a piss te — I mean a urine test, last month, and three in the past year. I passed them all. That should be in the file."

"You miss it?" Blaylock asked. "The booze?"

I honestly thought about it for a moment.

"Sometimes, yeah," I said. "More than I would've guessed, but not enough to freak me out or anything. Sometimes, you know, I just crave a cold beer. Or three. But if I had to quit eating Mexican food, I'd miss that, too. Maybe more than beer."

Blaylock slowly sat forward in his chair and dropped my file, closed, on his desk. "Here's the deal, son. Ninety-five percent of the people I deal with are shitbags who think the world is their personal litter box. I can't do them any good, and they don't want me to. Most of 'em are locked up again within a year, and all I can say is good riddance. Then I see guys like you who make a stupid mistake and get caught up in the system. You probably have a decent life ahead of you, but you don't need me to tell you that, and it really doesn't matter what I think anyway. So I'll just say this: Follow the rules and you can put all this behind you. If you need any help, I'll do what I can. I really will. But if you fuck up just one time, it's like tipping over a row of dominoes. Then it's out of your control, and mine, too. You follow me?"

~ ~ ~

After the meeting, I swung by a Jack-In-The-Box, then sat outside Wally Crouch's place for a few hours, just in case. He stayed put.

I got home just as the ten o'clock news was coming on. Howard Turner had been located in a motel in Yuma City, Arizona, there on business. Police had verified his alibi. He had been nowhere near Texas, and the cops had no reason to believe he was involved.

So Tracy Turner was still missing, and that fact created a void in my chest that I hadn't felt in years.

ABOUT THE AUTHOR

Ben Rehder lives with his wife near Austin, Texas, where he was born and raised. His novels have made best-of-the-year lists in *Publishers Weekly, Library Journal, Kirkus Reviews*, and *Field & Stream*. *Buck Fever* was a finalist for the Edgar Award, and *Get Busy Dying* was a finalist for the Shamus Award. For more information, visit www.benrehder.com.

OTHER NOVELS BY BEN REHDER

Buck Fever
Bone Dry
Flat Crazy
Guilt Trip
Gun Shy
Holy Moly
The Chicken Hanger
The Driving Lesson
Gone The Next
Hog Heaven
Get Busy Dying
Stag Party
Bum Steer
If I Had A Nickel
Point Taken
Now You See Him
Last Laugh
A Tooth For A Tooth
Lefty Loosey
Shake And Bake
Free Ride
Better To Be Lucky

For more information, visit www.benrehder.com.

Made in the USA
Monee, IL
04 December 2021

83844164R00157